FIRE OF THE FLESH

OF THE GODS - BOOK THREE

GINA STURINO

"She understands," Liam said solemnly. "She remembers. Tell us, who are you?"

The girl blinked again, releasing another wave of blazing tears down her face.

"Let her be. She will speak when she is ready." Lucille placed her arms over the child's shoulders and pulled her into her side.

"I can't stay long. I need to return tomorrow." Liam scratched his chin and glanced toward the bright window.

"I understand. I am glad you brought her to me. I will care for her. You can be assured of that. What she needs now is rest."

Lucille led the girl out of the room, up the worn stairs, and into the first bedroom, which contained only a wooden cot. The child didn't need prodding; she wordlessly climbed onto the bed and allowed Lucille to pull the colorful quilted blanket over her.

"Would you like a dolly, sweet girl? A little friend to keep you company?" Lucille asked, even though she didn't expect an answer. "I will make you one tonight. I have red silk for her dress and white yarn for her hair. She will look just like you. Would you like that?" Again, no reply. Lucille placed a gentle kiss on the child's forehead before leaving her for the night.

THE NEXT MORNING, the little girl climbed out of bed and padded downstairs to the great room below. Hearing her soft footsteps, Liam glanced up from his perch on the solid wooden chair in the kitchen.

"Morning, kid," he said by way of greeting. When the

child didn't reply, he nodded toward the fruit bowl on the table. "Hungry?"

Silently, she moved to the table and plucked an apple from the top of the pile. She rolled it over in her small hands, studying it as if it were a crystal ball. The longer she looked at the piece of fruit, the redder it became, ripening from a spotted yellow-and-red mix to a scarlet shade that glowed under her touch.

"Hey, what are you doing?" Liam muttered. "You're going to hurt yourself."

The skin of the apple began shriveling as wisps of smoke quivered around the girl's fingers. Sizzles and crackles reverberated from her palm.

"Stop that, kid. Fire is dangerous. You should know that," he cautioned.

The girl took no notice of his warning. Instead, she squeezed the fruit tighter. Roasted flesh oozed between her small fingers. A whiny noise mingled with the crackling, growing louder as more smoke floated above the girl's hand.

"Are you trying to get hurt?" Liam pushed from his seat and smacked the apple from the girl's hand. The scorched core fell to the floor. Ash danced around the girl's palm. She stared blankly at her blackened fingers.

Liam grabbed her chin and forced her face upward. "Look at me." Her eyes darted to meet his before shifting away. "Eyes of fire. You *are* a lumineer. What's your name?"

She didn't respond, but Liam saw her throat bob. "You understand, so answer me. What do they call you?" He released her chin. "If you won't speak, I'll ask your mama when I return to the mortal realm."

The girl's eyes jerked to Liam's mouth. She stared for a moment, then shifted her gaze to his eyes. Cocking her head, she hoarsely whispered, "Mama?"

"Ah. So, you do speak." He studied her. The intensity of her small, stern face almost made him chuckle. "What's your name?"

Her eyes blazed to an odd molten combination of yellow and red, resembling the apple that had ripened under her touch. Louder, she repeated, "Mama?"

He nodded. "Yes, your mama. If you won't tell me, I'll ask your mama."

The little girl's eyes welled with tears. Liam took a step back. He wasn't used to being around children, let alone a young lumineer who obviously lacked control over her emotions.

The child's arms flew around her torso, hugging her small frame. Thick tears rolled slowly from her eyes, streaking her cheeks with red welts, and it dawned on Liam.

"You thought your mama died? Is that why you're so quiet?"

She swallowed, trying to moisten her dry throat.

Liam released a sigh as he shoved his hands into his neatly pressed trouser pockets. "I'm sorry, kid. I should have made it clear. She's alive. Your mama is alive."

"But..." The word came out small and forlorn, much like the child herself. She didn't say more.

Liam watched her throat bob again as she swallowed. The fire of a lumineer could burn brighter than the sun, and after seeing the effects of her tears, he couldn't imagine the damage to her throat. He pulled his hands from his pockets and scratched the back of his neck. Even though the kid was a quarter of his size, she made him uncomfortable.

Meeting her sad eyes, he lightened his gruff voice and answered her unspoken question. "She's alive, but she's lost her light. She's no longer divine."

When you pass through the waters, I will be with you; and when you pass through the rivers, they will not sweep you over. When you walk through the fire, you will not be burned; the flames will not set you ablaze.

(Isaiah 43:2)

ONE

"When can you come?" Nova asked for the umpteenth time. "I really need your opinion. I know you love pink, but I'm thinking maybe a light green—celery, that's what they call it in the catalog. Maybe we can settle on a color, then you each can choose your own style of dress."

There was no nice way to put it. My friend had become Bridezilla. I held the phone away from my ear as Nova ranted on about colors, materials, flattering cuts, and heaven knows what else one could possibly say about a dress, especially one that would be worn once and *only* once. Bridesmaids' dresses were undoubtedly hideous.

Swallowing a groan, I planted a big smile on my face and hoped it relayed in my tone. "How about tomorrow?"

"Tomorrow? What time?" she squealed, and I pictured her bouncing up and down. Love had transformed my poised, polished, logical lawyer friend into a giggly teenager. "Can you come for lunch? I'll make lasagna, or Dane can grill. Or we can order take-out. Or—"

"I might be cutting it close for lunch. I teach my last

class at eleven, so I'm guessing I can be at your house around two. Does that work?" The fake smile lifted into a wide, genuine grin. Nova's cheerful enthusiasm was a welcome change after the last few weeks—one letdown after another. I'd been avoiding her, but suddenly, I couldn't wait to see her.

"Absolutely," she said. "Cam, I'm so excited for you to finally meet Dane."

"Feels like I already know him."

"I can't wait to show you the house, although it needs work. Maybe you can help me decorate after the remodel's complete. I need to pick out new sofas, a dining set. The previous owners left theirs, but we're getting everything new. Dane's letting me choose. His only request is no more grays and whites. He wants color. Oh! If there's time, maybe we can get a drink at Duffy's. I can't believe Dane and I now own a tavern. Wait until you see it. It's a townie bar with a backwoods vibe."

With a giggle, I said, "Me either. I can't wait to see everything, Nova. I'm so happy for you."

I meant it. Even though my life had been nothing short of chaotic the last few years, I was thrilled for Nova. She'd faced a destiny-altering decision head-on and found true love. Losing her station as a walking god certainly hadn't diminished her light. If anything, she seemed happier, content, at peace. Love looked good on Nova, even if it meant she carried on about hideous bridesmaids' dresses.

"Well, I have more good news to share. And a big favor to ask. Dane and I are working through the details, but we are planning a trip to see my family. I'll explain tomorrow."

"Okay." A lump formed in my throat. My only family— my mama—had been gone for decades.

After saying our goodbyes, I tossed my phone onto my

unmade bed, only to hear it buzz again as it hit the colorful, patchwork quilt. I plucked it up, figuring it was Nova calling back with some forgotten—and not-so-important—piece of information regarding her upcoming wedding. My eyes rolled when Liam Cross's name flashed on the caller ID.

"What?" I said after connecting the call. I couldn't even pretend with pleasantries.

"Where are you?" Liam wasn't good with them either.

"Excuse me?" My eyes again rolled. He brought out the worst in me. "That is none of your business."

"You're back in Milwaukee."

"Why'd you ask if you already knew?"

"You home?"

"Again, none of your business."

"Anything involving you is my business. Same place?"

"Like you don't already—" My words were cut off by a knock on the door. I yelped a startled, "Oh!" as my free hand pressed against my chest. The pounding resumed.

"Open up." Liam's voice sounded through both the earpiece and the door.

Releasing an exasperated huff, I unlocked the door and swung it open. There stood Liam, looking infuriatingly irresistible. He didn't smile; he rarely did.

"Liam. So good to see you," I said with exaggerated cheer. "And to what do I owe the pleasure?"

"Cut it out, kid. We've got to talk." He still didn't smile. Liam raked his hand through his shaggy hair, a sure sign he was irritated or distressed. He did it a lot around me.

"Kid?" I rolled my eyes for a third time, then let them roam around his face, taking in the rugged features that dominated way too many of my dreams. Steely gray eyes, dirty-blond hair, a square jaw that had a perpetual five o'clock shadow. And those lips... luscious, full, soft. If only they weren't permanently set in a scowl. "I suppose when you're like, ancient, I probably do seem a bit youthful." I grinned and fluffed my hair.

I stopped celebrating my mortal birthday long ago, not since Liam brought me to the Hark when I was nine years old. One of the many perks of being divine meant I didn't age, unless I wanted to, but what woman would willingly take on wrinkles? I eternally looked to be in my late twenties, although I was born over ten decades ago.

"Let me in," he commanded, nodding toward the apartment.

"No." My fingers clenched over the wooden edge. We locked eyes, playing our usual game—a staring contest. Although it was useless. Liam always won.

Blinking less than ten seconds in, I tried a different tactic, just to annoy him. "Ask nicely, and I'll invite you in."

"Why does it always have to be difficult with you?" His gray eyes narrowed, and he cocked his head. The simple gesture transformed him from breathtakingly handsome to dark and dangerous.

I surrendered with a sigh, pulling the door wider and stepping aside to allow him access. He brushed past me, and I took another step back to create more space between us. Touching him was like napalm to my skin.

"You're moving?" Liam hitched a thumb toward one of the cardboard boxes littering my tiny studio.

"I never unpacked." I waved him toward the bed. In my four-hundred-square-foot studio, there were not many places to sit—the bed or one of the moving boxes. Liam took a seat on top of the patchwork quilt, looking sorely out of place with his broad shoulders, black T-shirt, and distressed jeans that clashed against the cheerful pattern. I leaned against the wall, crossing my arms over my chest. "Why are you still here?"

Here meaning Milwaukee. Liam was based out of Chicago.

"Business."

"Okay. So why are you *here?*" I pointed to the worn carpet, now referring to my apartment. We'd kept our distance from one another the last several years.

"Business."

"I'm your business?" I raised a brow.

As a presiding angel, Liam held great power among gods and mortals. He was an enigma in the divine hierarchy, an angel who could exist on earth. People thought gods were myths, when in fact, they roamed the same streets as common folk every single day.

Angels, however, were a true rarity.

Most angels lost all ties to humanity once they were elevated to the station. Unlike what people saw in the movies, they didn't have halos or dress in all white; most never walked among mortals. They lived in a realm all of their own known as the Kingdom. Pure. Perfect. Cleansed of humanity's imperfections.

Liam didn't call the Kingdom home, and he kept his humanity. His station as a presider meant he was a peace-maker on earth, a liaison of sorts that helped keep order among the gods and mortals.

But Liam definitely didn't bring me any semblance of peace.

And he was far from perfect. He was bossy, arrogant, domineering, intense, infuriating—

"You're *always* my business, Cambria." Liam cut off my thoughts with his gruff sentiment.

I blushed, even though I knew what he meant. But his

tone seemed more intimate, more personal than simple concern. Then again, I never seemed to read Liam right.

Turning so he couldn't see my warm cheeks, I stared out the sole window of my cardboard-box-sized studio, then sighed and gave a shake of my head, desperately wishing he no longer had this effect on me.

"I heard you took a little trip." His gritty voice rubbed my skin like sandpaper.

"I didn't find her," I whispered. My breath hit the pane, creating a fog on the glass.

"Celia doesn't want to be found. Let her go."

I watched the fog dissipate, then murmured, "I can't. I need to right my wrongs."

"It's a suicide mission!" he growled, and I flinched. Liam had a darkness that could wilt the bravest of souls. It was the reason I always felt safest with him.

It was also why I was terrified of him.

"I thought by now you'd learn... you'd find your way. You're too damn emotional. One of these days it's going to *ruin* you, and there will be no going back. I won't always be here to help you."

A roll of anger shuddered through my body. For so long, I'd remained guarded around Liam, holding my emotions and feelings in check. Each run-in and unspoken word only added another brick to the wall between us. Pivoting, I faced him.

Years of teaching meditation and yoga still couldn't prepare me for Liam's stormy eyes that probed down to my soul. One look and he stole my breath.

The unwanted effect only made me angrier.

I flattened my left palm across the upper part of my chest, took a deep breath through my nose, filling my lungs, then counted to three and slowly released through my mouth. It was a simple soothing exercise I taught my students at Spirit of the Sky Yoga.

In a calm voice, I said, "I know you still think I'm a child who can't control herself, but it's my life, my choice. You no longer need to feel sorry for pathetic little me. I'm not your responsibility. Got it?"

He pushed from the bed, towering over me. His eyes pinned mine, and my resolve burst like a popped balloon. I shrank under his intensity, averting my gaze to the stain on the carpet—compliments of the previous tenant.

"For over one hundred years, I've watched out for you. I'm not going to let you spiral now."

"You mean for over one hundred years you've worn my scar, the burn that never heals. A reminder that no good deed goes unpunished. You don't get to play my hero anymore. You stepped out of the role decades ago."

"Play your hero?" Liam's eyes widened for a brief second before he gained his stoic composure.

I toed the carpet and lowered my voice to a whisper. "Have you ever stopped to think maybe I don't want your help? Maybe I don't want you to watch out for me?" I peeked up at him, trying to keep my voice level. "I'm not your responsibility, Liam. Not anymore."

"Not that easy, kid. I made a promise to your mother."

"Well, Mama's been dead a long time now. I'll find Celia, and when I do, I'll no longer be your problem." I turned my back on Liam again, blankly staring out the window until I heard the door click behind him.

TWO

Gwen had been on the verge of tears all morning. Her toned arms wrapped around my waist, tugging me into a hug. In a choked voice, she said for the third time, "We're going to miss you so much."

I returned Gwen's embrace, squeezing her tightly. A warm, fuzzy feeling ignited in my core, and her eyelids fluttered closed as she released a breathy sigh. She had no idea of what just transpired—my divine energy seeping into her, nurturing her—but when she pulled away, her face glowed, and she grinned.

I never purposely used my gift of touch, but sometimes it slipped out.

As a lumineer, a patron of hope and light, physical and emotional connections stroked the flame in my belly. Mama used to refer to it as a gift while Vann, my dear friend and fellow lumineer, described it as a transfer of spiritual endorphins, a catalyst of pleasure, hope, peace, and positivity.

Everyone had an inner light—gods and mortals—but the light of a lumineer could burn hotter than the brightest sun.

Our inner fire fed off others' energy, and like any flame, sometimes it was fueled involuntarily.

Sometimes it burned out of control.

I dropped my arms and took a step back, murmuring, "I'm taking your class on Monday. It'll be like I never left."

When I was hired on as a long-term substitute, I understood the teaching gig at Spirit of the Sky Yoga would be temporary. After Audrey returned from maternity leave, the studio gave me sporadic part-time hours, but they couldn't afford to keep me on full time, as much as Gwen tried. Today's class would be my last, at least in a teaching capacity.

I'd scoured online employment postings for a new job over the last several weeks. Unlike some of my divine friends, I couldn't make money materialize out of dust. My energy as a demigod didn't work like theirs. I had to earn a wage the old-fashioned way.

"You *better* be here on Monday," Gwen said in a motherly tone, tapping her foot against the wooden floor. "I want to hear about your interview."

I didn't have the heart to tell her it'd been canceled. Instead, I put on my best poker face and nodded. I'd perfected the happy façade. "Of course. With your glowing letter of recommendation, they'd be crazy not to hire me, right?"

"Oh, Cam, I wish you weren't leaving us. We're the crazy ones for letting you go." Gwen had a huge heart, which was how I knew she'd tried every measure to justify keeping me on. The money simply wasn't there. The studio had a loyal following, but ever since Mamaste—a competing yoga studio that targeted mothers and offered free childcare during classes—opened up across the street, Sky had lost a good chunk of business. Gwen had a lot more to worry about than me.

"And don't try waiving my membership fee. Audrey already warned me. When I take a class here, I'll pay just like everyone else," I added.

Gwen grimaced. "Cami—"

"Don't make me walk across the street and join—"

"Don't you dare say their name!" Audrey called from behind.

"We can't blame them for having a good business model." Gwen sighed and offered a limp smile. "Too bad I didn't think of it first."

"Yeah, but we *can* fault them for their choice of location. I mean, seriously, right across from us?" Audrey put a hand on her bony hip. She didn't advertise it, but she used to model. With legs for days and a perfect smile, she easily could return to the industry. "I should have said something. Now it's too late. They're *stealing* our business."

Over the last several months, I also had been tempted to jet across the street and speak with the new owner. A little nudge and I could've reshaped their entire business plan. It'd be simple, almost *too* easy, to sway them.

But influencing mortals—and gods—came with consequences. I learned that harsh truth at a young age.

"All right, ladies, I have to run." I grabbed the pink canvas duffel at my feet and slung it over my shoulder. "See you Monday."

AFTER A QUICK STOP AT HOME, I climbed back into my beat-up Volkswagen Beetle—fondly named Laverne—

and prayed she'd survive the drive to Dane and Nova's new home. With a dented driver's-side door, broken taillight, and permanently lit "Check Engine" light on the dusty dashboard, every trip could be her last. Until she died on the side of the road, I couldn't get rid of her.

Laverne was my one and only permanent, big-ticket purchase, earned from my sweat. *Literally*. Every job I'd taken in the last few decades involved physical activity, from teaching aerobics to the recent barre craze. It was how I shared my gift. I taught others how to tap into their inner light. Yoga was my favorite, mostly because it combined all elements of energy—spiritual, physical, emotional, and meditative.

The human body continued to fascinate me, specifically in what I could push myself and others to do. Tapping my inner strength helped me deal with my weaknesses.

And I'd never be weak again.

The feminine British voice over the GPS instructed me to make the next exit. I pulled onto a county road and followed the directions through farmland until I came to a four-way stop. Soybean crops stretched as far as I could see. Although I was in the middle of nowhere land, I double-checked for traffic before continuing straight. At least five miles passed before a sign welcomed me to Collins Grove, population 8,524.

I still couldn't believe Nova had quit her job, got engaged, and moved from the city to a tiny town in the middle of nowhere, all within a few months. Life could change in an instant—we were both examples of that.

The speed limit dropped from fifty-five to twenty-five as the highway wound onto Main Street. Victorian homes with sweeping verandas and manicured lawns lined the quaint street, eventually thinning out to bars and mom-and-pop shops as I entered the historic downtown district. The GPS voiced a warning as I approached the corner of Main and Charles Streets. Slowing down, I noticed a chalkboard sign in front of a coffee house, advertising the drinks of the day.

Hot or Cold: Oat Milk Honey Latte
Black Tea Infused with Lavender
Made with Collins Grove Local Lavender and Honey

They had me at local and lavender.

Pulling to the curb, I parked behind an old, blue pickup truck.

"Two matching rust buckets. You and Laverne will get along splendidly," I declared before cutting the engine.

I shot Nova a text, letting her know I'd be arriving soon, then headed into the coffee shop. A concrete placard plastered above the historic building's entryway read "EST 1894," and newly paved steps led to a glass door. The coffee shop's name, The Poppy Seed, and a list of its business hours were etched on the pane.

The bells above the door jingled as I stepped in. Several heads jerked my way, and multiple sets of eyes rolled over me. The stares that came with being different—in my case, having pure white hair and amber-colored eyes—used to bother me, but I learned from a young age to live with gawks and whispers. Mama said it was because I was special.

When I was a young child, she used to tell me bedtime stories of other *special* people—people like me. Divine, she had called us.

Her magical stories included tales of foreign lands where flowers blossomed at the snap of a finger and fruits ripened with the blink of an eye. The people in her stories never grew old, and they all had special gifts. She swore I was also one of them. I had a special gift. I was divine.

Until the day of the fire, I thought her stories were silly bedtime fairy tales.

THREE

As a child, before Liam brought me to the Hark, Mama and I lived alone in a small cabin, about an hour's walk from the nearest village. Since we didn't have a horse or buggy, we rarely traveled to town, further isolating us from the outside world. For the most part, it was just the two of us, although a few neighboring farmers helped on occasion with grunt work around the cabin. In turn, Mama gave them healing salves and tea leaves made from the herbs we grew in the garden next to our cabin.

Mama wanted us to keep to ourselves. She said the outside world wouldn't understand our gift. The cruel whispers and stares during our few trips to the village reinforced Mama's claims. We were different, and sometimes people didn't accept different.

After a particularly jarring altercation, I lost all desire to accompany Mama to town. People didn't think we were different—they thought we were freaks.

"Witches," the woman had called us, jabbing a finger at Mama and me as we walked into town. "Stay away from us." She'd yanked at her son's arm and turned in the opposite direction, scurrying down the dirt road as if we had the black plague.

I didn't know what a witch was, but from the woman's accusatory tone, I knew it had to be something bad. *Evil.*

Did that woman think we were bad? Dangerous like the black plague? My beautiful Mama a witch? A disease?

The idea made me so angry, I stomped my foot, leaving a blackened print on the green grass. Smoke wafted from the singed soil, stinging my nostrils. Lava-hot tears rolled down my cheeks.

Mama gasped and pulled me into her. When she looked down, my belly burned from the sadness in her eyes. "Don't mind them, Cambria. People are afraid of what they don't know. They don't know how very special you are. You are one of the chosen."

"Chosen?" I asked as another hot tear slipped down my cheek. It seared like the wax that sometimes dripped off our candles and onto my hands when Mama read to me at night.

"You're special. Very special. *Divine.* Remember the stories I told you? You have a gift. A light burns inside you, just as it burns inside of me. That light is called hope. It can brighten the darkest skies, bring warmth to the coldest days. But we must be careful. You must learn to use your gift wisely, control your emotions. Like a fire, your light can rage out of control. And like a candle, it can be snuffed out. Your gift must always be protected."

I nodded and made a promise to control my gift—the fire that burned in my belly.

It wasn't until Papa returned that I truly understood Mama's warning.

∾

HE CAME for me on an early fall evening, a few days after my ninth birthday. The sun had begun its descent over the lake in front of our cabin. Mama and I were pulling clothes from the line when the crunch of twigs sounded from the forest. The noises weren't unusual—plenty of animals roamed the woods. But as the sounds grew louder, the air shifted, turning thick and heavy, as if a storm were imminent. Clouds quickly rolled overhead, dimming the orange rays that had been warming our shoulders.

Reaching for the last pinafore, Mama's hand stopped over the fabric, and she went still.

"Mama?" I asked, pulling her skirt. "Think it's a bear?"

"Shush, child," she whispered. Her arm slowly retreated to her side, and she cocked her head, listening intently.

The hairs on the back of my neck rose as the crunching resumed. It grew louder and faster. Whatever it was, it was getting closer. From the heavy sounds, it had to be a big animal—no way could a bunny or squirrel make those loud snapping noises.

If it was a bear, we'd need the rifle that was propped against the wall within our two-room cabin, by the door where Mama always kept it for easy access. I was faster than Mama; it should be me to run and grab it. Bears were big and mean and had giant teeth and paws with nails as sharp as daggers. What if it attacked Mama? My heart raced, and searing droplets of sweat popped along my hairline.

I had no fear for myself, but I wouldn't let a bear get my mama.

"I'll get the rifle," I whispered before turning and fleeing for the cabin.

"Cambria! No!" Mama's plea rushed from her lips just

as a man's strong arms grasped me, lifting me from the ground and tossing me over his shoulder like a rag doll. The wind knocked from my chest.

"No!" Mama yelled. "Put her down! Don't you *dare* touch her!"

The sound of Mama's frantic voice gave fresh energy to my small body. I heaved in a breath of air, then beat my fists against the man's back. Each punch left an ashen hole in his dirty shirt until the entirety of it shriveled to shreds. Angry red welts blistered his back. He dropped his hold on my legs, and I fell to the ground.

The man snarled and stalked toward Mama. "Think you can hide her from me?"

Something hot and thick burned in me, so dense it made my limbs almost too heavy to lift. I clumsily pushed to my feet and staggered forward.

"Stay away! Get away from my mama!" I croaked. I desperately wanted to sound tough, but my saliva also felt hot and thick, making the words hard to form. They came out barely above a whisper, yet the man heard me. He went still, then slowly turned to face me.

When our eyes met, I nearly choked with despair. Blazing, amber-colored eyes clashed with my own. I recognized them. The uncanny resemblance made my tummy churn. I'd never met my father, but in that instant, I knew.

This deranged, scary man was *him*.

I was the daughter of a devil. No wonder the town shunned us. I finally knew what people saw when they looked at me.

Evil.

"Don't be afraid," the man said. "I've come to bring you home."

"Never!" Mama yelled, flying toward the man with her

fists raised. He jerked his chin, and she stumbled back, her head whipping as if she'd been slapped in the face.

The heaviness in my stomach gurgled and lurched, growing even hotter, even thicker. As Mama fell to the ground, the energy in my tummy erupted, shooting through my limbs and into my fingers and toes. My eyes burned with rage.

The man looked at me, calmly studying me with satisfaction. "Eyes of fire. Just like your papa. It's time to come home."

"Don't you dare touch her!" Mama yelled, pushing to her feet.

As the man turned in her direction with his hand raised, ready to lunge, a warrior's cry exploded from my soul, a shriek so loud the man's hands flew to cover his ears. I yelled over and over, primal, animalistic sounds that shook the ground. The air sizzled and crackled, vibrating from my screams. The whole world seemed to wobble.

Spiderwebs of fire emanated from my body. Flames flashed from my toes, zapping along the dirt and igniting the bushes and trees surrounding us. The grass shriveled into angry orange flames. Streaks of crimson traveled up the trunks of trees. Leaves wilted and turned black.

I was a fire-breathing dragon, slaying the beast in front of me—my father, my flesh, my blood. *A monster.* The flames consumed him, swallowed him whole, but I didn't stop screaming.

Even as the inferno scorched my throat raw, I still didn't stop. Over and over, I unleashed my fear, too far gone to care.

I set the world on fire and watched my father burn.

FOUR

"Welcome to The Poppy Seed!" a young woman called from behind the counter, hurling me into the present. She set a gooey brownie on top of a platter, replaced the glass dome, then met my eyes.

"Hi." I took a deep breath, planted a smile on my face, and stepped farther in. "Wow, those look heavenly."

Chocolate was a crack in my otherwise granola armor.

"We usually sell out before noon, but Denise had a special order and was in here earlier baking up a storm. They're our signature dessert. You must not be from CG." The barista wiped her hands against her black apron and grinned. "I'd recognize you, small town and all. We don't get a lot of out-of-towners after Labor Day."

"Yes, actually, I'm visiting a friend. She just moved here." I relaxed as the eyes around the shop fell away and people resumed their conversations.

"Oh! You must be Nova's friend," she said, propping her elbows on the countertop.

I chuckled, musing that Nova—of all people—now lived

in a nosy Hallmark-type town. "Yes. Still can't believe she ditched me and the city."

"Well, your loss for sure. We love Nova and Dane. Everyone is so happy with what they're doing for Duffy's, even keeping the name. That bar is a local landmark, so we were thrilled to see it saved." The woman brushed a glossy, chestnut lock off her shoulder, then pointed to my long, loose waves. "Your hair color is gorgeous. I'm a part-time cosmetology student at La Belle in Milwaukee. It's a commute, but the school is top-notch. We get instructors from Chicago, New York, Los Angeles—but I've never seen a white color so perfect and vibrant as yours. Seriously, that is hair life goals. I couldn't pull it off, but it's stunning on you."

"Would you believe me if I said this is my natural color?" I wiggled my eyebrows, which were dark brown, contrasting with the pure white of my hair.

"I'd say you have amazing genes." She giggled, then extended her hand. "I'm Nan."

And just like that, I found a kindred spirit in Collins Grove, a tiny town in the middle of nowhere.

After settling on the lavender-infused hot tea with a shot of local honey for myself, I ordered a black coffee for Nova, a mocha latte with whipped cream for Dane—Nova mentioned he had a sweet tooth—and three of the giant caramel fudge brownies. Nan packed the goodies in a pink bakery box, then slipped me the coffee shop's business card with her personal phone number and email address scribbled on the back. We parted ways with a promise to grab coffee when she was in Milwaukee next.

I juggled the drink caddy and the bakery box as I nudged the door open with my hip. The September sun bounced off the metal fender of the pickup in front of

Laverne. Squinting, I precariously climbed down the steps to the sidewalk, then placed the box and caddy on the roof of my car to fish for my keys.

The roar of a motorcycle had my head jerking upward. I caught the back of a flannel-clad driver before the bike turned and rumbled out of view.

It can't be.

As I unlocked the door and loaded the caddy and brownies into the bug, I reassured myself that it couldn't be *him*. Slipping into my seat, I tapped the GPS app on my cellphone and waited for the route to populate. I needed a new phone, but until I found another job, I'd have to make do with dinosaur service.

Finally, the route loaded, and I pulled out from the curb, only to stop at the sign a few yards up. The GPS indicated a righthand turn, the same direction as the motorcycle.

It is not him.

Besides, Nova would tell me if she were having someone join us for dinner. *Wouldn't she?*

The businesses and restaurants on Charles Street quickly thinned out to older homes. I passed a park where kids crowded the playground and fields, warming my core. I may not have had the ideal childhood experience, but seeing kids swinging and climbing reminded me of the good stuff—pushing Nova, Neal, and Celia on the swings and splashing with them in the pond behind our cottage in the Hark.

Being far older in age, I took on the big-sister role, although Neal, Nova, and Celia quickly surpassed me in power and energy. They were walking gods while I was a demigod—a lowly lumineer among the divine's most powerful.

We all had one thing in common—we were all raised by Lucille, a guardian in the Hark.

Lucille never treated me differently, and I was sure the children never noticed the plateau in my abilities. While Nova and her twin brother, Neal, could change the crystal-clear pond to a briny, pulsing ocean with a nod of their chin, it nearly wiped me out to summon a single cloud in the sky.

I never felt jealous. There was no room for that on my guilty conscience.

Past the park, I turned onto Lake Road where dense clusters of trees lined expansive lawns. The GPS voiced a warning for Nova and Dane's house, yet I missed it and had to turn back at the next driveway. From Nova's description, I knew they had a lot of land and were on a lake, but I couldn't see either from the road.

As Laverne chugged up their long drive, a sprawling, two-story white house with four pillars and a spacious veranda came into view. Eyeing the hanging baskets and rocking chairs on the porch, I double-checked the address on my phone. Nova's tastes certainly had evolved over the last few months, from a sophisticated loft in the city—a combination of white leather and fine art—to a sprawling country home in the middle of a forest.

Laverne sputtered to a stop, making a weird choking sound before releasing what I swear sounded like a cough. I scrunched my nose and turned the key in the ignition back and forth. Nothing happened. *Don't do this to me now, girl.* Maybe she needed time to cool down.

I knew how that felt.

My emotions used to burn out of control. Now, I could cool them with a smile. Coping mechanism, I supposed. A happy façade helped me balance the delicate flame that flickered in my belly.

Brushing my car woes aside, I climbed out and moved around to the passenger side to retrieve the drink caddy and bakery box. As I kicked the door shut and spun around, Nova appeared through the door with a large ball of brown fur squirming in her arms.

"What the—" I said under my breath as Nova simultaneously yelled, "Cami! You're here!"

She leaned over to set the wiggling furball down, then flew down the stairs and across the sidewalk to my side. Her arms were around my neck, pulling me in just as my warning to watch the hot drinks slipped out between giggles.

"So good to see you, friend," she said, drawing back. "Oh, you stopped at The Poppy Seed. Isn't it the cutest?"

"Yeah, I sent you a text. Took a guess on a drink for Dane." My smile widened as I took in Nova's sparkling blue eyes and shiny blonde curls that popped against her deep summer tan. She looked happy, healthy, carefree—a stark contrast to the last time I'd seen her.

"As long as it's loaded with sugar, you can't go wrong. I must've missed your message—" Nova was cut off by a high-pitched yap from the pup on the porch. "It's okay, Muffin!"

"And who is this?" I asked as Nova took the caddy from my hands. We walked to the veranda where she set the drinks on a small table tucked between two white rocking chairs, then bent and scooped up the dog.

"Cam, I'd like you to meet the newest member of the Nixon-Killbane household. This is Daisy, but I call her Muffin. Isn't that right, Muffie McMuffin." She pressed her nose into the fluff of fur on top of the dog's head.

Muffie McMuffin? My eyebrows raised as I watched her continue to nuzzle the dog, mentally making another addition to my "Who is this girl?" list.

"You got a dog?" I asked with obvious shock, then quickly added, "I mean, congratulations?" It sounded more like a question than a sentiment.

"I know, it's so crazy. We have a lot going on and definitely weren't looking to take on the role of fur-parents, but Daisy desperately needed to be rehomed, and when I met her, I just couldn't say no." Upon the mention of her name, the dog lifted her head and licked Nova's cheek. "She's actually not a puppy, but she's just so squishy and soft, and with these big brown eyes and her playful little personality, I think *she* still thinks she is."

"She's adorable," I said as Nova set the wiggling dog down. Daisy scooted to rub against my shins. I tucked the bakery box under my arm, crouched down and gave her belly a scratch. In turn, Daisy nestled farther into my leg. "Oh, she is sweet."

"Well, I'm glad you're taking a liking to her because *she* is the favor." Nova placed her hands on her hips and stared down at us.

I looked up. "What?"

"We've finally pulled it off. Neal agreed to come with us to Ireland to meet the rest of the family—Arthur, Anya, Mira, Nick, and Calla. All of us together." She blew out a sigh. "I know how you feel about Neal, and to be honest, I hope he doesn't chicken out last minute."

Nova rarely brought up her twin around me. I took most of the blame for Celia hightailing it out of our lives, but Neal shared a chunk of the burden too.

"What does Neal going to Ireland have to do with—" I eyed Nova, and her gaze dropped to Daisy, who yawned, bored with us. "You need a dog sitter?"

"Just for a week or two while Dane and I travel. I can't think of anyone I trust more for my fur-baby than her Aunt

Cami." Nova clasped her hands pleadingly. "It's a lot to ask, but we'll pay you, and really, Muffie isn't a lot of work at all. Just a walk twice a day, some love pats, and she's set. But we just got her, and I can't bear to board her. Her foster parents were going to watch her, but they have a new foster arriving soon who has aggression issues, so now we're in a bind. Our flight's in two days."

"Two days?" I stood up, shifted the bakery box to the other arm, and cocked my head, eyeing Daisy. She had soulful eyes that seemed to plead along with Nova. "You don't have to pay me."

"Ah, so you'll do it? Really?" She bounced up and down, clapping. Although, I'm sure she knew before asking that I'd agree to it. "You're the best! And we *will* pay you."

Nova also knew I was in a financial predicament. Extra money certainly wouldn't hurt. My mind flashed to my cardboard-box-sized studio, and I sighed. "Slight problem. Daisy might be small, but there's no way I'll be able to sneak her in and out of my apartment complex. They have a no-pet policy."

"Oh, I figured you'd stay here—if you don't mind, of course. Daisy is just settling in and getting used to a new routine." Nova grabbed the drink caddy from the table, then yanked open the screen door. "We have plenty of room for visitors. Come on, let me show you the house." Stepping through, she nodded to the wreath hanging in the center of the interior door. "I made that. The Pop—that's what locals call The Poppy Seed—hosted a class last week. This town is so adorable. Who knows, maybe after a week or two here, you'll decide to leave the city. Best decision I've made."

Nova's last few words mingled with the sounds of two distinct male voices—one I recognized.

No, no, no.

Nova flashed her megawatt smile. "That'll be the boys. I'll show you the house later. Let's get some plates for the goodies and sit on the back porch." She yelled through the screen, "Cami's here! She's already agreed to watch Daisy, and she brought treats from The Pop! Meet us out back!" I wearily looked to Nova, who beamed. "I have a sneaking suspicion you're going to love it here."

I had a sneaking suspicion I was being roped into something beyond pet sitting.

FIVE

"Novalee?" I asked, using her proper name with my big-sister voice as I trailed her into the kitchen. "Please tell me that wasn't Liam Cross's voice I heard."

"Speaking of Liam... I've been wondering forever, how exactly do you know him?"

Shifting my focus to the window above the kitchen sink, I sucked in a breath as Dane and Liam rounded the corner, coming into view. I blew out and muttered, "Great. Just great."

"What?"

Keeping my eyes on Liam, I shook my head. "I wish you would have warned me."

Outside the window, sensing my stare, Liam stopped walking and met my gaze. Our usual staring contest ensued. Nova asked a question, but I didn't really hear her. Liam held my attention hostage. To him, the game was a silly battle of wills—my way of showing defiance and challenging him. He thought I was a petulant child.

But to me, our staring contests weren't simply games. He didn't know how his eyes could paralyze me—how, sometimes, I couldn't move, think, breathe when he looked my way.

"Cam?" Nova asked, tapping my shoulder.

Liam's eyes snapped away, and he continued walking. I looked over my shoulder to Nova, who frowned.

"You okay?"

"Yeah. But Liam can be so... *Liam.*"

"You really don't like him, huh? I thought..." She trailed off.

"No. He's fine." I waved my hand and smiled. "But you know how he can be—all judgy and grumpy. I wasn't expecting to see him here."

Had I known, I possibly wouldn't have come. Maybe Nova guessed that.

"He's taking a sabbatical. Spending a lot of time fishing with Dane. Helping at the bar too." Her chin jutted toward the window where a sparkling lake lay beyond the perfectly manicured lawn.

"Really?" My brows rose. Work defined the all-mighty, all-powerful Liam. "A sabbatical? I didn't know there was such a thing for his... *kind.* He's choosing to spend it here? I mean, no offense, but he can literally go anywhere."

As a presiding angel, Liam could transcend the realms as easily as mortals crossed state lines, taking himself to the magical lands Mama used to tell me about, including the Hark.

"Yeah. This break has been really good for him. He's definitely more relaxed."

I tried not to roll my eyes. "Until he sees me. Did he know I was coming?"

Nova pivoted away to grab a knife from a drawer. She cut the brownies into halves, making six smaller pieces, and arranged them on a platter. "Can you grab those plates and napkins? Dane has a cooler of beer and water outside."

"Well, I take it from your non-answer, Liam didn't know."

"Actually, he did." Nova lifted the three to-go cups from the caddy and placed them on a tray along with the platter of brownies. "Set those on here," she directed, pointing to the plates and napkins in my hand. She spun and called over her shoulder, "Come on, Daisy."

At the mention of her name, Daisy lifted her head from within her donut curl. She climbed off her plush bed under the built-in desk and followed us to the sliding glass door that led to the back patio. Nova barely had the door open before Daisy escaped through the crack. Her tail wagged wildly as she stopped in front of Dane, who'd just come to the top of the staircase. Liam lagged a few feet behind.

As I stepped onto the patio, I squared my shoulders and took a breath. It was my first time meeting Dane, and I didn't want to come across as a grump. Although, with Liam hanging around, Dane was probably accustomed to sour moods.

"Cam, this is Dane," Nova said with a wave of her hand after setting the tray on the glass tabletop. She grinned up at Dane, who beamed back, obviously smitten with his fiancé. "Dane, this is Cami."

Dane took three steps to me and extended his hand. "Feels like I already know you."

"Same! So nice to finally meet you." My voice came out artificially high. I knew Liam's eyes were on me. I felt them, like lasers probing my skin. "I haven't gotten the official tour, but from what I've seen, the house is amazing. Congratulations—on this and, well, everything."

Our arms dropped to our sides. He motioned to Liam, and his smile widened. "You know Liam, right?"

Unfortunately. Instead of giving an obnoxious reply, I nodded and peeked over Dane's shoulder to Liam, who stood at the top of the stairs, still staring with his steely gray eyes.

"Well, let's sit down. Cam brought coffee and some treats from The Pop." Nova moved to the cooler, pulled out a water bottle, and pointed it at Liam. "You don't drink coffee, right?"

"Don't put that mud in my body."

Typical Liam, so righteous. I snorted. Liam's eyes narrowed.

"Cam's always getting on my case about eating better." Nova ignored my reaction and handed out plates, then gestured toward the platter. "Today must be her cheat day because she usually brings homemade granola." She twisted one of the to-go cups on the tray to view the name on the drink, then handed it to me. "Lavender tea—good choice."

"Cheat day?" Liam said in his low, growly voice. He eyed me, and my cheeks flamed. "The girl that survived on ice cream and soda is giving lectures on eating right?"

I clenched my jaw as I wrapped my fingers around the cup, glad to have something in my hands... before they went over Liam's mouth.

Or around his neck.

"How long have you known each other?" Dane asked. He leaned back in his chair and linked his hands behind his head. He looked almost pleased, as if he were greatly enjoying our caustic banter.

I shoved a brownie into my mouth and chewed. "Long enough." I swiped the corner of my mouth and jerked my chin toward my tea. "Think I'm going to need something stronger to get through this. Got wine?"

Nova's brows knitted. She looked from me to Dane, then lifted from her chair. "Sure. I'll grab a bottle."

After she disappeared through the patio door, I sucked in my lower lip and stared down at my plate, not feeling particularly chatty considering the company. Liam's proximity seemed to have a significant impact on my maturity level, lowering it several notches.

Dane broke the awkward silence. "Hey, guys, just want to say thanks for doing this for us. You have no idea how much it means to Nova and me."

"Hmm?" My eyes flickered to his face.

"Watching Daisy and supervising the construction crew for our remodel. We have projects here and at Duffy's. Liam's also helping manage things there while we're gone." Dane fit Nova's description—striking blue eyes, shaggy black hair, and a sinfully wicked smile. Tall, dark, and handsome. Being a former hunter, Dane had a gritty edge that made him seem dangerous—but in an exciting way, unlike Liam who just seemed *dangerous*. "We appreciate you guys pitching in. Plenty of space at the house here for you both."

"B-both?" I stuttered. My eyes shifted to Liam, then back to Dane. "Here?"

Dane nodded. "I know it's a crazy time to sneak away, but Nick and Mira can't stay in Ireland much longer. Calla's growing stronger by the day. They need to head to the Land sooner rather than later."

Before I could stumble over another one-word reply, Nova came through the sliding door with a bottle of wine in one hand and two long-stemmed glasses in the other. With my lower jaw practically hitting the table, I tilted my head up to meet her bewildered eyes.

"Uh, everything okay?" she said, glancing at Dane.

He shook his head and shrugged. "Yeah, fine. Why?"

Nova set the bottle down and began dispensing wine into a glass. "Cam?"

"B-both of us staying here—at the house?" I managed to get the words out as I tapped my fingertips against the glass tabletop.

Oblivious, Dane nodded enthusiastically. "Four bedrooms. Plenty of space."

"An entire city isn't enough space," I muttered, shaking my head.

"You're such a child," Liam said under his breath.

"Oh, stop. Just because you're ancient doesn't make me a kid, Uilliam." I glared at him, then grabbed the wine glass off the tabletop.

"Uilliam?" Dane's brows rose. His lip twitched, suppressing a smile. "Really? And you made fun of *my* name?" He looked at Nova. "Remember, he mocked Dane *Kill*-bane? Said I should change it to In-sane. Or was it No-brain? 'Member that?"

"How exactly do you two know one another?" Nova asked, ignoring Dane and giving an obviously annoyed nudge to his arm. She brought her wine glass to her lips and took a sip.

I chugged mine.

"Long story from a long time ago," Liam answered.

"Apparently not long enough," I grumbled. Sighing, I set my emptied wine glass back down and clasped my hands together. "Listen, Nova, I wish I could help you guys out, but this isn't going to work. As you can see, Liam and I can't even get through a drink without wanting to kill one another."

"Don't want to kill you," Liam mumbled.

"Isn't there anyone else you can ask?" I rested my hands in my lap and looked to the sky, as if it could send down someone—*anyone*—else to take my place. "If Liam's staying here, can't he watch Daisy?"

"No," Nova replied, vehemently shaking her head. "I mean, no offense, Liam, but I think Daisy is a bit terrified of you."

"Aren't we all?" I murmured.

"What was that?" Liam griped.

Nova's lower lip jutted out as her shoulders slumped. "We can delay our trip. It's no big deal."

As heat crawled from the back of my neck to my cheeks, I averted my eyes. I really didn't want to let her down. Her family had gone through so much in the past few months; they deserved this reunion.

Nova blew out a puff of air, then placed her palms flat against the table, resolving herself to the disappointment. "Really, it's probably better if we plan for another time. With the bar and home remodels, and Daisy finally warming up to us, the timing is all wrong."

Dane set his hand over Nova's. "Babe, what about Calla? If you don't see her now, it might be a while before they all can return. And Neal finally agreed to meet your parents. You go. I'll stay home. I can join the next time everyone can make the journey—"

"I'll do it." Shaking my head, I said firmly, "I can do it."

Dane looked expectantly at Liam, who shrugged and said, "Never had a problem with it."

I rolled my eyes.

"Really?" Dane grinned and rubbed his palms together. "Thanks, Cami. I knew I'd like you. You too, *Uilliam*. I knew I could always count on you."

Picking up and wiggling my glass, I planted a smile on my lips. "How long did you say you'll be away?"

"Um, a week. Two at most?" Nova poured a splash of wine into the outstretched glass.

"I'm going to need much, *much* more of this." I swallowed the entirety of Nova's pour in one gulp, then set the glass down. Racking my brain for a solution, I reasoned for an alternate plan that didn't include Liam and me sleeping under the same roof. "Well, I can't take Daisy to my apartment, so I guess Liam will have to stay at a hotel. There's got to be a hotel in this tiny town."

"It's probably easier for Liam to stay here. Once they get started, the foreman said his crew will be coming as early as six in the morning and may stay until sundown. This house has good bones, but it needs work." Dane looked admiringly to the brick wall behind him. "We got it for a steal. And the bar is about two miles from here. Liam's going to manage things for us there too while we're gone."

Nova shook her head. "Oh, come on, Cam. The house is big enough for the two of you. It'll only be a week... maybe two."

A week seemed like an eternity, even when immortal.

Dane and Nova excused themselves from the table to start dinner, although it most likely was their way to escape the awkward tension and side-eyed glares between Liam and me.

With the two of us left alone, the silence only made things worse. Tension overshadowed the warm September sun. I stared down at my plate. Liam cleared his throat, maybe his attempt at getting my attention since I'd been avoiding eye contact. I plucked a crumb from the tabletop and flicked it onto my plate, then started stacking the cups and dirty plates onto the tray Nova left behind.

"Need a hand?" he asked, pushing his chair back.

I paused with the heavy tray gripped in my two hands and slowly tilted my head toward Liam's outstretched arm, remembering a time when he first asked me to take his hand.

Don't be afraid... Take my hand... Don't let go.

SIX

Mama always said fate brought Liam to us the day Papa came for me. I regarded fate as an ironic, formidable force.

Maybe it was fate's hand. Or maybe it was the ethereal fires igniting the darkened sky. Whatever drew Liam to our remote cabin in the woods brought him with only minutes to spare. He worked to contain the raging fire as Mama cradled my spent body.

"Open your eyes," she'd pleaded. "Please, Cambria. Let me see your eyes."

I was so weak, and my lids felt like sandpaper, but I peeked them open.

"Oh, my baby. My sweet child. Your light is gone." Mama wept as she cupped my cheeks.

While my memories of the events that followed were foggy, I'd never, *ever* forget the soothing sensation of Mama's divine light seeping into my skin as it left her, tempering my quenched soul. She fed me her energy, reigniting my extinguished light. Liam stumbled to us just as Mama went limp.

"Take my hand. Take my hand..." The echoey, gravelly voice rang in my head as unconsciousness blackened my vision.

I woke in a strange cottage with a strange woman peering over me. Muddied memories flittered in and out of my young mind, but when I saw the strange man from the fire, I realized the terrible night had to have been real.

Days later, Liam entrusted me into Lucille's care, and then he left without a goodbye, seeming to disappear into thin air. Weeks passed, and I wondered if I'd ever see my mama or the mysterious stranger again.

Lucille and I quickly developed a new routine in the glorious land she called the Hark. Just like the fairytales Mama used to tell me at bedtime, this surreal world defied imagination. Every color shone crisper, brighter, purer—from the emerald-green grass in the endless fields and the powder-soft clouds in a baby-blue sky to the crystal-clear waters of the pond. Mama's bedtime stories did not do this magical land justice.

I was too shy to ask Lucille if the Hark was indeed one of the mystical lands Mama had told me about. Instead, I would wordlessly follow her around during the day as she gardened and cooked. We'd gather the fruits and vegetables that ripened before our eyes. One bite into an apple from Lucille's orchard and I *knew* I somehow must've traveled to the place Mama had promised existed.

The Hark simply was too perfect, too pure, too sweet, too intense, *too everything* to be part of the harsh world I'd just escaped.

But my poor Mama was still *there*. And here I was, experiencing the beauty and glory of the Hark. The thought of Mama suffering would bring instant, scorching tears to my eyes that welted my cheeks over and over.

Every night, Lucille would tuck me into my small wooden cot, place my handsewn dolly under my arm, and pull the quilt to my chin, ending with the promise, "Uilliam will be back, and then I will learn your name." I still hadn't spoken more than a word or two.

She'd kiss my forehead and sing me to sleep. Lucille's gentle voice soothed my fears, but nightmares of the fire and Mama's limp body continued to plague me. I'd never forget the raging-red glow of Papa's eyes when he lunged for Mama or my own surge of uncontrollable fear and hatred as I fought back.

That's all I really remembered of the minutes that followed Papa's attack—all-consuming rage, overwhelming fear and red-hot fire.

Sometimes, when I closed my eyes, I could still see it. Waves of fire rolling over and over and over...

The terrible dreams came nightly, but one morning, I blinked awake to find Mama's amber-colored teary eyes carefully studying me. Over her shoulder, the wooden cross I'd whittled out of driftwood dangled precariously from a rusted nail. I was no longer in my cozy cot in the beautiful cottage with Lucille. My small mind worked to find a reason.

Was the fire a terrible dream? A nightmare?

"Shh, shh," she cooed as I began twisting frantically in her hold. "It was a long trip. Settle now." Mama ran her hand through my hair and down my cheek. I melded into her hold. Minutes passed, and my heart settled. In Mama's arms, I felt whole again.

I'd almost convinced myself the Hark was a dream when a deep, gravelly voice broke the silence. "Told you I'd find out your name."

I stiffened in Mama's arms, recognizing the voice.

"Cambria, I hope you didn't give Uilliam a hard time. He says you aren't speaking. That can't be true now. Not my chatty cat."

The air in my lungs deflated. The fire was *real*. Mama had lost her light. And Papa...

Fear twisted my stomach, turning my skin hot and sweaty.

"Settle now, Cambria," Mama hushed. "You're safe now. Uilliam saved us."

The horror of what I'd done hit my body in waves of grief. Shame burned my cheeks. Sweat sprouted along the back of my neck as tears welled in my eyes.

"No, no," Mama whispered, swiping the fiery droplets from my cheeks. "You must control your gift, child."

But it was too late. I couldn't control the darkness that simmered under the surface of my skin. It ran through my veins, mingling with the blood that made me divine.

For as long as I could remember, I'd heard the whispers and felt the stares, but I never knew what other people saw in me... until I met my papa. He unleashed the part of me that was from him.

I was like him. *Bad*. Maybe even worse.

"You're gonna hurt yourself again," Uilliam said, pushing from his seat and moving to the window against the farthest wall. "Was afraid of this."

My eyes darted up as he leaned against the sill and looked outside. Sunshine danced along his sandy hair. His crisp white blouse stretched across his strong, broad shoulders and tapered at his waist. I wondered if the blisters had healed yet.

Glancing from the sill, Uilliam sighed. "She can't stay."

Mama didn't reply, but from the subtle quake of her body, I knew she was nodding. A jolt of panic shot from my stomach to my limbs. A light fizzling noise sounded as my anxiety burst from my fingertips and into Mama's arm. She gasped and loosened her hold.

"Now, now, Cambria," she scolded, clasping my hand. "It will be okay. Uilliam's given me his word. He'll help you. You must trust him."

I shook my head. Hot tears poured from my eyes, burning my cheeks as they rolled over the contours of my small face and down my neck. The wetness singed like magma, yet I barely felt the pain.

"Please don't cry," Mama pleaded. "Please, Cambria."

"Look at me," Uilliam commanded. I couldn't help but do what he said, even though I was terrified. "You must control your energy. You can never allow your emotions to take over again. Your mama and I made a deal." He stopped when he noted my wide eyes. His harsh voice gentled. "I'll help you, but you have to do your part too. Okay?"

I didn't say anything, just blinked. Mama nudged me. "Answer him."

I buried my head into the crux of her arm. Mama didn't know how badly my throat still hurt or how desperately I tried to keep my emotions under control.

The physical pain of my scorched throat didn't hold a candle to the pain that burned my heart—knowing *I* was the reason for the fire.

I was the reason Mama had lost her gift—her light.

I had no idea what'd happened to Papa, but I wished he was dead. I wished it was *him*, not Mama, who'd lost their divinity.

"Cambria," Mama coaxed, "come on now. Don't be rude to Mr. Uilliam."

I begrudgingly looked up, catching Uilliam's unyielding

gaze. The fire in my belly cooled by the chill in his stern eyes.

"Until you learn to control your gift, you'll live in the Hark. Lucille will be your guardian. Mind your manners with her. She's a good teacher. I've promised your mama that I'll bring you for visits. Maybe one day you'll be able to make the journey and transcend the realms yourself, but I will be the judge of when and if that time comes. You have a powerful gift, Cambria. There's a light that burns in your soul, and if you let it, it'll ignite the darkest sky, warm the coldest night. That light is called hope." Uilliam's voice lowered. "That light can also ignite for other reasons, as you are well aware. No more fires."

Mama shifted me in her arms. "You're safe now. No more need for fires."

I swallowed, trying to moisten my scratchy throat. "You?"

"I'm safe too. He's gone," Mama replied softly.

Nodding, I searched Mama's face. It'd only been a few weeks since the fire, but she seemed to have aged. Lines I hadn't noticed before etched along her forehead and at the corners of her eyes and mouth. They reminded me of spider webs, and I hated spiders. Her eyes no longer sparkled like sunshine. The energy that had once glowed within her soul now burned in mine.

"It'll be okay," Mama promised. "Thanks to Uilliam, we will be okay."

"We need to go soon," Uilliam said. He shifted from foot to foot, glancing toward the door. He was a big man, even bigger than Papa. Maybe he *could* keep us safe.

Mama stroked my hair. "He'll bring you to see me again. You get better now, okay?"

"Lucille will treat her well." Uilliam returned to the

window to stare outside. The cottage stunk like a stale campfire, and I wondered if Uilliam was assessing the forest behind our cabin. I didn't know how much of it'd burned, and I was too ashamed to ask. "It's time."

My arms wrapped around Mama's neck, and I squeezed. Maybe if I held on tight enough, Uilliam wouldn't be able to take me back.

But Mama easily peeled my arms away and kissed the top of my head. "How does it work, Uilliam?"

"We'll walk that way." He hitched his thumb toward the forest beyond the window. "Then we'll be gone. She'll wake in the Hark, like coming out of a dream."

"That doesn't sound so scary, right?" Mama asked me.

My lower lip jutted out and trembled.

"Normally I'd wait till she's asleep." He shrugged. "Don't have the time."

Mama pulled me in for another squeeze and whispered into my hair, "I love you. No tears now, okay?" I nodded, even as my eyes filled with them. "Uilliam, tell Lucille to stroke her hair when she's upset. Calms her down."

A broken sob spilled out, and my small hands flew to my mouth to cover the sound. I didn't want Mama to see me sad, not after everything I'd already put her through.

"Control," Uilliam coaxed. He crossed the room and turned around. "I promise you, your mama will be okay. Now, it's time to go." He opened the door and stepped out.

Somehow, I knew Uilliam was the type of person who meant what he said. I slipped from Mama's lap and followed him. Mama stayed in her seat. I didn't look back. If I saw she was crying, I'd run back into her arms, and that might make Uilliam mad.

Wordlessly, I followed him out of the door and to the blackened clearing in front of our cabin. Ash and dust floated at our feet and wafted up to my nostrils. I hated its stench.

"You trust me?" he asked as he glanced to the forest. "Speak up. No more silent treatment."

"Yes, Mr. Uilliam," I whispered hoarsely.

He looked down at me and grinned, transforming from a scary stranger to the most beautiful man I'd ever laid eyes on. "Call me Liam, kid."

The corners of my lips lifted into a hint of a smile. I nodded but stopped walking as we approached the end of the burnt clearing. I didn't want to go into the forest. What if a bear was in there? Worse, what if *Papa* was in there, hiding? Waiting for me?

"Don't be afraid. Take my hand," Liam urged.

He waited for me to move. My wary eyes traveled from his palm to his face. I studied him, noticing the formidable features of a man who surely wasn't of this world. I'd only heard of the gods and goddesses who walked among us from Mama during bedtime stories when she would tell me her fairy tales. She always said I was special, but I was nothing like Liam.

He was breathtakingly beautiful.

"Go on," Liam said with a smile. "Take my hand and don't let go."

I hesitated, looking from Liam to the forest. Papa wouldn't dare cross a man like Liam. No, he'd get one look and run.

I reached for Liam's outstretched hand and made a silent, solemn promise to never let go.

SEVEN

"Cambria?" Liam asked, placing his outstretched hand on my bicep. I jerked back to reality.

Shrugging off his hold, I set the tray back onto the table and straightened. "Listen, I don't know what those two are trying to pull, but we both know this"—I waved my arm toward the house— "is not going to work. After they leave, we'll figure out how to get through the week they're gone."

One to two weeks. One to two weeks. I repeated the mantra in my head, then muttered out loud, "It better be only one."

As a child, I'd counted the days until I saw Liam again, although I never knew exactly when to expect him. Unlike the mortal world, time in the Hark didn't follow calendars or rely on watches. Now, the idea of spending time with Liam set my heart racing for a different reason.

"Let's just get through this for them." I picked up the tray again and pivoted away, but Liam was in front of me in a flash. The man was big and bulky, yet he somehow could move like a ballerina. Rolling my eyes, I asked, "Now what?"

"Your car."

"What?" I tightened my grip on the tray.

"Sounds bad."

I blinked. He either had bionic hearing, which was possible considering his strength, or more than likely, he had one of his birds following me. I'd gotten used to them over the years, hardly noticing the strange creatures he used to keep tabs on my whereabouts.

Liam stepped in front of the patio door, blocking my way. His gray eyes narrowed as he glared down at me. "Don't leave before I check it out."

"It's fine," I muttered. "You wanted to give me a hand? Well, get the door."

Liam never showed vulnerability, but his gruff voice lowered almost pleadingly. "Hate what we've become."

I brought my eyes up to meet his, startled by his confession. Liam used to be my world, my dream, my future.

I hated what we'd become too.

"Never wanted it to be like this." He leaned in, and his breathy words brushed my forehead, just as his calloused hands used to when I was younger. Whenever I was upset, Liam did as Mama had suggested long ago, caressing my hair to calm away my fears.

Before I could reply, the door behind Liam slid open.

"Cami!" Nova exclaimed from within the kitchen, Daisy at her heels. "You're a guest here. You don't need to clean up. I was just coming to grab that."

"It's no problem." I broke away from Liam's stare and slipped past him. My elbow brushed against his forearm. Any contact with Liam evoked a physical reaction—an almost visible energy that seemed to buzz between us. I shivered and prayed Nova and Liam didn't notice the little quake of my body. I hated that he still had that effect on me.

"Here, give me that. I'll take care of this later. First, I want to give you a tour." Nova took the tray from my hands and placed it on the kitchen counter. "Come on. I'll show you the lower level first."

Daisy and I followed her to the adjoining dining room while Liam stayed behind with Dane in the kitchen. I didn't look back, but I knew his eyes were on me.

"We'll be stripping the wallpaper in here and having it painted." Nova wrinkled her nose, eyeing the floral monstrosity that caked the walls. "No idea what the previous owners were thinking with this print."

I trailed Nova through the two-story house, only half hearing her chatter about the ongoing home renovation and changes at the bar. Apparently, Liam would not only keep an eye on the construction at the house, but he'd also be overseeing Duffy's, which had recently changed into Nova and Dane's ownership.

"It's a townie bar. The kind where everyone knows everyone—like Cheers—but with deer antlers and stuffed fish on the walls. You walk in and the whole place turns to see who's there."

I chuckled, recalling the coffee shop. "Yeah, I got a taste of that at The Poppy Seed. Nan seems really great. We exchanged numbers."

"She's a sweetheart. The whole town has welcomed us with open arms. You'll like it here. Much less chaotic than the city." She smiled faintly as she stopped in front of the first door at the top of the staircase. "I know it's been a rough couple of years. Maybe a change of scenery will do you good."

My grin faded. "Not if the 'scenery' includes Liam."

Nova's hand lingered over the knob. She turned to face me. "Honestly, Cam, I don't want you to do anything you don't feel comfortable with. If staying here with him makes you uneasy, we can reschedule." She looked me in the eye, watching for my reaction. "What's your deal with him anyway?"

I sighed, knowing Nova would eventually get it out of me. It was the lawyer in her. Once she set her mind to something, she wouldn't stop until she heard the whole complicated story.

"Where do I start?" I gestured toward the door, and she pushed it open. Daisy stayed at Nova's side as we stepped into a guest bedroom decorated in shades of blue. I went to the window, pretending to check out the view of the backyard.

I'd never share all the intimate details of my past with her, yet my cheeks flushed as I considered what to say. Thinking about Liam brought up a palette of emotions, from lust and passion to betrayal and pain.

Unsure where to start, I stared outside and rolled over the series of events that wove our stories together. Nova's backyard reminded me a bit of Mama's cabin. Plush green shrubs and bushes lined the perimeter, allowing peeks of the lake. A long wooden pier jutted from an opening along the shoreline.

I couldn't imagine Liam out there fishing, although he used to fish with me when we visited Mama.

Now, he never relaxed. He didn't have time for that.

Exhaling long and slow through my nose, I turned in Nova's direction. "I lived a lifetime before Neal and you came to the Hark. Liam was a part of that life. He was different then. Still Liam, but softer. Gentler. Funny and kind. You know how this world changes us. It certainly changed him."

Nova's brow furrowed as she moved from the doorway

to my side. Gazing out the window, she said quietly, "I don't know if it's the fresh air, lake life, or Dane's cheesy jokes, but Liam's changing again. He even has some cheesy jokes of his own. He's actually quite funny."

"I really don't foresee any comedy routines between us. We seem to bring out the worst in each other."

We watched as Dane and Liam strutted into the back-yard. They stopped in front of a pristine white shed that looked like a tiny replica of the main house. Dane gestured toward the building before unlatching the door and disappearing inside.

I sighed. "We'll make it work. And who knows, maybe you're right. Maybe I do need a change of scenery."

Dane reappeared with a lawn mower. He pushed it next to Liam, leaned over, and yanked the pull string. The engine roared to life. Dane stepped aside, and Liam took hold of the mower. Dane pointed around the yard, then bent to cut the engine. Next, Dane motioned to the mani-cured flowerbed lining one side of the shed. They both crouched down to look closer at the garden.

"You have to admit, the scenery here isn't bad," Nova said as she elbowed my side.

As if hearing the compliment, Liam glanced up to our window. Nova gave a little wave.

"If I want nice scenery, I'll check out Vann," I said. Liam looked away. He couldn't possibly have heard me, yet I felt a twinge of satisfaction. Liam despised my friend and fellow lumineer, Vann.

"Oh, so Vann and you are on again?" Nova asked, cocking her head. "I forget since your status with him changes weekly. He's a flake."

Vann and I had never dated. And he had a boyfriend.

But I wouldn't let Nova in on either fact. I grinned. "A hot flake."

"Does he still do gigs?" she asked lightly.

"Yeah." Guilt and sadness tinged my voice, and I gave a shake of my head, trying to sweep away the emotions.

Nova's twin, Neal, and Vann were both musicians, but that's where their similarities began and ended. While Vann was serious about his divine calling, utilizing music to spread hope, Neal exploited his. Neal used his gift—his words—to influence Celia. He wrote poetry and songs to manipulate her—just like my father had used his divine charms to deceive my mother. When Vann realized it, he told me, and I freaked out.

I'd rushed to Celia before thinking things through, before calming myself. It was all too similar to my parents' story. In my heightened emotional state, my touch—the touch of a lumineer—shattered her trust and crushed her heart. I projected my pain, fear, and insecurities onto her. She fled, shunning her divine responsibilities. I'd been looking for her since, knowing I could finally use my gift for good.

I'd return her hope. I'd give her the light that burned in me—Mama's light. I never deserved it anyway.

"Speaking of gigs," Nova said, interrupting my thoughts, "Duffy's has live music every weekend. Can't wait for you to see the place. Think you'll have time to walk over there tonight after dinner?"

"Walk there? Didn't Dane say it was like two miles away?"

"There's a trail we catch up the street that follows Sully's Creek. It's a beautiful, winding path through the woods. The creek eventually empties into the lake by Duffy's. I've been walking or biking to work."

"Wait, you're *working* at the bar?" My brows shot up. Before Nova and Dane hooked up, she was a corporate attorney at a hotshot law firm in the city. "That's quite a change."

"Yep. I went from taking the bar to working *in* a bar." Nova laughed and tucked a blonde curl behind her ear. With her stunning looks, I could only imagine how often she got hit on at the bar. I wondered how Dane put up with it. "I'm telling you, Cam, life is different here. Being surrounded by nature, having a community that treats us like family... Dane and I are home. We've *finally* found home." She gently grasped my elbow, and her voice lowered. "Maybe you can too."

I shrugged off her hold and turned away. Any talk of home brought a knee-jerk reaction, an instant jab to my heart. While I'd come a long way from the little girl whose tears seared flesh, I still battled to control my insecurities. I'd lost more than my home.

I had lost it all.

"Cami?" Nova asked, placing her hand on my elbow again. "Want to talk about it?"

I shook my head. I'd known Nova her entire life, yet she knew little of mine. Shame prevented me from sharing the details of my past.

Nova studied me for a second, then turned and continued the tour of the upper level, chattering on as if nothing had happened. I let her lead the way out of the bedroom to the hallway. Daisy obediently followed at our heels.

"We painted this ourselves. The cosmetic stuff is easy. Construction starts Wednesday."

The lingering scent of fresh paint wafted from pristine white walls. Nova gestured toward the door at the end of the hall. "Why don't you take our room while we're gone? You probably won't even run into Liam, but at the least, you won't have to share a bathroom." We moved inside the room, and Nova opened one of the interior doors to reveal a spacious en suite. She pointed to the giant whirlpool tub built for two that occupied the farthest wall. The window above it glowed from the late afternoon sun. "Great for relaxing with bubbles, candles, and wine."

"I'll need it." *Especially with him in the house.*

I didn't say it aloud, but Nova must've caught the insinuation because she said, "You probably won't even see him. He'll be busy here, or he'll be at Duffy's, managing things there."

"So, is everyone working at the bar?" I chuckled.

"There's a job there for you too. We always need help. As great as the staff is, they're young and unreliable. You know how it goes." Nova absently waved a hand as she led me out of the bedroom and to the top of the stairs. "Liam will be filling in as needed while we're gone."

"It was a stretch picturing you working at a bar, but Liam?" I ran my fingers over the smooth, gleaming banister. "I just can't."

"Well, it's not like he's making a career of it. He's been staying with us off and on the last month—helping Dane. They've become thick as thieves. They're good for each other. Kinda balance each other out. Liam's keeping Dane levelheaded with all the chaos of construction and taking over the bar, and Dane's helping Liam to not take everything so seriously."

"Yeah, good luck with that."

"Really. He even almost got Liam to do karaoke at Duffy's."

My jaw dropped. "No."

"This close." Nova held up her thumb and pointer finger, leaving a small gap between the two digits. "Another beer and a star would've been born."

"Now that I'd have to see." I giggled and continued down the carpeted stairs.

"Oh, there's more." Nova hit the landing and turned around. "There's a group of seniors that comes in on Thursday afternoons for Euchre—it's a card game that's popular around here. Sometimes they stay for happy hour. One night, this little eighty-year-old lady went up to Liam and asked him to dance. The two of them had the entire bar line dancing by the end of the night!"

The more Nova spoke of Liam, the more the memory of the man I used to know came back to life. The man whose eyes glimmered like molten metal when he looked my way. The man whose voice soothed my aching soul.

The man whose lips ruined me for any other.

"Well, that's it," Nova said, freeing me from the memory. She placed one hand on her hip and waved around the foyer with the other. "Our new home. What do you think?"

There was that word again.

Home.

EIGHT

The Hark remained my home well into adulthood. Liam kept his promise to my mother. He would come to Lucille's cottage several times a year to help me transcend the realms and see Mama.

Decades went by. Automobiles replaced the horse and buggy. Electricity and indoor plumbing became standard. Radios, television, telephones, cars, and airplanes linked a vast world. Life moved on, and Mama grew older along with it while at some point, I stopped aging.

During our earlier visits, Liam would tell me all about the world's newest innovations while we fished from the shoreline in front of Mama's cabin. He'd take me to the fair when it came to town or to a matinee movie at the cinema or for candy at the five-and-dime. We'd end our trips with ice cream or hamburgers at the local diner.

Mama never joined us. Roads and highways connected the cities surrounding Mama's land, but she was content to remain isolated in her small, remote cabin on the lake. I don't think she ever left.

As time passed, Liam's responsibilities grew, and the

months between our visits stretched longer. When I'd see Mama, the changes in her became more obvious. Wrinkles etched her face. Her skin turned as fragile as crepe paper. She grew softer, her movements slower. I'd hug her, feel her frailty, and desperately wish I could return her light, give her the eternal youth I'd been afforded from her sacrifice.

During my last visit with Mama, she leaned in and whispered in a weak voice, "My sweet girl."

She seemed to have shrunk another inch and was as thin as a rail. Although I wasn't a tall woman, I dwarfed her. She spoke hoarsely, as if each labored word scratched her throat.

"Look at you. My girl is all grown up. A woman now, huh, Uilliam? You'll have to beat them off with a stick. I know you'll keep her safe. I trust you with her, Uilliam. I've always trusted you. Fate brought you to us that day."

His eyes flickered from Mama to me, then to the ground. Crimson spotted his cheeks. If I didn't know better, I'd have thought he was embarrassed, taken aback by Mama's comment. But that didn't make sense. Nothing fazed the almighty Liam anymore. Whatever warmth he once held for me had simmered out to a cool awareness, a barely there acknowledgment.

I'd become a burden to the formidable presider.

With a heavy breath, Liam lifted his head and squared his shoulders. "You have my word, Miss Beal. I'll always keep her safe."

"I know. It's what makes this easier." Mama smiled as I clutched her limp hand. "Darling child, I know you are sad. I see the weight of your guilt. I have no regrets, my love. I live on in you. Our fire burns as one. Be good now." Her eyes fluttered closed as her voice trailed off.

Liam's chin dropped to his chest, and he went still for a

few seconds before his body jerked. Even though I had no idea what was happening, my lungs deflated and my stomach lurched. The air seemed to have thinned to nothing. Seconds passed, and I still wasn't able to breathe. My skin slickened with sweat, and I swayed into the wall.

Something was wrong. *Very* wrong.

Liam finally looked up, but he wouldn't meet my eyes, and I knew.

Mama was gone.

"Mama!" I cried and grasped her limp hand. "No, no! Liam! What did you do?"

I twisted in his direction, and he hunched over, moaning. His left hand flew to his side, clutching the burn that still scarred his body.

"Bring her back!" I shouted through tears.

"She's gone, Cambria. I'm sorry," he muttered between groans. "I had no choice. She was called. It was her time."

"I didn't get to say goodbye." My breath turned hot as fire. Sweat dripped from my forehead. The temperature in the small bedroom notched up. Liam grabbed me by the elbow and led me out of Mama's room and through the front door of the cabin. He stopped only when I jerked from his hold. "How could you? I didn't get to say goodbye. I didn't get to tell her how sorry I am!"

Liam took a few steps back, then doubled over as I wept. Each time he tried to stand upright, my sobs would send him to his knees. He looked up with imploring eyes. "I had no choice. It was her time. There was nothing I could do."

The ground beneath my bare feet sizzled as my anger surged. "You should have brought me to her sooner! You could have let me make the journey on my own. I would have had more time with her. You can take me to her now!"

"No, Cambria." Liam shook his head. His fingers dug into his thighs as he whispered, "She's home."

"Take me to her!" I pleaded as I walked up to him. Each step left a black imprint on the green grass. I grabbed his arm, and he flinched. "Take me to see her!"

"Not possible," Liam said through clenched teeth.

"I know you can!" I screamed, stomping my foot.

"Not poss—" He broke off as a wave of pain took his breath away. Liam panted along with me. Smoke floated from his shirt, and the material near his scar blackened. He groaned into his legs, doubled over.

Heat traveled from the pit of my stomach and through each limb. I balled my hands, then slowly splayed my fingers. The tips of my fingers trembled, and my vision blurred. I took a step back, appalled at what I was quickly becoming. I hadn't felt or seen this raging-red fire since *him*.

Papa.

A ball of fury. A pit of anger. Boiling and simmering.

An outcast. A stain. A sinner.

Evil.

"Why?" I cried. Scorching tears leaked from my eyes. "Why did she do it? Why did Mama do it? Why did she give me her light? I can't control it. I can't control it because a part of me is bad. Evil."

"Don't say that. Don't ever say that again," he whispered through gritted teeth.

"I was born from sin and deceit. There's no way for me to rid myself of him. His blood flows through my every cell. It carries into my thoughts. It darkens my light. Do you see me? Look at me!" I banged my fists against his solid chest, but he didn't budge. He took my assault just as he took my pain.

Just as he wore my scar.

"I don't want to feel like this. I hate it. Mama said it was a gift. But I don't want it. Please take it. Take it away." My pleas fell in weepy mumbles. I covered my eyes, barely feeling the intense heat of my molten tears. "I can't control it. I can't control it."

Liam grabbed my wrists and gently pulled my hands from my face. He guided me into his arms, drawing me against his solid chest where I rested my scorched cheeks. The wild thumping of his heart almost drowned out my racing thoughts. He whispered into my hair, "Give it to me, Cambria. I will take your pain. Let it out. Let it out."

Over and over, he whispered into my hair, stroking my forehead with his gentle, calloused hands, calming me until my crying finally subsided.

Looking up through wet eyelashes, I whispered, "Nothing good has come from me. I'm bad. A burden. A burden to everyone. Mama, Lucille, *you*. I know that scar won't heal, even for you, the great Uilliam. My sins burn your back."

Liam released his hold. He took a step back, then reached to cup my cheeks. He held my face steady, staring into my red eyes. His thumbs rubbed away the hot tears. "I will carry your pain."

"No." I shook my head. "Mama's gone now. I can't be your burden anymore."

"You are not my burden. You have never been a burden."

But that couldn't be true. Over the last several years, when Liam and I visited Mama, he had stopped taking me to get ice cream. He no longer brought me to the lake to fish. We didn't catch matinee movies together or get hamburgers at the diner. Our trips to see Mama were made with only a few words spoken to one another. Most of the time, he wouldn't even look at me.

No matter what he said, I knew I was a burden.

A burden to everyone.

Lucille may have cared for me like I was her own, but the Hark had never felt like home. I didn't fit in there. I was a scarred demigod among gods and goddesses of great strength and purpose.

I was an outcast living above my means.

"What will I do now?" I whispered as fresh tears welted my cheeks. "Mama's gone. I have no place, no home. Mama was my *home*."

"Look at me," Liam said, lifting my chin with a finger. "You have a place. You have a home. With me. I will be yours, and you will be mine."

With his proclamation, he grabbed my elbows and pulled me in. I fell against him just as his lips smashed into mine, devouring me with an intensity that made my blood sizzle for an entirely different reason than before.

He kissed me like the men kissed their leading ladies in the matinee movies we used to watch together. With a ferocity that claimed me. With a passion that made my belly burn like the fires of a million suns.

But unlike the emotion that burst from me when I was young, this heat radiated from his sweet promise.

I am his. I am his home.

We clung to one another, our hands grasping as if we couldn't get close enough. His arms wrapped around me, pulling me into him so tightly I could hardly breathe. But I didn't care. I didn't need to breathe. I only needed him.

Liam suddenly broke away, only to lean in and connect again, slow and tender—a kiss that unlocked another part of my soul.

Papa may have unleashed a darkness in me, but Liam released a light so blindingly bright, it felt as if a part of my heart had detonated.

For the briefest of seconds, Liam and I transcended the fields outside of Mama's cabin, landing in a new place of pure perfection. Every cell in my body radiated with pleasure, purging the evil I thought had blemished my soul.

The sun. The stars. The moon.

Hope. Beauty. Peace.

A field. A lake. A kiss.

Passion. Desire. Fire.

I pulled away, gasping and heaving for air.

"Home," Liam whispered into my parted lips.

At his singular word, the world that had flashed as bright as a million suns faded into the deepest dark. A chill swept into my bones, but I barely felt it as my lids drifted closed.

I woke back in the Hark, tucked under the quilted covers in my wooden cot at Lucille's cottage. No note. No goodbye. Liam had once again left without a trace. Only this time, he never returned.

NINE

Although Nova and Dane had prepared a feast for dinner, I pushed around the food on my plate until I finally set my fork down and threw my napkin over the hardly touched steak. Liam, on the other hand, ate with the ferocity of a runner preparing for a marathon.

"Not hungry?" he said, pointing his fork at my plate.

"I'm waiting till I get home so I can stuff my face with ice cream and candy. You know me." I smiled sweetly. "It's how I survive."

"Can I have that then?" He pushed the napkin away with his fork and jabbed at my steak.

"All yours." I hated that he could go through dinner unfazed by the odd tension. My stomach was in knots. I could hardly choke down water. I had no idea how I'd survive being under the same roof as him for a full week.

One week. Two at most.

"—maybe fifteen minutes or so, if that's okay?"

Blinking, I asked, "Sorry, what was that?"

"Daisy's walks. She only needs a short one in the

morning and afternoon. Fifteen minutes or so. I'll have everything written down, but she's really quite easy to care for." Nova repeated the instructions I apparently had missed while zoned out.

Hearing her name, Daisy lifted her head.

"Do you not have return tickets?" I asked, changing lanes in our conversation. I could possibly survive one week. But two?

"We don't," Dane replied. He linked hands with Nova. "We were hoping to spend an extra week, just the two of us. But if things get hairy here, we'll come home early."

"Bar'll be fine," Liam said, waving his fork. The man was a bottomless pit. Then again, being grumpy and intense all the time probably burned a lot of energy. "The reno too. I can handle it. No problem."

"Me too. No problem," I said, swatting a hand as all eyes turned back to me. "Easy-peasy. Daisy and I will be just fine." I smiled brightly. "Just curious, why not use your gifts?" I wiggled my fingers, indicating their divine abilities. "You can probably knock out the reno in an hour, especially with *him* around." I gave a nod toward Liam. As a presider, he could build an entire house in the matter of a day using just his mind and a dab of dust.

"We need to blend in. Besides, it's a good way to connect with the community, putting some of the guys around here to work. They get a paycheck, and we're building relationships." Dane jerked his thumb toward the kitchen. "But Liam and I did cheat in there. It was a disgusting shade of green. Looked like puke."

"Speaking of puke," Nova said, scrunching her nose. "Liam, you have to watch Jonny—the guy at Duffy's who always wears tank tops with cut-off jeans. He made a mess of the bathroom twice last week. When he starts talking about the great fishing trip of 2006, he's had enough. Cut him off."

Nova and Dane carried the conversation, mainly chatting on about the bar and its quirky patrons. Talk switched to Liam's responsibilities at Duffy's while Dane was gone.

"Try to keep things civil. I'm building a reputation in this town." Dane took a swig of his beer.

"I'm always civil." Liam shoved a forkful of food into his mouth and chewed loudly.

Dane gave an eye roll and nodded. "Sure, right. Just don't give them the look."

"What look? I don't have a look," he said with wide, innocent eyes.

"Oh, you have a look." I couldn't help chiming in. His head jerked in my direction, and I tilted my chin defiantly. "You're giving it to me now."

"*What* look?" He put his fork down, the first break in his incessant face-stuffing since dinner began.

"The one that makes grown men pee their pants." Nova laughed, shaking her head. She picked up her wineglass and brought it to her lips, adding, "True story. Saw it at Duffy's," before taking a gulp.

Liam shook his head, grimacing. "I won't give them the look."

"No talking down to them either. I don't want to come back and find half the crew has quit." Dane arched a brow.

"Huh?" Liam made a bewildered jerk of his head toward Dane and flipped his palm upward. "Talking down?"

I snorted, nearly splattering my mouthful of water everywhere. Oh, this was getting fun.

"You have this way of making people feel tiny and small

and—" Dane was cut off by his fiancée, who tapped his muscley bicep.

"Honey, don't worry. Liam will do just fine. If he scares anyone away, Cami can charm them back." She then patted my hand.

I shook my head furiously. "Oh, no, no, no. You said the dog is my responsibility. You never mentioned anything about managing Liam and his bad attitude."

"I don't have a bad attitude!" Liam yelled, scooting his chair back. "And I'm sitting right here, in case you all have forgotten."

"It's just, you know," I said, pushing bread crumbs around my plate with my finger, goading him. "You can be a bit intense. No filter. Rude, demeaning, insensitive, judgmental."

"Leave anything out?" His eyes narrowed to slits of steel.

"Patronizing, condescending, abrupt." I held up a finger with each character flaw I could think of. "Controlling, domineering."

Liam's lip snarled. He shifted his focus to Dane and Nova. "You two have anything to add?"

Dane scratched his forehead in thought. "Think she pretty well covered it."

"Oh, Liam. They're just teasing you." Nova pushed from her chair and patted his back like a concerned mother. "You know we love you. You've been a huge help at Duffy's —and they love you there too. For the most part. But I guess, just, you know, watch your tone."

Liam raked his hand through his hair, then brought both arms to rest on the table. He muttered, "My tone's just fine. Mrs. Martins has no problem with my tone."

"Mrs. Martins is at least eighty. She probably can't *hear*

your tone," Dane teased. He joined Nova in stacking dinner plates. "Speaking of, we should get down there soon. Band will be setting up around seven, and I want to introduce myself to them. They'll be playing the next two Saturdays while we're gone. You going to join us, Cami?"

"Yes, please come?" Nova clasped her hands together. "Eighties cover band. I've heard they're awesome."

I looked at my wrist, checking my imaginary watch. "I should get home. Long day, and I still have to stop at the Metro Mart. Need to pick up a few things before they close." I stood and gathered my plate and cup. "Let me help clean up, then I should hit the road."

"No, I got it," Dane said, taking the contents from my hands. "You'll be cutting it close as it is. Think they close at nine. Don't buy too much—we'll have everything stocked for your stay. Really appreciate you helping."

"No problem," I lied. "I'm so happy for you guys."

We said our goodbyes on the front porch with promises to touch base in the morning on the details of their trip. Dane and Nova slipped back inside, but light footsteps trailed me to my car. I didn't need to look back to know Liam was behind me. His presence was tangible, a touch to my skin without physical contact.

Reaching for the door handle of my car, I suddenly stopped and let my arms fall to my side. With my back to him, I asked in a quiet voice, "So, is it just me?"

"Hmm?" he replied. I swear I could feel the heat of his breath, even though he was a few feet away.

"You're kind and funny and nice to everyone else. So, is it just *me*?" He didn't say anything, so I continued. "You said you hate what we've become. Well, I hate it more. But I'll never be good enough. Will I?"

"What are you talking about?" He put a hand on my

shoulder, and I shrugged it off. His touch made all thoughts flee my brain.

Gathering my wits, I turned to face him. Quietly, I said, "I heard you. The visit before Mama died. You and Lucille thought I was asleep, but I heard everything. I wasn't good enough. I'd never be good enough for the almighty Uilliam."

"What the hell are you talking about?" He leaned in closer, and I caught his unique scent—wind, wood, and mint. Liam never wore cologne; he didn't need to.

"Lucille said I could make the journey myself. She thought I was strong enough, that I had the control, but you didn't, did you?" I tried to steady my voice. *It's not safe. She's not safe.* The pain of Liam's words still stung decades later. "I'd never be good enough. You held it over me."

"That's what you think?"

"I heard you!"

He pressed his palm against his eye, as if pushing away a headache. "You heard wrong." He took a step closer.

"So, you remember?" I took a step back. My butt bumped against my car door. Liam was always formidable, but this close, he made it difficult to breathe.

He lifted a hand to brush a chunk of my snow-white hair over my shoulder. His hand grazed my neck, and I shivered. If I had problems breathing before, air became impossible. My heart thumped as I looked at my feet, unable to meet his eyes.

"This ugly world never deserved you." Liam's tender voice made my stomach flip.

Focusing on my sandals, I asked, "What happened to you? I thought... I thought you really cared."

"You." He groaned, then added quietly, "*You* are what happened to me."

His words lanced my heart. Silent seconds passed

before I gained enough composure to look at him. Before I could respond, he spoke so softly I had to watch his lips. Those darn lips that continued to haunt my dreams.

"You happened to me. I watched you grow from a scared child to an alluring adult. Into a woman. I saw your scars heal and rip open, and each time, my own scars burned with your pain. I wanted to take it away, to take you away so you'd never need to face it again. But I had no way to help you. I hated feeling helpless, and you make me feel that way."

"I didn't need you to help me. I didn't want your help. All I wanted was for you to believe in me, to be my friend."

"I didn't want friendship."

I was a burden he'd been carrying for far too long. Hearing him say it out loud stung more than I cared to admit. I averted my eyes and sniffed. "I know."

"Don't think you do."

With a nod of his head, my car started, although the keys were still tightly clutched in my sweaty hand. My body gave a startled jerk as Liam's arm brushed against me to pull open the car door. Molten steel eyes pierced me when he looked down.

In the distance, a black bird cawed as it swooped over the roof of the house, jolting my attention from Liam. I watched as it circled the darkening sky, then landed on the rail of the veranda.

"Drive safe, Cambria."

I swallowed and wordlessly climbed into my car. He shut the door, keeping his eyes on mine.

As a child, I had a crush on Liam, the man who saved me. Later, somewhere along the way, I fell in love with him. But I was never meant to love him.

He may have saved me when I was a broken child, but he left me broken as an adult.

TEN

D ane lugged the last, overstuffed suitcase to the trunk of his red Audi TT. Nova stood on the veranda with a wiggling Daisy in her arms. She pressed her face into the dog's neck for the millionth time.

"I'll miss you, Muffin," she said, on the verge of tears.

"It's just a week," I offered, giving the same pep talk I'd been replaying over and over in my head.

"Maybe two," Dane called. "We'll check in when we can. Got to go, babe!"

"Okay, okay." Nova set Daisy down, then smoothed her cotton shirt. "She needs to be fed—"

"It's all written down. Don't worry," I interrupted. Not only had we discussed everything in detail on the phone, but that morning, Nova had given me another tour of the house and had gone over Daisy's schedule with me again. "She'll be fine." *It's me I'm worried about.*

"Cathy's phone number is on the contact list on the counter."

"Cathy?"

"She was Daisy's foster mom—she and her husband live

up the road. They're wonderful. If you have any problems, call her."

"I think I'll be okay." But from Nova's nervous face, my confidence quickly faltered. I'd never cared for an animal before; I hoped I wasn't getting in over my head.

"Liam can help with her too. Daisy's kind of warming up to him."

My stomach further twisted at the mention of Liam's name. We'd left things so awkwardly on Saturday night, and I hadn't seen him or talked to him since—not that I expected him to call or stop over to rehash things.

In the week to come, avoidance was my motto. Maybe it was his, too, because according to Dane, he'd gotten up at six and had been on the rowboat fishing ever since, even knowing Dane and Nova would be leaving before lunch.

A big part of me was relieved Liam and I wouldn't face each other again with our friends as witnesses. Nova looked nervous enough leaving Daisy; she didn't need our added stress.

"Sure you don't want me to bring your bags up?" Dane asked, linking arms with Nova. "It'll only take me a minute."

I waved a hand. "No, no. I don't have much. Besides, the stairs will be good exercise. I like to keep moving."

"I've heard. What was it you taught, yoga? You know, this town could use a studio. It's small now, but I've heard rumors that a business park is being built off the highway. It's going to bring in a lot of folks."

"Seriously!" Nova chimed in. "A yoga studio in Collins Grove would be amazing. You should totally look into it while you're here."

"Sounds fun and all, but starting a business takes money." Money I didn't have.

"I'd invest in it." Nova rubbed her palms together in front of her nose.

"Personally, I think it's a great idea." Dane started toward the car, then called over his shoulder, "Babe, we've got to roll. Cam, thanks again for everything. Keep an eye on Liam!"

"No way. He's your mess to deal with!" I hollered back as Nova wrapped her arms around my neck and squeezed.

"You're the best, Cam." She leaned away. "I hope this week goes well. I have a good feeling about it."

I sighed.

She released her hold and crouched to give Daisy a final pat on the head. "You be a good girl, Muffie."

"We'll be fine," I replied calmly. "Go on, before you guys miss your flight."

Nova offered a wan smile before turning toward the car. She climbed in and gave a half-wave as the car roared to life. Daisy and I watched the car back up, then roll forward to head down the long drive. They disappeared into the thick, green foliage.

"It's just you and me now, Muffie." The dog lifted her head toward me and made a whiny noise. "You don't like the nickname either? Daisy it is. Come on, girl. Let's get my bags."

She obediently trailed me to Laverne. The car hadn't given me any more trouble since Saturday night. I'm sure I had Liam to thank for that. I wouldn't complain. Money was tight as it was, and car repairs weren't in my limited budget.

If only I had a nest egg. A yoga studio of my own would be a dream come true. I loved helping people find peace and healing through their mind and body. Heaven knew how much it helped me cope through the years.

After Mama died, I didn't leave the Hark for a long time. Liam's abandonment caused almost as much pain as her death. I didn't understand it. How could he kiss me with a passion that made my belly burn like the fires of a million suns one minute, only to abandon me to the dark the next?

What did I do wrong? Why was I *always* doing something wrong? I asked myself those questions over and over, even though I knew the answer.

I was bad. I was like Papa. *Evil.*

During the fire, Mama may have reignited the pilot light to my soul, but Papa was the darkness forever threatening to snuff it out.

ELEVEN

I emptied my toiletry bag in the expansive master bathroom, setting my shampoo, conditioner, soap, and razor in the shower, and my toothbrush, toothpaste, lotion, and hairbrush on the countertop. In my cardboard-box-sized apartment, all that stuff was crammed into a Tupperware and shoved under the tiny sink next to my toilet. Nova and Dane's master bath was possibly as big as my entire studio.

I moved to the Jacuzzi tub and lifted the basket Nova had left on the ledge. Lavender-scented bath oils, a candle, and a bottle of wine had been set in it, along with an envelope bearing my name. I flicked it open and pulled a note-card with Nova's neat handwriting.

Kick your feet up, relax, and enjoy!

I grinned, then moved to the connecting master suite to finish unpacking, Daisy at my heels. I was quickly growing used to my new sidekick.

Nova had cleared out part of the closet for me. I almost laughed when she told me. She knew I rarely wore anything other than yoga gear—certainly nothing that needed to be hung up. Instead of emptying the suitcase, I dragged it into the closet and rummaged through to find a tank top to change into. Although it was mid-September, a heat wave had hit the Midwest, and temps were expected to reach the high eighties over the next week. I pulled the tank over my head, then moved to the window.

The afternoon sun shone brightly in a cloudless sky, smattering rays of light that sparkled like little diamonds on the water's surface. Only a slice of lake peeked through the thick trees lining the shore. From the window, a part of the pier was visible.

The rowboat was tied to the cleat at the end. Liam stood on the opposite side, fishing from the pier. A white bucket and brown tackle box lay at his feet. I watched him cast out a line, then furiously reel it in. His muscles flexed and relaxed as he repeated the motion. After a few unsuccessful attempts, he fixed his pole, leaned down to grab his bucket and the box, and moved up the pier and into the shed.

Before he reemerged, I pushed from the window and hurried back to the bathroom to smooth my hair and apply a layer of lip gloss, then I cringed, annoyed part of me instinctively wanted to look good for Liam.

With my odd white hair and unusual eyes, I wasn't a conventional beauty. Unique was a better description. At least when I looked in the mirror now, I didn't see the amber flames that used to burn in my retinas.

Papa's eyes. I'd never forget the moment I saw myself in those horrid eyes.

The reflection staring back at me looked composed, but the memory of Papa left me on pins and needles. I needed to expend energy.

"Come on, Daisy," I said as I ambled out of the bathroom. "Let's go for a walk. We can visit Nan." Daisy gave an annoyed yelp and laid her head back down. "Got to hurry, girl. Come on."

I also needed to escape before Liam returned.

Nan and I had texted a few times since meeting two days before, quickly bonding over a mutual love of tea, yoga, and romance movies. We'd already made several plans for the week I'd be in Collins Grove. I'd decided to embrace the place, make the best of it while I was here. Having a new friend to explore this new town certainly was a bonus. Besides, keeping busy meant I'd be less likely to run into Liam around the house.

A reluctant Daisy followed me downstairs to the laundry room where I grabbed my crossbody bag and clipped a leash onto Daisy's collar. We exited through the attached garage. Dane and Nova kept the interior door unlocked and used a keypad for the garage door to access the house. They'd given me the code that morning, repro-gramming it to my birthday to make it easy to remember, although I didn't celebrate birthdays.

After pushing the button on the wall and watching the wide garage door creep up, I led Daisy out and punched in the code, 0514. The door retreated, slowly lurching down. Dane had warned me to keep an eye on it and make sure it closed fully. Apparently, the garage door was on the fritz. He'd given me a rundown of the house's faults, also mentioning that the screen door in the front didn't latch and the toilet in the half bath on the first floor sometimes continued to run after flushing.

Again, I wondered why Liam, Dane, or Nova didn't use their divine energy to make those quick fixes. It'd be as easy as snapping their fingers.

Then again, of all people, I shouldn't be one to question how people used their gifts.

Laverne rested in the shade, having survived another trip from the city. Along with a new cellphone, a new—or more accurately, a new-to-me because it'd have to be used—car would soon be added to my list of upcoming expenditures. I sighed, not wanting to think about my financial troubles on top of my Liam troubles.

The driveway tapered as Daisy and I neared the street. I checked for traffic at the mouth, then led Daisy to the southbound lane. The gravel shoulder of the road was narrow, dropping to a deep ditch spotted with yellow and purple wildflowers.

"Let's gather some on our way home," I said to Daisy. "I bet Liam hates flowers. Anything cheery annoys that man." Her tail wagged, as if agreeing. "You've got to help me if I'm going to survive this week, okay?"

I stopped walking and looked expectantly at Daisy. Her tail again thumped wildly. I patted my new accomplice, then fished in my crossbody bag to grab a doggie treat. Before Nova left, she'd made me stash a baggie full of them to have on hand in case Daisy petered out on a walk. Apparently, it happened often, and only a dog biscuit would get her going again.

After turning onto Charles Street, I pulled out my vibrating cell. A text from Gwen flashed on the screen.

"Shoot!" I exclaimed, slapping my free hand to my forehead as I realized I'd forgotten all about her class at the studio that morning. I shot her a quick apology, then slipped the phone back into my bag. With the flurry of activity over the past few days, Saturday seemed so long ago.

I already missed the energy and healing yoga brought— not just to me, but to my classes. I loved seeing bodies strengthen and spirits shine as my students learned the practice. Providing hope and light was my divine calling, no matter the tragic events of the past.

The flame in my belly continued to flicker, even if it was now Mama's light.

Daisy must've noticed the sudden change in my mood. She abruptly stopped, circled my legs, then leaned into me. I crouched down and hugged her neck.

"Thanks, girl," I whispered. "I needed that. You and I are going to be just fine this week. Come on."

As we continued our walk, we passed the empty park. At this time of day, kids were probably still in school. The vacant swings swayed in the gentle breeze, tempting me. I used to push Nova, Neal, and Celia, but I was so much bigger and older than them. No one pushed me in return.

I was always the outcast.

Lost in my thoughts, I hardly heard the throttle of a motorcycle until it was too late. Liam pulled up beside us.

"Where you going?" he yelled over the sound of his bike.

"To get tea!"

"Why you walking?"

"Daisy needs exercise!"

"Not safe!"

"Huh?"

He finally cut the engine so we didn't have to shout over the noise. "Lake Road's not safe. No shoulder to walk on. You shoulda drove."

I held up my hand. "Stop, Liam. I don't need a lecture. We're fine. I can take care of myself. I'm a big girl now."

His eyes roamed my face, landing on my lips. "I can see that."

One look and I went from loathing him to desiring him. My heart ticked faster. Inhaling deeply through my nose, I held it in for three seconds, then slowly released it through my mouth, just like I taught in class. I repeated the exercise, but when Liam's eyes jerked from my lips to my rising chest, I took a flustered step back.

Tightening my grip on Daisy's leash and crossing my arms over my chest, I asked, "Did you come out here just to tell me that? Didn't send one of your birds to follow me?"

"Do I need to? Gonna do anything stupid?"

"Goodbye, Liam," I said, rolling my eyes as I began walking away.

"See you at home," he called.

My steps faltered, and my shoulders fell. *Home.* Once upon a time, he'd promised to be my home. Now, we'd be eating, sleeping, breathing under the same roof, but unlike my dreams of the past, we wouldn't be playing house.

TWELVE

"I'll only be a few minutes," I promised Daisy as I looped her leash around the leg of the bench outside of The Poppy Seed. "Look, Nan already put out water for you." With my foot, I slid the bowl in front of Daisy, who eyed me, then it. She plopped to the ground and rested her head on her front legs. "Be right back."

Grinning at how quickly I was becoming a dog person, I spun on my heel and skipped up the steps. A blast of cold air welcomed me.

"Cami!" Nan called from behind the counter. An older woman stood next to her. "Denise, this is the friend I was telling you about. She's watching Daisy while Nova and Dane are out of town."

"Oh, yes!" Denise came from around the back counter and pulled me into a hug. "I'm thrilled to meet you! Welcome to our sweet little town."

"Thank you." My belly warmed from the instant friendship. At Dark Beans, the packed coffee shop I usually frequented in the city, I would be crowded by people, yet I always felt alone. "I'm definitely feeling the welcoming vibes—especially here. And your treats," I said, smacking my lips. "Out of this world."

"Speaking of treats, have you eaten?" Denise stepped behind the counter and pushed open the lower display's glass partition. "Do you like spinach and feta? I have one mini quiche from breakfast left. It's a new recipe using fresh herbs from my garden. Want me to bag it up for you?"

"I haven't eaten. Sounds amazing. Yes, please do!" I ticked off answers to her questions, then reached into my bag to fish for my wallet.

Denise waved her hand. "No, keep your money. Consider this a little welcome treat." She pulled the quiche from a platter, placed it into a plastic container, and set it into a bag along with a plastic fork and napkin.

"And how about an Arnold Palmer? Freshly brewed iced tea with freshly squeezed lemonade," Nan said, plucking a cup from the tower beside the cash register.

"Sounds fresh." I giggled.

"With this heat wave, you need something refreshing. Nan mentioned you walked here? That's kind of a hike." Denise handed me the bag.

"Yeah, I like the exercise."

"Your friend didn't join?"

"My friend?" My brows knitted, then I snapped my fingers. "Oh, Daisy. She's right out front."

"No, no. I mean that hunka hunka burning man staying with you. We call him Li-*yum*." Denise emphasized the last syllable while fanning her cheeks. "Heard you all know one another. Liam, Dane, Nova, and you."

Nan flipped up her hands. "Didn't hear it from me. Apparently, Libby at the library filled Denise in. But seriously, give us the scoop on Li-yum. He's like, the hottest catch in Collins Grove right now."

I frowned and shrugged. "I guess. If you like the grumpy judgmental type."

"They call that brooding in romance novels." Denise nudged Nan in the ribs and wiggled her brows.

"Always seems pleasant when he stops in," Nan offered as she swatted Denise's arm away.

"He comes here?" I asked, cocking my head and looking around the empty coffeehouse.

"Yeah, at least a few times a week. He's hooked on our hibiscus maple lattes." Denise nodded and started combining pastries from the near-empty platters onto one large serving tray.

"Really?" My eyes widened.

"Has a sweet tooth too. Makes me set aside two of the giant snickerdoodle cookies on days I make them. I never thought a man eating a cookie could look so erotic, but..." Denise looked up and fanned herself again.

"That pompous..." I trailed off, shaking my head. Both ladies' eyes narrowed in on me.

"You like him, don't you?" Denise jabbed a finger toward me as a wide smile stretched across her cheeks.

"No." I took a step back.

"You're blushing." Now it was Nan pointing a finger at my pinkened cheeks.

"Because it's so absurd!" I croaked, taking another step back.

"What's not to like? He's hot. Like scorching." For the third time, Denise fanned her face. "If only I was twenty years younger!"

I snorted. Little did she know, Liam had centuries on her.

"Seriously, Cami," Nan said. "You should hear the buzz around town. First, it was all about Nova and Dane, who look like they stepped out of the pages of *People Magazine*, and now Liam. Think half the ladies in town go to Duffy's just to get a glimpse of him and that fine ass of his. Me included." She fluffed her chestnut curls. "If I was sleeping under the same roof as him, I'd 'accidentally' get lost on my way to my bedroom." She hooked two fingers into air quotes as she emphasized the word "accidentally."

Denise added in a high-pitched, girly voice, "Oops, sorry. This isn't *my* bed?"

"You two are impossible!" I groaned.

"Impossibly fun!" Nan laughed and hooked arms with Denise. "Okay, no more teasing about Liam and his sexy butt. What are you up to for the rest of the day?"

Before I could answer, the bell above the door chimed as a group of teenagers pushed through.

"Oh, school's out," Denise said, looking at her watch.

"I should check on Daisy anyways." I twisted my head toward the window, but Daisy was too low to the ground for me to catch a glimpse of her.

"The puppy outside?" one of the high schoolers interjected. "She's adorable! But she does kinda look sad."

"Oh, here," Nan said, handing me a bone-shaped cookie. "For Daisy. They're homemade dog treats, something new Denise is trying."

Shaking my head, I grabbed the bone and dropped it into the bag. "You guys are too generous. Thank you. I was nervous about my stay here, but I think I'm going to really love it." I wiggled the bag. "Hopefully Daisy will forgive me for taking so long when she sees this."

Denise looked at Nan and waved her hand, shooshing her toward the door. "Take a break—I've got things covered in here for a bit. And don't forget Cami's tea."

The bell jingled again when we stepped out. Daisy did a slight jerk at the sound.

"Miss me, girl?" Walking down the steps, I pulled the doggie treat from the bag and held it up for her to see. Her tail smashed against the concrete.

After Nan and I sat down on the bench, I unpeeled the wrapper and handed Daisy the bone, then rubbed my hands on my shorts to wipe away the drool from her sloppy tongue.

"Here." Nan offered the tea. "Man, it's hot out."

Nodding in agreement, I took a sip, then placed the cup on the ground before pulling the quiche from the bag and ripping open the plastic container. Suddenly ravenous, I shoved it into my mouth, moaning as I chewed. "This is delicious. *What* does she put in these?"

"Oh, she'll never tell." Nan laughed and leaned over to scratch Daisy's ear. "I've been working here since it opened, and I still don't know what kind of addictive crack she adds to her goodies. Everything she makes is amazing."

"Wow. Does she do catering?"

"She'd love to expand into it—people are always ordering in bulk for parties, but she can hardly keep up. She'd need to move into a bigger space. But more pressing, she really needs to hire a few more people. Hey! Aren't you looking for work?"

Devouring the quiche in record time, I rubbed my hands together over the empty container, ridding them of crumbs. "I have no experience working in a bakery or coffeehouse, but I do dabble with baking at home. Just granola, simple stuff." I looked vacantly to the building across the way. A large "For Sale" banner stretched across the glass window. "What was in there?" I pointed to the building.

"That was an antique shop. Owner retired. It's been gutted down to the bones. Personally, I think it looks better now, all brick and beams. Very industrial. It'll get snagged up quick." Nan nudged my arm with her elbow. "Would make an amazing yoga studio. Perfect location."

"That's funny. Just this morning, before Dane and Nova left, they said Collins Grove needs a yoga studio. I'm not sure I'm ready to leave the city just yet." I laughed, although it sounded very tempting. My brain stirred with the possibilities. What if I could save enough to open my own studio? "Besides, I'm practically broke and currently unemployed."

"Yeah, I guess starting a business is a big step. But if you need a job, you should consider talking to Denise. She can always use extra help at The Pop." Nan stood and stretched her arms over her head, sighing. "Speaking of, I should probably get back in. I don't know where high schoolers get all this money for fancy coffee drinks, but we are about to have our after-school rush."

Behind her, a group of girls walking in pairs rounded Charles Street, backpacks slung over their shoulders.

As we said our goodbyes, my voice was cut off by the rumble of a motorcycle. I glared, fully expecting Liam, but it was a stranger who slowly passed, his eyes intently focused on Nan.

"Ugh," she muttered after the air quieted. "Wish he'd just stop."

"Who's that?" I watched the man's blond hair fade into the distance.

"My ex. He won't quit. Stalker drives by here at least twice a day. During summer, I used to get off at three, so he probably still expects me to be leaving around this time." She rolled her eyes and waved a hand. "Idiot."

"Aren't they all?" I laughed as I unhooked Daisy's leash from the leg of the bench, waking her from her nap. Ah, the life of a dog—treats and afternoon naps.

"I'd like to think there's more good ones out there than bad. Not going to let *him* win by punishing other men for his bad behavior though." Her eyes widened, and she leaned in, lowering her voice. "I just started seeing someone. That stays between you and me. Gossip travels like wildfire here."

I giggled. "You don't have to worry about me. Besides Nova, I literally have one friend here, which would be you. Well, and maybe Denise now too."

Nan adjusted her black apron, then brushed her hands over the stiff canvas fabric. "Well, seems like I'll need to introduce you to more people around here, especially if you'll be here for at least the next two weeks."

I held up a finger. "Hopefully just one."

"You know Nova just said that to get you to agree. Patty Tomlinson at the post office told Denise that Dane and Nova put their mail on hold for *three* weeks." Nan wiggled three fingers.

My jaw dropped, and my hands flew to my hips. "You've got to be kidding me."

And I didn't mean about all the gossip in this nosy little town. I would *kill* Nova.

"We'll see, I guess." She crooked her fingers into a wave. "I gotta get back inside. We on for tomorrow—trivia night at Duffy's?"

"Not Duffy's." I moaned. Avoiding Liam seemed like Mission Impossible. "Anywhere but there. Nova said there's a microbrewery up the road from here?"

"Trivia at Duffy's is the Tuesday thing to do," Nan

singsonged, then clucked her tongue. "Now that is a tongue twister."

I sighed and gently tugged at Daisy's leash. "It's just..."

"Li-yum?" A grin overtook Nan's cheerful face. Her eyes twinkled mischievously. "You do like him, don't you? Just admit it already."

"I said it once, and I'll say it again. *No*. He's impossible. Arrogant. Bossy." I started backing away.

"Girl, you like him so bad!" Nan bounced up and down while clapping her hands.

I stuck my tongue out and continued with Daisy obediently at my heels.

Now I understood why dogs were considered the perfect companion. Loyal to a fault, dutiful, and they never talked back.

THIRTEEN

Crowds of kids filled the sidewalk on Charles Street. A few stopped to pet Daisy, some calling her by name. We wove through the hordes, making our way past the park. Every swing was occupied, and laughter rang through the air.

Maybe it was a symbol of what was to come. A park that only hours before sat lonely and abandoned now bustled with youthful cheer. The smiles and giggles made my tummy warm, the little light inside me flickering from their happiness.

Maybe, just maybe, Collins Grove was my landing place. Being around people fed my energy, my light, but perhaps instead of the hordes of faceless people in the city, what I needed was the closeness of a community. I'd already made fast friends in Nan and Denise, and then there was Nova and Dane, who were essentially family.

My pace picked up, an optimistic hop in my step.

But as I turned onto Lake Road, I abruptly came to a stop, practically skidding in my Converse sneakers. In the middle of the street, an ominous fat black bird perched, calmly waiting for me.

"Liam," I muttered, looking to the sky. "You've got to be kidding me." Facing the bird, I placed my hands on my hips and stared him down. "Shoo. Go tell your master to mind his own business."

The bird's head twitched, then he cawed and took flight.

Huffing, I walked the rest of the way home with the bird circling above me, staying high in the sky, remaining within eyesight. The lightness in my step from a few minutes before was replaced by the angry stomp of my sneakers against gravel.

When I got to the mouth of the driveway, I yelled to the sky, "Go on now. I'm fine, see!"

I bounded up the drive, not bothering to check if the bird was still there, and punched the keypad on the garage. Poor Daisy whined and tugged at the leash, obviously needing a potty break. I gave her an apologetic smile as I unclipped her. Nova said Daisy didn't need to be leashed while in their yard, only on walks.

Watching her roam the front lawn gave me a few minutes to let my anger cool. I plopped onto one of the rocking chairs and blew out a breath. Maybe Liam's intentions were good, and maybe I was overreacting, but I didn't need a babysitter. What could happen in the middle of small-town USA with nothing but nature surrounding me? Did he have that little faith in me, always thinking I was going to mess up?

But danger can be anywhere, just like Mama's remote cabin.

The front door whooshed open, and Liam grumbled from behind the screen. "What took so long?"

Flinching from the sudden sound of his voice, I reflexively released an "Oh!" as my hand covered my heart. "Darn it, Liam! Don't sneak up on me like that."

He yanked the screen door open and stepped out, running a hand through his mussed hair. It was longer than usual, and his skin had darkened to a sun-kissed tan from hours spent fishing on the rowboat. It somehow made him look even sexier. Life surely wasn't fair. He looked hotter than ever, and now I was stuck seeing him every darn day for the next week. Possibly more.

Nova owed me. Big time. At least enough money for a new smart phone.

I pulled at the hem of my shorts and scooted back against the rocking chair, looking ahead at Daisy. Eye contact with Liam would only make my racing heart pound faster. I needed to stay calm, show him he couldn't ruffle my feathers, not even with one of his messengers tailing me.

"I saw one of your *friends*. What do you think's going to happen around here? Collins Grove is like a modern-day Mayberry," I said, referring to the fictional town in the 1960s *Andy Griffith Show*. "You worried a kid might try to steal my iced tea on my walk home?"

Liam took a seat in the rocking chair next to me and gazed ahead, also watching Daisy as she romped around the front yard. "Road's got potholes and no shoulder. And I've seen how that mutt drags Nova on walks."

"Muffie McMufferson is *not* a mutt. No wonder Nova didn't trust you to watch her." I chanced a glance at him. His strong forearms rested against the rocking chair's armrests. Annoyed by how relaxed he appeared, I added, "Oh, by the way, Denise said she'll have your hibiscus maple latte ready for you at the usual time tomorrow." I waited for him to look my way, then widened my eyes, batted my lashes, and smiled sweetly. "I simply don't understand how you can put that mud in your body."

"This whole town is too nosy for its own good." Liam grunted, and his forearms tensed, rippling his muscles. As much as I hated to admit it, Nan and Denise were right. Liam was scorching hot. And I did have a crush on him. Always had and, unfortunately, probably always would.

"Well, I kind of like it." I leaned back against the wooden headrest. "They look out for each other here."

"Was just looking out for you," Liam said quietly. "On your walk."

Usually, his overbearing treatment would make my blood boil, but the sincerity in his voice softened the blow. I peeked over at him and said quietly, "I can take care of myself. I've been doing it for years."

"I wear your mark," he replied, referring to his burn marks from the fire, which sort of bound us together. Back when I lacked control, my pain and emotions caused his scars to reopen, welt, and blister all over again. I hadn't seen the ugly blemishes in years, yet I knew they were still there —a forever reminder of the day I lost control. The day I lost my light.

"And you never let me forget it," I whispered back, humiliation stinging my cheeks.

"I wear your mark," he repeated, hitching his thumb toward his heart. "I carry you with me. If anything happened to you..." He shuddered, and my stomach flipped. Leaning forward in his chair, he looked ahead and solemnly asked, "Why did you leave the Hark? You were safe there."

The question caught me off guard, and my breath hitched in my throat. Silent seconds ticked by before I said in a wobbly voice, "To see you."

His Adam's apple bobbed as he swallowed. "I was going to come back."

"But you didn't."

Mama died, and Liam abandoned me. I lost my Mama, and I lost my Liam.

After Liam ditched me in the Hark, I replayed our kiss. Over and over. If my emotions branded his back, then his kiss branded my heart. Did he not feel it too?

His rejection stung. It grated on me. I wanted—*needed*—to confront him. I needed closure.

The desire and drive to find Liam allowed me the energy to transcend the boundaries and travel from the Hark to the mortal realm. The taxing journey nearly wiped me out. It took weeks to recover, then months to find Liam.

Little had I known at the time, but Liam felt my presence the instant I transcended the realms. He didn't care enough to come himself. Instead, he sent one of his birds to watch over me.

"You needed time to heal from your mama's death." Liam sighed and leaned forward, propping his thick forearms on his thighs.

"You left me!" I blurted out.

"I *never* left you. I carry you with me. Always. Your passion, your pain, the palette of emotions that consumes your heart and burns like a match to your soul. It's more than the scar that marks my body. You are seared into my skin. I'm branded by *you*."

Eyes wide, cheeks burning from shame, I whispered, "Someday it'll be gone, Liam. I won't be the constant burden that burns on your back."

"You don't get it, do you? Silly girl. Here or gone, you're with me. Whether or not the reminder of you marks my skin, you're here." He thumped his chest.

Shocked silent, I stared at him, unable to respond. Liam barely spoke in complete sentences, usually spitting out three-word commands. The sudden severity of our conversation and the rehashing of old wounds made my pulse spike.

Liam stared at me for a few seconds, then said quietly, "You have all this good in you, but instead, you focus on the dark corners, the shadows of your past. You carry guilt over something for which you are not responsible."

Fat tears swelled in my eyes. I took a heavy breath. With age and experience, I'd learned to cry without overwhelming the fire in me. Still, I didn't want Liam to see my tears. Inhaling and holding my breath for several seconds, I desperately willed them away.

"It's hard to watch, Cambria. You have this gift, this divine light, but you're too stubborn, too scared to face the truth, to let the good outshine the bad. Your Mama lives on in you, but you're hell-bent on giving her gift away. I can't watch you spiral."

A tear escaped my eye, trailing down my cheek and plopping onto my thigh. I lowered my eyes, focusing on the wet spot. Guilt ate at me from the inside out; I didn't feel worthy of the second chance gifted to me by my mother.

"Mama died because of me. Because a part of me is bad. I've learned to control myself, but it doesn't matter now. When it mattered, I failed. How can I live with that?" My voice was so low, I didn't know if Liam could even hear me. Then again, Liam was superb at everything, hearing included. I didn't look at him or wait for an answer to my rhetorical question. "Mama never talked about Papa, even after the fire. I don't know much about him, but I pieced some things together. When she was young, he manipulated her, twisted her thoughts so she'd fall in love with him. He wanted to sire a lumineer so he could use me—use his *own* child—for evil." I shook my head, scattering more tears against my cheeks.

I'd never forget the burning amber flames of his irises when we locked eyes... what I saw... hellfire. I shivered.

Most chilling was recognizing myself in those eyes.

If eyes were the windows to the soul, then mine was bad, born of deceit and sin. There was no way to rid myself of my father, even after he turned to ash. I carried his bloodline, his genetic makeup. Part of him flowed through me, soiling my thoughts, darkening my light.

"I never deserved Mama's gift."

"Your Mama gave you her light because she loved you. A perfect love. A selfless love. The most powerful love." Liam lifted a hand, reaching for my arm, but then let it drop back to his lap. His gruff voice lowered. "This scar is more than a reminder of the night I found you. It's the moment I learned the truth of light and love. How love drives the light, fuels the flame, burns the flesh."

I winced, knowing the scar still pained him. Because he was divine—a presider, one of the most powerful beings to walk the earth—the wound should have healed in seconds. But he was touched by evil.

He was touched by me.

"I promise, Liam, I'll make things right," I whispered.

"I don't want you to make things right!" Liam pushed to his feet. "I want you to understand!"

"Then help me!" I cried. "Help me understand."

"You need to heal. And healing is not something you can get from me or anyone else. Knowing your worth, your purpose—that comes from here." He thumped his chest, just above his heart, with his fist. "You think giving away your light will somehow free you of your guilt, of all that you carry? You think it'll heal this scar on my back, free me of you?"

I pushed to my feet and faced Liam, looking up at him through wet eyelashes. *He* didn't understand—guilt consumed me because my mama sacrificed herself so I could go on. Helping Celia was the one way I could redeem myself. "It's my fault my mother died. My fault my father died. My fault Celia left. My fault."

As my words turned to sobs, Liam pulled me into his chest, and I collapsed against him. His chin dipped to rest on my head, and he murmured softly into my hair, instantly calming me. I didn't hear his whispered words, but it didn't matter. Having his arms around me brought comfort and security.

After regaining composure, I took a step back and sniffed. "Sorry," I mumbled, averting my eyes and focusing on the wooden planks of the shiny, polished floor.

Liam used a finger to lift my chin. His tender tone grabbed my attention. "When people look at you, they see hope, joy, peace. They see *you*. I wish you'd see it too."

"That's on my outside, not my inside." My soul was stained, a part of it burnt and blackened.

He shook his head and released an annoyed sigh.

"I need to see Celia, to talk to her. I was so wrong in thinking Neal was manipulating her, using her like Papa controlled Mama."

"She'll figure it out. She's a smart girl."

"You know where she is." My eyes narrowed on Liam as his face hardened. "But you'll never tell me. When you look at me, you still see that little girl who lost control and killed in a fit of rage. You talk about my good, yet when it comes down to it, you don't believe in me." When Liam didn't respond, didn't defend his belief in me, I shook my head and pushed past him. "I'll always be *that* monster to you."

FOURTEEN

Later that evening, I holed away in Nova and Dane's master suite—my bedroom for the time being—while Liam escaped to the rowboat. I knew he was somewhere on the lake because I caught a glimpse of him from the window while filling the Jacuzzi tub.

It'd never made sense why windows were placed above tubs, but the confirmation that Liam wasn't right down the hall allowed me time to truly decompress. I dumped a third of the bottle of lavender-scented bath oil into the stream of hot water as I sat on the ledge of the tub. Music from my phone's speaker drowned out my pounding thoughts. I uncorked the wine and slugged straight from the bottle as I sank into the hot water.

Nova had left a candle in the basket, not knowing how terrified I was of fire. As romantic as candle-lit dinners or fireside drinks sounded, the orange flames caused an immediate post-traumatic response.

By the time the tub filled, half the wine bottle was gone, and my eyes felt heavy. I submersed myself in the soothing water and let the soft songs from my meditation playlist lull me. Daisy's yapping woke me an hour later.

"Sorry, girl," I muttered, lifting my head from the tub. "But I really needed that."

I dried off using one of Nova's extra thick, extra fluffy towels, then slipped into pastel pink sleep shorts and a white tank top, not bothering with a bra since it was almost bedtime.

After pulling my hair out of its towel wrap and into a wet, messy bun, I grabbed my cell from the tub's ledge. The screen flashed to life, blaring the time. It was well past dinnertime. I peeked out the window, checking to see if the rowboat was back—I didn't spot it—before running downstairs to grab a quick snack to eat in my room while watching Netflix. After calming down, I wouldn't chance another run-in with Liam.

Head down, immersed in reading Nan's text about her plans for the next day, I didn't notice Liam emerge from the hallway bathroom until it was too late. I crashed into him.

The phone went flying, and my hands instinctively went up to grab the nearest object to steady myself, landing flat against Liam's damp, bare chest.

My eyes moved slowly upward to meet his. Molten steel. We stood motionless. Seconds passed, and his heart thumped wildly under my fingertips. My palms remained firmly glued against his warm skin. His nostrils flared, although his solid chest barely budged. My own, however, heaved with labored breaths.

I swallowed, and Liam's gaze flashed to my mouth, then back up. With our eyes locked, my hands began to move of their own accord, roaming from his solid chest up to his broad shoulders, down his arms, then to his sides. My fingers skimmed the pink-and-white welted skin above his hip, grazing it before he twisted his palms and grasped my wrists, pulling me into him.

A throaty sigh escaped my parted lips, and my lashes fluttered upward.

"Can I see it?" I whispered, meeting Liam's blazing eyes.

His pupils dilated. He slowly released his hold on my wrists. "Yes."

My breath hitched. My eyes darted from his chest to his lips, then dropped to the floor. I swallowed again, my throat drier than the desert. Liam took a half step away as he turned his torso, bearing his scars.

Pink-and-white welts swirled above his hip and part of his back, not in a pattern, yet beautiful, as if purposely marked. Mesmerized by the lines that seemed to sweep up and out like the burst of a firework, I reached out my hand, pulled back slightly, then moved closer again until my fingertips touched his flesh. I heard Liam's intake of air just as his body flinched. Startled, I snatched my hand back and looked up.

"Sorry," I whispered, curling my fingers into a loose fist. "Did that hurt?"

He shook his head.

I cocked my head. "Then why...?"

Now it was Liam swallowing, composing himself. "That wasn't from pain."

The air stood still. A throaty noise sounded, either from him or me. Time ticked on, but we were paralyzed, frozen from the intimacy of a simple touch.

Finally, Liam broke his gaze. "Good night, Cambria."

He turned and disappeared into his room—the one decorated in blue accents—two doors down from where I'd be sleeping.

∽

IF ONLY I COULD SLEEP...

Hours later, I lay in bed, staring at the ceiling, thinking of the intricate lines of Liam's scar. Daisy snoozed in her little doggy bed by the door. Darn dog slept most of the day and now was back at it, snoring peacefully.

Checking my phone and realizing it was past one in the morning, I pushed from bed and moved to the bathroom to grab melatonin from my toiletry bag. Usually, I had no problem falling asleep; the nightmares that came after, waking me and keeping me up for the rest of the night, were the problem. A doctor had suggested the low-dose supplement to get back to sleep.

I popped one in my mouth, then returned to bed and waited for sleep to take over. The melatonin worked its magic. My lids felt heavy, and I drifted off. Then the nightmare came, as it did most nights.

Rustling sounded from the forest. A bear? No, a monster. *Papa.*

He lurched from the dark woods, chasing me under the moonless sky. I couldn't see anything except his glowing eyes. I ran and ran, stumbling over sticks and twigs, falling and getting up. He was closing in... so close I felt the heat of his eyes... the heat of hellfire.

I screamed and jerked upright.

Sweat dotted my head, and my heart pounded, but the gentle caress of a hand over my forehead swept away the terror. I quickly calmed, lowering my head back against a feather-stuffed pillow, sinking back into the plush mattress. Strong arms circled me, pulling me in. A calming voice shushed me. Calloused hands brushed over my hair, cradling my head. I was blanketed in comfort. Secure and safe. I closed my eyes and drifted off to a dreamless sleep.

When I blinked awake the next morning to warm, yellow rays splattering the room, I was alone. The other side of the bed was untouched, the pillow plumped and the comforter pulled tautly.

I searched the room. Daisy slept in her dog bed, still curled into a donut, still snoring. Giving a shake of my head, I reached for the remote and flipped on the morning news.

I must've dreamed it, but I swore Liam was in my bed during the night.

FIFTEEN

After finally emerging from bed, I brushed my hair and teeth and headed downstairs to make tea and get Daisy her breakfast. I set a mug in the microwave to heat, opened the back door to let her out, then filled her bowl with a scoop of dog food. Daisy let herself back in through the gap in the sliding glass door and immediately lapped up the contents of the bowl. Her tongue gave a final lick, and she looked up expectantly with big brown soulful eyes.

"Still hungry? Want a treat?"

Her tail thumped against the floor.

"Nova said they are for walks only, but I'll sneak you one. Just don't tell on me, okay, girl?" I scratched her head and leaned over to give her a kiss.

"That is one spoiled dog," a man's voice called with a laugh.

I shrieked and jumped up, crooking my arms out in front of my chest as if I were about to go ninja on him.

"Oh, sorry!" the guy said, taking a step back. "Didn't mean to scare you. I'm here for the wallpaper. Well, and everything else this place needs."

I put my hand over my heart and looked to the ceiling, calming myself. "Oh, I thought I was alone."

"Cambria!" Liam bellowed from the other side of the sliding glass door, pushing it open with a puffed chest and crazy eyes. He stopped when he saw the man. "Dammit, Tom. What are you doing here?"

"Um, I'm working?" He hitched his thumb toward the dining room. "Stripping wallpaper today. Dane gave you my schedule, right?"

"What the hell did you do to her?" Liam's eyes blazed— not the evil amber glow like Papa's but still scary, especially knowing his immense strength. One deliberate jerk of Liam's chin and this poor man's windpipe would be crushed. "Why'd she scream?"

"Liam," I said, folding my arms over my chest. "*You* didn't tell me renovations would start this morning. I wasn't expecting anyone here." I tapped my foot and looked at him.

"Right. Yeah." Liam grunted out the words. He cocked his head at Tom. "Don't talk to her."

"Liam!" I shrieked, appalled at his behavior.

"Don't look at her either."

"Oh my God!" I buried my face in my hands. "Stop, just stop. Tom, I'm so sorry." I extended my hand. "I'm Cami, a friend of Nova's. I'm watching Daisy while they're gone."

Tom didn't take my hand. Instead, he just stared at it, then looked at Liam. I shook my head.

"Don't worry about Liam. He's all bark." I dropped my arm to my side, glared at Liam and silently mouthed the word, "Bully."

Liam's eyes roamed over me. "Get dressed."

My mouth dropped open. I hadn't bothered with a bra and suddenly realized it when Liam's eyes landed on my chest.

If he was going to act like a jerk in front of Tom, I'd give it right back to him. "I *am* dressed." I put my hands on my hips. The shorts were short, and the white tank top stretched snugly across my chest.

Tom's gaze shifted from me to Liam then to the ground. He started backing away as Liam prowled toward me.

"You can't tell me what to wear," I said, biting my lower lip as he stalked closer.

He placed a hand under my elbow and leaned in. "Come with me."

Poor Tom was beet-red, either embarrassed or frightened. Most likely both. To save him from further distress, I allowed Liam to guide me out of the kitchen.

"What the hell?" I said, shrugging off his hold.

"What the hell?" he mocked in a high-pitched voice. "What the hell are you wearing? Prancing around here half-naked."

"Seriously? Half-naked?" I waved my arm down my body. "This is what I sleep in. Maybe if you would've told me the renovation guy was going to be here, I would have put on a bra. But you didn't, so how was I supposed to know?"

He just continued to stare at me with those steely gray eyes.

Looking up to the ceiling, I balled my hands into fists. "You're impossible. Seriously."

I turned and ran up the stairs. I wouldn't let Liam bully me. No way. Not now, not ever. He would not tell me what to wear or who to talk to.

Don't talk to her. Don't look at her. Who did he think he was? I stomped around the bedroom, getting hotter and angrier, and... I stopped as a smile spread across my face. Today's forecast called for sunny skies and unseasonably warm temperatures. And I had my adorable yellow bikini packed just in case it got hot enough to swim in the lake or try out Nova's new paddleboard.

With a plan of attack formed, I rubbed my palms together.

Game on.

~

FROM A BEDROOM WINDOW, I watched Liam climb onto his motorcycle and rumble down the drive. I slipped downstairs and into the kitchen.

"Hey, Tom!" I called as I poured a glass of lemonade. "Thirsty? I made some lemonade from scratch. Want some?"

He yelled back, "No, thanks!" but I brought him a glass anyway. He probably was terrified of Liam catching him talking to me.

"Hey, I'm sorry about Liam. He's kind of protective of me. Big-brother type and all. Here." I handed him the glass and grinned, hoping my megawatt lumineer smile would relax him. "I'll be out back if you need anything."

I ran back upstairs to gather a towel, a book, my yoga mat, and my phone, then swung through the kitchen to fill a thermos with water. Daisy followed me through the sliding glass door to the back patio.

The scent of mowed grass permeated the air. Its earthy freshness floated on the soft breeze, reminding me of my surreal time spent in the Hark. There, gods and goddesses controlled the weather like one would control the air conditioner or furnace. If we wanted the lulling sound of a summer storm, one of them would crook a finger, and the sky would immediately swell with rain.

Growing up in a place as surreal and serene as the Hark should have been the greatest blessing bestowed upon a lowly demigod like me. But I never fit in.

The gods weren't judgmental or mean-spirited. In fact, they welcomed me with open arms and never treated me differently. But many of them never experienced or understood the harsh reality of humanity.

They didn't understand *me*.

On the morning I left the Hark to find Liam, Lucille had desperately tried to convince me to stay. But it wasn't *home*. I didn't belong. I'd never belong. Besides, she didn't understand my need to leave. She didn't know about Liam's kiss or how greatly his abandonment hurt me.

Realizing I was determined to go, Lucille warned me— even if I were able to successfully transcend the realms, there was no guarantee I'd have the energy or strength to return on my own. I'd need another god to help me make the journey back. I gave a sad, silent nod, knowing my decision to leave would have long-term consequences. Lucille then left me to concentrate.

Transcending the realms took intense focus and immense energy. I'd seen Liam do it hundreds of times, although he'd often take me while I was sleeping since it was easier on him.

I squeezed my eyes shut, envisioning Mama's cabin, forcing myself to recall each wall, window, corner, crack, and floorboard. They illuminated in my mind, as crisp as a picture, then they slowly fell out of focus. My hazy vision began to swirl, spinning so fast everything became a blur. My eyes popped open. The air twisted and thickened, cocooning my arms and legs. I couldn't breathe or see or move. My chest constricted, and my eyes snapped shut again.

Then I was there, standing in Mama's cabin. Flesh and bones, I'd been transported from the beautiful realm known as the Hark to the middle of the dilapidated two-room cabin I used to call home. Realizing I'd succeeded in making the journey, I gasped for air, clutching my chest as I dropped to my knees. My muscles spasmed, and my head pounded. Exhaustion hit me like a wave of water, grounding me. I laid on the dusty floor and closed my eyes.

I didn't know how much time passed or how long I slept, but when I woke, the headache was gone. I clumsily used my heavy limbs to sit upright. Emotion swelled in my throat as I absorbed the room. At one time, it'd held so much love and life, but it appeared no one had been there in months, maybe even years. Cobwebs stretched across corners, and grime covered the floor.

On the wall, the cross I'd whittled out of driftwood still dangled from its rusted nail. I sat rooted in place, spell-bound by the memories. *Mama and I baking, reading, knit-ting, singing, sewing, dancing, laughing, crying.* I sniffed away tears as I slowly crawled to the door of Mama's bedroom—the room we shared before I was sent to live in the Hark.

Her bed was made. The last time I saw Mama, the colorful quilt I'd helped her sew had been wrapped around her frail body. Now, it was pulled taut and neatly tucked in the corners under the mattress. I wondered if Liam had come back to bury her—if he had placed Mama into the ground. Had he then returned to fix up her bed?

Liam may not have come back to the Hark for me, but I prayed he had at least come back here to give Mama a proper burial—a final resting place for her mortal body.

Curiosity got the best of me. I shuffled out of the cabin to the front lawn, scanning for a headstone. The lake sparkled in the distance, and behind me, the forest that had burnt to a crisp decades before had regrown, plush and thick. Long gone was the lingering, stale stench of fire that used to burn my nostrils. Now, the clean, earthy breeze carried the promise of a fresh start, new beginnings.

I took two steps toward the lake, but a small black bird's caw stopped me. As it swooped in front of me, I followed its movements until it landed on a beautiful, red granite head-stone. The bird gave another croak, then took off.

My heart thudded as my feet wearily carried me forward. As I neared, Mama's given name and her date of death came into focus. I moved closer to read the words etched on the bottom of the stone monument.

"When you pass through the waters, I will be with you; and when you pass through the rivers, they will not sweep you over. When you walk through the fire, you will not be burned..."

"The flames will not set you ablaze." I spoke the last line out loud.

"What's that?" Tom said from behind the screen door.

My head jerked in his direction as I jolted from the memory. "What? Oh, sorry. Was talking to myself. Bad habit."

Tom looked at the ground, not making eye contact. "Thanks for the lemonade. It was really good. Left the glass by the sink."

"Oh, glad you liked it." I smiled brightly, waving a hand. "Help yourself to more. There's a pitcher in the fridge."

"Okay, cool." Tom spun around and disappeared into the house.

I breathed in and out to settle my nerves. Reliving the memory of my first solo trip from the Hark had me worked up. Daisy gave me a nudge with her wet nose, then barreled down the steps. I followed behind.

While Daisy romped in the yard, I dropped the yoga mat, phone, thermos, book, and towel onto the pier, then circled back to the miniature house-shaped shed. People in Collins Grove must've been pretty trustworthy—the shed had no lock and was stocked with all sorts of expensive-looking equipment. I quickly located the paddleboard; its hot-pink-and-yellow wave pattern made it easy to spot against the gray walls.

I laid the board on the grass, then called for Daisy to follow me to the end of the T-shaped dock. I lifted off my cover-up and adjusted my yellow bikini top. Part of me felt a little guilty for pushing Liam.

But part of me couldn't wait to see his reaction.

I turned on a new age music station on my radio app and rolled out my mat. It'd been only three days since I'd taught my last yoga class, but my muscles ached as I stretched.

After my solo journey to the mortal realm, it'd taken weeks for my body to fully recover. I'd vowed to build my physical and spiritual strength. Ever since, I'd rarely skipped a day of exercise or meditation.

Daisy wandered up and down the pier before yawning with an exaggerated stretch and plopping down. She curled into a donut and closed her eyes.

"Nice downward dog, Dais." I giggled and lifted from the mat. "You're a quick learner."

The sun grew hotter and brighter. Sweat dotted the back of my neck. I took a slug of water, then walked down the pier to lug the paddleboard from the grass to the water.

"I can do this," I said, wading into the shallow shore.

My toes hit the refreshing water, instantly cooling me. I

dragged the paddleboard beside me as I padded farther out. Gentle waves hit my shins.

"Here goes nothing," I whispered as I climbed on top of the board, effortlessly mounting it. "Well, that was easy enough."

Sitting crisscross, I breathed in, holding my breath for several seconds before slowly releasing it. I repeated the exercise until I felt balanced and centered even as the waves swayed the board.

Being my first time attempting yoga on a paddleboard, I started with beginner poses, first shifting to a kneeling position with my hands in front of me. After I found my equilibrium, I lifted my hips toward the sky, held the pose for a minute, then brought my left leg to my chest, breathing in and out as I again held the position. I repeated the exercise with my right leg. Lowering my body flat against the board, I grinned.

The lake's current and the light breeze heightened the meditative aspect of yoga. My senses felt alive as my head worked in harmony with my muscles and nature.

As I continued the exercises and acclimated to the board, I shifted into a more demanding pose. Starting from a standing position, my feet together, I transferred my weight to my left foot, then bent my right knee behind me, bringing my heel toward my butt. I reached my right hand behind to grab the inside of my foot, steadied myself, inhaled slowly, and kicked my foot upward until my thigh was parallel with the board. Looking up, I stretched my left arm forward and focused on the lake's horizon, breathing deeply as I held the pose.

"Cambria!"

My body jerked, the board wobbled, and I toppled over, splashing into the water with a squeal.

"Cambria!" Liam roared again when I clamored to my feet.

I brushed my sopping locks from my face and adjusted my bikini top. Lake water stung my nostrils. The calm and serenity from yoga quickly dissipated, replaced by anger. I settled my startled heart, then glared at Liam, who stood at the bottom of the porch stairs with his hands on his hips.

With exaggerated force, I smacked my hands on my hips, imitating his pose.

"What do you think you're doing?" Liam yelled as he stomped through the yard.

"Me?" Anger flashed through me. "What did it look like I was doing when you snapped me from my pose?" I grabbed the board and waded to the shore where I stopped a few feet from a red-faced Liam. Pushing the board into his chest, I lowered my voice. "You made me fall, you big jerk."

Liam tossed the board to the ground and glared at me. "I told you to..." His eyes roamed to my dripping bikini top. "I said..."

A sweet smile spread across my lips. "Yes? You told me to what?"

I popped my hip and cocked my head, looking at him expectantly, blinking my wet lashes. The yellow bikini contrasted nicely against my summer tan, although I wasn't nearly as dark as Liam.

Clearly struggling to keep his attention on my face, he drew in his bottom lip and ran his hand through his already tousled hair. Stepping forward, he leaned close enough that I could feel his warm breath against my wet skin. "Don't push me, Cambria."

"Don't treat me like a child, Uilliam."

"Act like a child, get treated like a child." As he inched closer, his pupils dilated.

"I grew up a long time ago," I whispered throatily, losing my cool. Goosebumps freckled my arms and chest, either from his nearness or the breeze hitting my wet body.

"I know." He lowered his face until his nose brushed against my forehead, grazing my hairline. My skin tingled as he traced a finger along my jawline.

Even if I could move, I wouldn't. I savored his closeness, the way my body reacted to him, and the way his body reacted to me. The electric current between us spoke louder than words, louder than his obvious hesitation.

In a husky, pleading voice, Liam said softly, "Get dressed."

He broke the spell, twisting and bending to pick up the abandoned paddleboard, and then disappeared with it into the shed.

SIXTEEN

Daisy nudged my legs, and I realized I'd been rooted in place since Liam had walked away minutes before. I scratched her head, then gathered everything from the pier and returned to the house, hearing Liam banging and rustling with equipment in the shed as I passed.

The dining room, which Tom had begun to strip of wallpaper that morning, had a perfect fresh coat of eggshell-white paint. Cocking my head, I looked over the room. Tom's equipment, including the drop cloths that had covered the table and chairs, had been cleared out.

Shaking my head, I stomped to the sliding glass door and spotted Liam by the shed. "*What* did you do?" I yelled as I stepped onto the deck. "Where's Tom?"

"Finished early," Liam called back in his usual gruff tone. He didn't look up as he worked on his fishing pole. "Sent him home."

"He just started."

"Fast worker."

"Liam!" I groaned. He'd used his divine magic to complete the makeover. "You fired him, didn't you?"

"He got paid."

"Ugh!" I stomped my foot. "I can't believe you!"

Liam continued to focus on the pole. "He'll be working on the bathroom at the bar tomorrow. Should be happy to get paid and have a day off. What's the big deal?"

Rolling my eyes, I shook my head and stepped back inside. "He's impossible," I said to Daisy, who plopped down next to her food bowl. "Hungry again?"

I poured dog chow into one bowl, filled the other with water, then went upstairs to change out of my bikini. The air conditioner made my wet swimsuit icy and sticky against my skin. I peeled it off and slipped into a white fluffy robe from Nova's closet. Several dresses caught my eye. Before Nova moved from the city, she'd had a wardrobe to die for.

She did say I was welcome to use whatever I needed in the house... I dropped my hold on a silky red dress. All these beautiful clothes and nowhere to go.

Sighing, I slipped down the stairs and into the kitchen. Daisy's bowl had been lapped up.

"Want a treat?" I asked as she stared at me expectantly. Her tail wagged, and I swear she smiled. "Remember, this stays between us."

After giving her a dog biscuit, I searched the fridge for something for myself. Dane wasn't joking when he said they'd leave it stocked. Each shelf was crammed, top to bottom, with fresh fruit, meats wrapped in white paper, various artisan cheeses, three kinds of non-dairy milk, plastic containers of deli salads, and enough vegetables to host my own farmers' market. I pulled out the ingredients to fix a lettuce wrap.

As I rolled honey ham and aged white cheddar in a large butter lettuce leaf, my cell pinged with a text alert. I grabbed it, along with my plate, and called for Daisy to follow me up the stairs.

Nova and Dane's spacious master suite had to be at least double the size of my entire studio apartment. It fit a king-sized bed with nightstands flanking each side, two lounge chairs facing a fireplace, two dressers that were probably bursting with more of Nova's designer labels, and a treadmill tucked in one corner. A wide-screen television was mounted above the gas fireplace.

Although fire terrified me, the idea of a drink by the fire *did* sound romantic. When I read or watched cozy scenes like that in books and movies, I'd always get a pang of jealousy. Sighing, I realized I was missing out on both the fire *and* the romance. I hadn't been on a date in months. No one really interested me.

Except him.

I groaned, annoyed at how easily and quickly Liam was getting under my skin. Daisy sat at my feet as I sank into one of the chairs. I turned on a show, ate my lunch, and checked my messages, trying to keep my mind off the impossible man in the backyard.

Nan: *I can pick you up at 6 for trivia*

The bar was closed on Sundays and Mondays, so I assumed Liam would be heading in at some point today to get it open and ready for the bartenders and waitstaff after the break. Would he stay? Dare I chance going? What if he embarrassed me again? If an innocent conversation with Tom sent Liam into overprotective, big-brother mode, I didn't even want to imagine the scene he'd make at the bar.

Me: *Seriously, anywhere but there.*

Nan: *Chaz will be at trivia*

Me: *And who's Chaz?*

Nan: *The new guy*

Me: *Fine. But you owe me!!!*

Nan sent back a kissy face emoji. I groaned and tossed my phone onto the seat of the other chair. "Can't get away from him, can I?"

Daisy looked up, then set her head back down on her front paws.

"You okay, girl?" I leaned over to study Daisy. Nova said she was a well-behaved, chill dog, but her energy seemed off. As I scratched behind Daisy's ears with both hands, she looked up with sad eyes. "After lunch, I promise we'll walk."

Keeping my promise, I finished eating, then threw on a workout outfit, figuring I'd shower off the lake water once we returned—no use cleaning up if I would just get sweaty again on a walk.

It took a few prompts to get Daisy downstairs, but as we entered the laundry room, she perked up at the sight of her leash.

"Happy, girl?" I asked, clipping it on.

We exited through the garage. At the end of the driveway, I shifted our course, going north toward the path that Nova had mentioned led to Duffy's. Daisy kept pulling at her leash, however, leading me to a side street. Several houses dotted the route. She tugged and yanked me along until she stopped in front of a small, yellow bungalow. Her head jerked up, and her tail wagged.

"You know this house?" I tilted my head and waited for a reply, which came seconds later from a black furball barreling from around the back of the house. I was unprepared for Daisy's sudden jolt, and her leash slipped out of my hands. The two dogs ran to each other, jumping, tackling, and rolling around like boxers in a ring.

"Daisy, no!" I yelled, rushing forward.

"Oh, Daisy's back for a visit!" a woman called from the side of the house.

I stopped and turned toward the woman, who didn't seem concerned that the dogs were nipping at one another. "Oh my gosh, are they okay? Looks like they're fighting!"

"Oh, that's how dogs play." The woman laughed, waving a hand as she walked to my side. "You must be Nova's friend. I'm Cathy."

"Oh, yes! Nova mentioned you fostered Daisy." I released a shaky breath and held out my hand. "I'm Cami. Jeez, that really scared me. I'm obviously not a dog person."

"Nova told me." Cathy grinned. "I offered for Daisy to stay with us while they took their trip. We fostered her for a few months before they adopted her. Such a sweet girl."

Heat crept up my neck. "You offered..." My voice trailed off. "She mentioned you were getting a new foster?"

"Hm, she did? No, no new dogs coming any time soon."

I inhaled. *Nova! You sneaky liar!*

"Bruno and Daisy are best buddies. We usually get them together a few times a week to play."

"B-Bruno?" I stuttered, still flaming from Nova's deception. *How could she? She tricked me!*

"Think he's been missing her, being all mopey."

"Daisy too. She practically dragged me here." I rubbed the sweat off the back of my neck—from anger, not the unusually warm temperature.

"Hot as heck, especially for this time of year. Want something to drink?" Cathy swatted at the back of her arm where a fly had landed.

I shook my head and smiled, loving how friendly Collins Grove was. Nan, Denise, Cathy—everyone I met was warm, welcoming, and genuine.

Maybe that's why Nova did it, a nagging voice whispered in my head. *You need a little kindness.*

I couldn't argue with my inner voice. People's energy helped feed my light, my soul, and the last few years had drained quite a bit from me. Guilt could be a vacuum, sucking time, energy, and purpose.

There was no way to right what had happened to Mama. And even though my father was evil to the core, what I did was wrong. I'd turned him to ash out of rage and retribution.

Now, guilt ravaged me, much like the fire had ravaged Papa. I didn't deserve Mama's gift. I couldn't control it. I hurt Mama, Papa, and Celia.

I couldn't change what happened to Mama or Papa, but I could make things right with Celia. I could restore her hope.

Maybe I didn't deserve Mama's gift, but Celia did.

CATHY and I exchanged numbers before we departed. Daisy walked home with a bounce in her step, rejuvenated from seeing her buddy Bruno.

"That's all you needed, huh, girl? Some time with your friend?" I let her lead the way home as my mind wandered. "Know how you feel. I had a friend who was like a sister to me. My baby sister. I watched her grow up into a sweet, shy woman."

I stopped walking and looked to the sky. *I'm talking to a dog.* But Daisy also stopped and sat. She looked at me with her big sweet soulful eyes, as if waiting for me to go on.

"Okay, okay. I'll tell you the rest, but I'm not proud of myself, Daisy. Celia, that's the girl, she fell in love with a boy, Neal—he's your new mama's twin. Nova and Neal also were like siblings to me. I watched them all grow from little tiny babies into strong powerful gods." I shook my head. "It's why what I did is so wrong. I *knew* Neal. He's immature, but he's good. He's *nothing* like Papa."

When I learned Neal was manipulating Celia, I'd lost control of my emotions. I'd never forget the image of sweet Celia's face crumbling when I told her how Neal was using his divine gift to twist her thoughts.

"Really, Daisy, I was scared." My voice wobbled, but I grew angrier. "I was scared, and it made everything so much worse. When I touched Celia, my panic seeped into her. I couldn't control my emotions, and now I worry Celia carries my pain, my fear."

Daisy made a whiny noise and licked my hand.

"You're a good listener, girl." I sniffed and rubbed an eye. "I want to fix it. I want Celia to have hope, to know that Neal's love is real. I want to take back the pain I caused her. She's lost, and I'm so worried she won't find her way. I *can* help her."

A noise rustled from above us. Both Daisy and I looked to the crown of the trees where a black bird circled before landing on a branch about ten feet away. Daisy growled, but I rested a hand on her back, and she settled.

"It's okay. Time for us to get home anyway." I wasn't about to push any more boundaries today.

SEVENTEEN

After showering and drying off, I fingered through Nova's wardrobe, searching for something to wear to Duffy's. Whatever remorse I'd possibly feel for borrowing one of her designer duds without asking was wiped away by her little white lie—she had other options for watching Daisy, yet she'd tricked me into coming.

Yanking a silk sundress off the hanger, I slid it over my head. The smooth material felt cool and feather-soft against my warm skin. It probably cost more than my monthly rent and was definitely too classy for a townie bar, but once I had it on, there was no way I'd take it off until the night ended.

The doorbell rang just as I slipped my foot into a black leather sandal. I blew Daisy a kiss, then hurried down the stairs.

"Wow!" Nan's eyes widened when I opened the door. "Dang. You look hot. Wait till the locals get a look at you!"

"Courtesy of Nova's fabulous wardrobe," I said, pinching the corners of my hem and dropping into a slight curtsy.

"Um, I think we need to play dress-up in her closet

sometime soon." Nan's hand skimmed the fabric. "This color looks *so* good on you. Really highlights your eyes."

"Seriously, we can skip trivia and have a fashion show." I hitched a thumb toward the stairs, still reeling from the thought that Nova had conned me.

Nan laughed and swatted her hand. "I was kidding. I'm sure Nova doesn't care having you, her *friend*, trying on her clothes, but she barely knows me. Besides, you are not getting out of trivia night."

"Fine. We'll do it another time." I linked arms with Nan and led her to the laundry room. "You look pretty hot yourself. Love the top."

The emerald-green tank Nan wore complimented her chestnut hair, which had been expertly styled into loose beachy waves. She wore black shorts and chunky high-heeled sandals that accented her toned legs. Nan's makeup was done up to perfection. A shimmery taupe eyeshadow highlighted her brown eyes, and a rosy-pink gloss made her full lips look pouty yet sweet.

"Maybe you can do my makeup and hair when we play dress-up. You've got talent."

Nan twisted a curl between her manicured fingers. "Just call me the queen of cosmetology." A perfect brow lifted. "But absolutely! It's a date."

I didn't have a house key since Nova and Dane usually exited and entered through the garage. I plugged in the code and watched the garage door creep lower, making sure it completely closed as Dane requested.

Liam's motorcycle was already gone. I'd heard him leave for Duffy's a few hours before.

Patting my hair, I followed Nan to her Ford Escape. It was an older model but pristinely kept, unlike Laverne who was littered with gum wrappers and gas receipts and hadn't had a proper wash in over a year. I wasn't a total slob, but I certainly wasn't as tidy as Nan.

"Duffy's is close, right?" I asked as Nan backed up, her eyes glued to the rearview camera screen. "Nova said I can walk there."

"Oh, you haven't been yet?" Nan flashed me a look, then refocused on the screen. "Yeah, really close."

I shook my head. "She said there's a path that follows some creek and takes you right there."

"Yep, Sully's Creek. I'll point it out when we pass it."

Nan maneuvered onto Lake Road. About three lots over, she pointed to a clearing. "You can catch the path there. It twists around, but if you keep walking that way, you'll eventually see the boat ramps and back patio of Duffy's. The creek empties into the lake. Duffy's has some awesome water frontage. Lots of people boat there."

Continuing straight, we passed the street Bruno lived on. Nan swung a left, heading in the opposite direction. She glanced my way and shrugged. "I'd guess it's a two-mile walk? Totally doable, but who wants to get all sweaty, especially in a dress like that."

A few minutes later, we pulled into the packed, gravel parking lot for Duffy's. Besides tinted glass doors, the front of the brown building was windowless. But inside, Duffy's was far from dark and dingy. A row of windows lined the back, offering a perfect view of the patio and lake. A long bar occupied the wall to our right while tables filled the middle and booths lined the left. People were everywhere—on the patio, sitting at tables, and lined up near the bar.

Happy, cheerful energy bounced from person to person, springing off the walls and hitting me in warm waves. A tingling sensation burned in my belly, the fire in me fed by the room's jovial atmosphere.

I noticed a familiar face a few steps in.

"Tom?" I asked, tapping the man I'd met briefly earlier in the day on the arm.

"Oh, hey." His eyes darted away and landed on Nan. "Hi, Nan."

"Hi, Tom!" Nan replied with a half-wave.

"I want to apologize about Liam," I said.

"Apologize?" His gaze jerked back to me. "What for?"

"For earlier today," I answered awkwardly. My fingers nervously pinched the edge of my silk dress's strap by my shoulder.

"Did something happen after I left?" Confusion creased his brow. He scratched his forehead and cocked his head in thought. "Crap, did I forget to do something?"

Shaking my head, I muttered, "No, no. Nothing. Never mind."

"Well, when you see Liam, tell him I appreciate everything he did for me today."

Now confusion drew my brows together, and I was the one cocking my head.

"Paid me extra and gave me the day off. I got to finish two things on my wife's 'honey-do' list."

"How is Cindy?" Nan interrupted. "Baby's coming soon, right?"

"Yep. Two weeks till her due date." Tom's eyes lit up as he held up two fingers, making a V. "Finished painting the nursery and put together the crib after Liam gave me the day off. He's a good dude. Paid me more than double and said it was a bonus for the baby. Cindy's sitting over there—wouldn't miss trivia even if she was in labor. Tell Liam she sends her thanks too."

"Cambria," a voice mumbled over my shoulder.

"Hey, Liam, thanks again." Tom patted Liam on the

arm, then hitched his thumb toward his wife. "Stop over when you get a chance. Cindy wants to thank you for today."

Tom walked away, leaving me alone with Liam since Nan was immersed in conversation with another patron.

I slowly turned and met Liam's gray eyes. "That was nice of you."

"Hmm?" Liam's mouth barely moved as the murmur left his lips. His eyes remained locked intently on me, paralyzing me in place.

It took a few seconds for me to be able to speak again. "Giving Tom the day off and some extra cash," I said, unblinking.

"I can be nice, Cambria."

"I know," I whispered. "I remember."

As if a magnet was pulling us together, we each took a step forward.

"I'm still that... man." Liam's breath hit my cheeks.

Time seemed to stand still as we stared at each other. His mouth was inches from mine, but I felt his lips as if they'd brushed over my own. I slowly dragged my arm up, bringing two fingers to touch my lower lip.

Liam's breath hitched, and he made a slight sound— a groan, but not from pain.

"Doesn't she look hot?" Nan squealed, looping her arm through mine, breaking our spell.

I blinked from the interruption, but my eyes still didn't leave Liam's.

An awkward silence followed until Liam severed it, saying, "Yes. She does. Have fun, ladies." He gave a nod and walked away.

"Oh my God. That was the hottest thing I've ever seen." Nan jabbed me in the side. "I knew you liked him."

A woman I didn't know came to my other side. "Seriously, I want a man who looks at me like that."

"Huh?" I turned to look at her. She was around Nan's age, late twenties.

"Like he wants to eat you up." She popped the P in "up" and grinned. "I can see why. You're the hottest thing in here tonight."

"Cam, this is Tori, my roommate." Nan pointed at her friend with her free hand. "Tor, Cam insists nothing is going on between those two." She tilted her head and wagged her brow. "*Right*. I don't believe it either."

"Nan!" I huffed. "Nice to meet you, Tori. And to clarify, *nothing* is going on between us. Liam is like a cranky old man."

"God, he's hot. Seriously. He's earned the nickname Li-yum." Tori fanned herself, just as Denise had at The Poppy Seed. "Think he and Dane single-handedly saved this bar just by bringing the eye candy." She cupped her mouth with one hand and silently mouthed, "Themselves."

"The guys around here don't want to hear any more about Dane and Liam and their fine asses. So, no talk about them at the table," Nan warned.

The girls led me to a half-full table. Three guys dressed in preppy polo shirts and pressed chinos were sitting back in their chairs, engrossed in their cell phones. They didn't seem to notice our arrival until Nan cleared her throat.

Tori rolled her eyes. "Typical."

"Guys, this is Cami," Nan said, putting her arm around my waist. Three sets of eyes roamed up and down my body, eyeing me like I was a piece of juicy steak.

"Nice." The one sitting to the left nodded his blond head and licked his lower lip.

"Umm. Nice to meet you too?" I half asked, half stated,

confused by the man's weird greeting. A fake, tight smile awkwardly lifted the corners of my mouth.

"Doesn't look like you know much about sports." The guy in the middle snickered. "But you can be on my team." He gave a cocky grin and held up a tablet. "Just logged our table on for trivia."

Huh? Who were these guys?

My distaste must've been obvious because Tori knocked the blond guy on the arm. "Eyes off. She's taken."

Taken? As in... Liam's girlfriend? I was about to correct her when the last guy pushed from his chair and moved around the table to Nan's side, bumping into me. He pulled Nan in, but as he grabbed her with one arm, his free hand brushed against my butt. I froze, praying Liam didn't see. It was a jerk move, but I didn't need or want a scene.

"Sorry." He extended the offending hand to shake. "I'm Chaz." A smirk spread across his thin lips as he squeezed my hand tightly—a little too tightly.

Oh, no. This isn't happening. Sweet Nan is not dating this disgusting jock.

The blond guy spoke up, introducing himself. "I'm Matt, and that ugly mug goes by Meatballs. We call him that because—well, I'll leave the *why* to your imagination." He wagged his eyebrows and threw his head back, laughing.

"You're a neanderthal." Chaz laughed with his friend. He had immaculately styled thick, dark blond hair. His baby-blue polo bore the logo and name of the Collins Grove Community Bank. He looked like a typical frat boy—lots of spending money and the arrogant attitude that came with it.

Nan and Tori took a seat while I remained standing. The only empty chair left was between the guy Matt had so tactfully referred to as Meatballs and Tori.

"I'm going to run to the bathroom," I said, needing a

moment to compose myself before joining the table. I looked around and waved a finger. "Which way is it?"

"I can show you!" Tori offered, scooching her chair back.

"Oh, that's okay. Just point the way."

"That way. Can't miss it. There're fake deer antlers on the door for the men's room, so look for the sign that says 'Doe.' Come to think of it, the antlers might be real." Tori looked expectantly at Meatballs.

"Naw, fake." He took a swig from his beer. "Game's starting in ten. Don't be late."

"Right." I cringed as I walked away. Their table dripped with toxic masculinity. I glanced back, wondering *what* Nan saw in Chaz.

Mind your own business, Cambria. The deep voice whispering in my head sounded an awful lot like Liam.

But it was sound advice. I'd meddled before, and it'd ended in disaster.

As I headed toward the bathroom, passing the bar, several eyes darted my way—assessing me, reminding me I was different. An outsider.

Nova and Nan warned me Duffy's was a townie bar; maybe it was simple curiosity.

But still, it reinforced one fact: I'd *always* be the outcast.

EIGHTEEN

Because I was a lumineer, positivity warmed my belly. Negativity ignited the same flame, but it felt different, and something about our table set my inner light ablaze. After I returned from the bathroom, I took a seat and tried to cool myself down.

My stomach twisted, as if lava were rolling and swooshing inside of me. It had to be nerves from meeting a new group of people.

I thought a glass of wine would help calm me, but it made me feel warmer instead. The silk dress stuck to my sweaty back. I scanned the room, hoping to see Liam. The man was infuriating, but something had me feeling off, and his familiarity would be comforting.

Spotting him, I inhaled long and slow. His head jerked my way as if sensing my stare. I gave a wan smile.

The group didn't seem to notice my building trepidation. They were in a deep debate, answering trivia questions, but Chaz's eyes would shift to me, making me squirm each time I caught him ogling.

Around the bar, patrons engaged in excited conversation as the trivia competition got underway. Happy chatter and laughter floated from the tables surrounding us, but a foreboding weight sat on my chest, making it hard to breathe. My foot tapped against the floor. I twisted and pinched the hem of my silk dress, pulling the material away from my clammy skin, unable to keep my hands still.

"I need air," I blurted out, pushing from my seat. I stood and made my way toward the door, stumbling as I wove between tables, but Liam was to me in a flash, steadying me.

"What's going on?" he asked, searching my face. I shook my head. I couldn't explain it. "I'm here," he said gruffly. "Everything's okay. Let's go outside."

Still unable to answer, I nodded. Liam positioned his hand under my elbow and guided me to the door.

Nan stopped us, placing a hand on my shoulder. "Cami? What's wrong?"

"Think I had too much sun earlier today. Not feeling well."

"Oh, hope you're okay. Can I help?"

"I got her." Liam kept his hand under my elbow. "Gonna get her fresh air."

"Okay, good. Thanks, Liam." She rubbed my shoulder, easing some of my tension.

Liam guided me out the front door and into the parking lot. The warm breeze brushed my cheeks, clearing my head of the fog. I splayed my fingers out in front of me, then wiggled them. My stomach uncoiled. I breathed in and out, slowly relieving the weight on my chest. The unease fell away in layers.

I shivered, and Liam started to unbutton the flannel he wore over a plain white T-shirt.

"Here," he said, offering it to me.

"I'm okay. Actually, I feel fine." I took a step back and placed a finger at my temple. "That was weird. Maybe it was too many people, too much energy... with the game and all. You know how competitive people can get. I think it just hit me. In the city, I'm used to being around people, but in the last two days since I've been here, the solitude may have thrown me off balance." I was rambling, but Liam kept staring at me so I kept talking. "I'm fine."

He tilted his head and probed my face with his intense eyes.

"I think I'm going to head home. You should get back in there. Looks busy. I can walk. Nan showed me the path."

"I'll take you." He started toward his motorcycle, which was parked in the first stall to the immediate right of the front entrance. He turned and shoved the flannel into my arms. "Put this on. Wind'll feel cold."

"Okay." I slipped into the shirt. He had the sleeves rolled up, which made it the perfect length for my arms. Nearing the bike, I stopped and tugged at his arm. "Wait! I'm wearing a dress." I pointed to the hem of Nova's silk dress.

His eyes flashed to my legs. "See that."

"I'm not getting on *that* wearing *this*." I pointed to his bike, then to myself.

"Fine. We'll walk." He turned and stomped toward the back of the building.

I followed. "You don't have to walk me home. Have one of your little birds follow me if you're worried."

"Gonna walk with you."

Already feeling like a burden, I didn't argue and followed him to the back lawn of the bar. An expansive flat, grassy area led to the lake. A few pontoon boats and speedboats were docked along the piers. Patrons mulled around the back, walking to and from the crowded patio—some had to-go containers while others ate at picnic tables.

"I didn't know they served food here," I said as I followed him to the shoreline. A clear-cut path had been made through the trees that flanked each side of Duffy's yard.

"Yep." Liam wasn't known for small talk or idle chatter, but his clipped responses seemed purposeful, annoyed.

On the path, the trees above us offered a natural umbrella from the warm September sun, which had begun its descent. The trail hugged the shoreline but quickly split from the lake to the creek. Dense shrubs and wildflowers provided a barrier, keeping pedestrians on the path while not obstructing the spectacular view. Crystal-clear water bubbled over jagged rocks. The setting was as peaceful and perfect as Nova had described it. Now I understood why she opted to walk versus drive the two miles.

"So, this is what is meant by the phrase 'babbling brook'?" I asked, needing to break the awkward silence.

Liam grunted in response.

At our pace, the trail to Nova's house would take at least half an hour to walk. I sighed. "I can see this is gonna be a fun walk."

Liam stopped in his tracks, eyeing me. The muscles in his jaw tensed.

"Yes?" I offered after he stood silently, still staring at me.

"You shouldn't have left."

"The bar? I didn't feel well. Something's off." I shrugged.

Liam shook his head. "Not talking about leaving the bar."

"The house? Nan invited me to trivia." I pulled the

flannel tighter around my body and continued walking. "Do you seriously expect me to just sit at the house this next week? God, Liam, you're impossible. By the way, I found out Nova *tricked* me into staying. Daisy's foster parents *could* have watched her. But no, for some stupid reason, Nova lied to get me to stay here. Under the same roof as *you*."

I was babbling again, just like the brook. I kept going and going. "I am going to have a word with her when she calls. I can't believe it. Why in the world did she think this was a good idea?" I threw up my arms, exasperated.

"Stop," Liam said gruffly, and I realized I'd been walking and talking, landing me several feet ahead of him. I turned to face him. His blank face was unreadable, but the stiffness of his shoulders spoke volumes. "Not tonight. I meant the Hark. You should not have left the Hark."

Caught off guard, I let out a low "Oh" and looked down to the pebbled trail.

He walked to my side. "You should have stayed with Lucille."

My face warmed from embarrassment. I balled my hands. "I can walk the rest of the way myself."

"You were impatient. Always so impatient."

I turned and clomped away. His footsteps followed. We walked silently for at least ten minutes before he spoke again.

"Lucille could have helped you. You would have healed much faster."

"Healed from what?" I yelled, whipping around to face him. "From you kissing me, then ditching me? No note, no goodbye. *Nothing.*"

He grabbed my arms and pulled me in, keeping enough space so I could still see his face, but not enough room where I could ignore his intoxicating scent—the woodsy, earthy, sexy scent that had my insides flipping. I already wore his shirt, but it smelled of detergent—not *him*. Not the distinct scent that was Liam. *My* Liam.

In a choked voice, I said, "Maybe I should be asking *you* —why did *you* kiss me? You kissed me, and the next thing I know, I'm waking up in the Hark. If you want to know why I left, it was to find *you*. To find out *why*. So tell me, Liam, why?"

We stared at each other as the creek lulled in the background, settling my pounding pulse. After several long seconds, he blinked. I counted it as a win—one of the few times I'd actually won one of our silly staring contests.

"I shouldn't have kissed you," he confessed, releasing his hold and jamming his hands into the pockets of his jeans. "That kiss should not have happened. I was caught in the moment, not thinking right."

My heart shattered, and the heat in my stomach cooled. I lowered my eyes. Liam's rejection stung as much now as it had then.

We walked the rest of the way in silence with Liam keeping a few steps behind me.

At the top of the drive, Liam punched in the garage code, and we watched the door creep up. I didn't say goodbye or look back as I walked through the garage to the interior door. Once inside, I leaned against the wall, listening to the creaking sound of the door closing. I exhaled, releasing a mile's worth of breath.

"Why, oh why did you do this to me, Nova?" I asked the question out loud.

Daisy, upon hearing my voice, barreled down the stairs. She ran to my side and licked my hand as I held it out to scratch her.

"Your mama is in big trouble," I told her. "Come on, let's see if big bad Liam has left the building." I walked through the dark laundry room to the kitchen, then headed to the foyer to peek out the window. Liam's head slowly faded as he treaded down the steep drive. Just as I lost sight of him, a black bird swooped above, landing on the veranda where I assumed he'd stand watch until Liam returned.

"Need to go out, girl?" I asked. Daisy cocked her head, which I took as a yes. "Let's go to the back."

Daisy followed me through the kitchen. I slid open the glass door and stepped out behind her onto the porch. A bird circled above us before taking a perch on the top of the shed. I assumed it was the same messenger from the veranda. Daisy didn't bark at the bird or pay any notice of it. She did her business, then padded up the stairs to my side.

"Nice night out. Want to sit out here for a bit?" I asked, waiting for her to answer. She yawned and stretched. I sighed. "You're right. Let's go to bed."

Once upstairs, I yanked the silk dress over my head, giving another sigh as I threw it in the closet next to my unpacked suitcase. Groaning, I glared at the silken puddle, realizing I'd have to dry-clean the dress, even though I'd only worn it for a few hours. Deep wrinkles etched the delicate fabric.

"Come on, Daisy-girl, let's find a show." She looked up from her doggy bed, then laid her head back down on her front legs and closed her eyes. "Even rejected by a dog. Wow, I must be some kind of special."

I flipped on the TV, responded to a few text messages from Nan and Gwen, then settled into the mound of silk-covered pillows on the bed. The events of the evening slipped away as I drifted in and out of sleep, finally plummeting into a deep state of slumber.

Nan wandered into my dreams, strolling along the same path Liam and I had taken earlier in the night from Duffy's to Nova and Dane's house. With each step she took, the sky grew darker. Her feet crunched over pebbles. She wrapped her arms over her chest, as if she were either cold or anxious. She kept walking and picked up her pace, glancing back every so often. Another crunching noise sounded above her footsteps.

It's a bunny, I whispered to her, but she couldn't hear me.

The crunching grew louder. Nan twisted her head to look behind her as her walk turned into a jog. Branches snapped. The wind whistled. Leaves rustled.

Nan, it might be a bear! I tried to yell to her in my dream, but she still couldn't hear me. She scanned the forest, her eyes darting and widening, then she started running, horror filling her face as Papa lunged from the bushes.

"No!" I yelled, bolting upright and panting. Sweat trickled between my cleavage and behind my knees. The sheets were cold and wet from my nightmare.

Liam was through the door and to my side before I had a chance to rub away the tears painting my cheeks. "Cambria," he said softly as he kneeled beside my bed. "Another nightmare?"

I nodded, sniffing and swiping away my emotions.

"Move over," he commanded softly.

I did as told, and he climbed in beside me, wrapping his arms around me. My head hit his chest, and my eyes grew tired and heavy. They drifted closed, and I returned to a deep state of sleep, this time dreaming of Lucille's beautiful cottage and the butterflies that danced above the flowers.

When I woke the next morning, Liam was gone. The

other side of the bed looked untouched. As my mind replayed the foggy memory of my night terror, I couldn't decipher fact from fiction. I didn't know if Liam had once again come in the night or if it was another figment of my wishful imagination.

NINETEEN

Daisy and I left for a morning walk without running into Liam. His motorcycle was parked in the garage, so I assumed he was fishing.

At the bottom of the drive, Daisy tugged at the leash, pulling me northbound onto Lake Road.

"No, Daisy, we'll see Bruno later. Let's get a treat at The Poppy Seed. Nan's worried about me." I wondered if everyone slipped so easily into one-sided conversations with pets.

After a short stand-off, Daisy relented. Feeling a little guilty, I allowed her extra time to sniff the grass along the way, which meant our thirty-minute walk turned to forty-five.

"Almost there," I said to Daisy, although the pep talk was more for my benefit. With no breakfast or morning caffeine, I was operating on fumes by the time we turned onto Main Street.

A motorcycle slowly passed us, snapping my attention to the model and driver. It wasn't Liam, but I recognized the blond hair—Nan's ex. He slowed down as he passed the coffee shop.

"Give it up, pal," I muttered. "She's moved on."

Take your own advice, Cam.

Liam's kiss happened decades before, yet the torch I desperately clung to still flickered. His confession last night snuffed out the remnants of hope—he regretted it happened. *I shouldn't have kissed you.* My cheeks flamed.

I must've still looked red in the face when I stepped into The Poppy Seed because Nan immediately filled a plastic cup with ice and water.

"The heat wave continues, huh?" she asked, handing it to me. "How are you feeling? Make sure you stay hydrated today."

I gulped half of it down, saving the rest for Daisy. "I'm going to give Daisy-girl a drink. Think she's holding a little grudge—she has a doggy pal she wanted to visit this morning. Don't want to leave her thirsty too. Be right back."

"Oh, here." Nan plucked a bone-shaped dog biscuit from below the counter. "This should help win back her good graces."

I grinned and grabbed the treat. "You're the best."

I was back a few minutes later, wiping off the slobber from Daisy's affectionate kisses upon seeing the treat. "Worked like a charm. If only people could be won over so easily."

"Yeah. So, tell me about your night with Liam." Nan wagged her eyebrows as she dropped her elbows onto the counter and rested her chin in her hands.

"Oh, no. No. Nothing is going on between us. I promise." I held up two fingers, flashing what I thought was the Girl Scouts' honor sign.

"What's that—you a *Hunger Games* fan?" Nan laughed

and swatted my hand. "It looked pretty clear to our table—and the bar for that matter—that Liam and you have something going on. He was on you like a fly on poo."

"He's really overprotective of me. Big-brother type stuff." I absently waved a hand and changed the subject. I didn't need that little flame of hope reigniting from Nan's nonsense. "Speaking of a fly on poo—that's a really gross visual by the way—I saw your ex pass the shop this morning. What's the story with you two?"

Nan rolled her eyes. "That's a story that should be told over coffee. What do you want?"

"Tea, actually. Any kind as long as it has caffeine. And please add a little of your local honey." I took a seat as Nan prepared tea for me and coffee for herself. The walls of The Poppy Seed's cozy interior were painted a light shade of blue and decorated with artwork made by locals, all available for purchase. "This place is so cute. Love that you guys support local artists too. Where's Denise?"

"Oh, you just missed her. She was in at five this morning, helping our main baker, Medine. Med's here with her until I get in, then Denise usually goes home for a nap after we have our morning rush and gets back around two to help with the after-school crowd. We close shop at four. It's crazy on afternoons when I have school. I have to leave on the nose, although my instructor is pretty understanding if I'm a little late. I just feel bad leaving the clean-up and close-down all on Denise."

"Right. You'll be in Milwaukee tonight, huh?"

"Yep. It's a four-hour class tonight." She blew out a puff of air, sending a few of her chestnut strands dancing.

"Sounds like an exhausting day."

"It is. I left my house at quarter to eight and won't get

home until after ten tonight. I wasn't joking when I said we could use extra help."

Nan handed me my tea, then sank into the seat across from me. She propped her feet up on the chair between us with a sigh. "So, you want to hear about Aaron." I tilted my head. Noting my quizzical expression, she added, "My annoying ex."

"Oh, right." I leaned back and took a sip. My cell pinged. The screen illuminated with a notification of a new text from Liam. "Talk about annoying. Hang on, I should check this."

She grinned. "Right, nothing going on between you two. Sure."

Liam: *Where are you?*

Me: *NOYB*

Liam: *Where's that?*

I tilted the screen so Nan could read the messages.

Me: *It means none of your business*

Liam: *You're my business.*

Nan laughed, cupping her cheeks. "Wow!"

Three dots appeared, indicating Liam was typing. I shot him a final message—*At The Poppy Seed*—then flipped the phone facedown and set it on the table, not bothering to wait for his reply.

Rolling my eyes, I gave a shake of my head and said, "Okay, so Aaron. Tell me all about the stalker on the Harley."

Nan sipped her coffee, then offered a small smile, pulling in her lower lip as if thinking, then slowly exhaled. "Maybe 'stalker' is a bit harsh. We dated off and on for the last decade—since high school. But the last three years, we were solid. He worked his ass off to put himself through college. Got his bachelor's degree in mechanical engineering, so no walk in the park. And he did it with no support from his family." Her eyes flashed to the wall. "It's what makes what happened so hard to believe." She focused blankly on an abstract painting for a few more seconds, then said, "You are so easy to talk to. I don't get the judgy vibe from you at all."

"I'm here to listen, not judge." I held no room on my guilty conscience for judgment.

She smiled weakly as she adjusted herself in the chair, uncrossing and recrossing her legs. "Well, see, the thing is, my brother's an addict, and Aaron comes from a family of abusers. I thought we were on the same page, both not wanting to go down that path." She wrinkled her nose and looked at me. Tears glistened in her eyes. "I found coke on him—well, tucked in the saddlebag of his bike. I thought we were going to get married. I thought he was serious about committing to me, to a better future—not the destructive life that comes with drugs."

Nan's raw hurt and honesty had me reflexively reaching for her hand and squeezing it gently, exerting my positive energy. It seeped slowly into her, like aloe on a sunburn. Her hot, sweaty hand cooled under my touch. A warm glow lit her cheeks. She pulled her hand away and looked at it.

After what happened with Celia, I avoided using my gift of touch at all costs. Instead, I taught others how to tap their internal light with yoga or meditation. I'd forgotten how good it felt to physically share my energy.

The benefit of my gift was mutual—as much to me, the healer, as to Nan, the receiver. We both sat silently for a few seconds, each stunned and curious about the sensations that had passed between us. She tilted her head and looked from her hand to me. I averted my eyes. How would I explain what just happened?

"So, um, what about the guy from the bar last night?" I asked, hoping to take the attention off me. Besides, I genuinely was curious about Chaz... and what she could possibly see in him.

"Oh, Chaz?" She rubbed her hands together, then tucked them in her lap. "We're not serious, but he asked me out, and I figured why not. I've known him forever. He comes from one of Collins Groves' founding families. His dad is president of the bank, and his mom's on the city council. He's... Well, he's the opposite of Aaron in pretty much every way. Grew up with both parents, always had money, played college ball. That sort of thing." The corners of her lips turned down, and she lowered her voice. "Aaron doesn't know his dad. His mom's had druggie boyfriends in and out of the picture. Didn't do sports or anything in high school because he had to work. That kind of thing."

"So, kind of the jock versus the bad boy?" Calling Chaz a jock was being polite.

"Thing is, Aaron has done so much to break from his mom's destructive cycle—college, dream job. I don't know why he'd touch that stuff, and he knows how I feel about it. Yet, he chose drugs over me." She shrugged and smiled brightly, obviously faking it. "It's sad, but what am I going to do? He offered no explanation, no apology. Now he drives by looking all sad and pathetic."

"You haven't talked to him about it?"

She shook her head. "Nope. When I found the stuff, I blew up. We haven't spoken since. If only he would've—" The bell above the door jingled, and Nan's head whipped around, then back to me. "We'll talk more later." She pushed back from her chair, leaned in, and whispered, "Small town with big mouths."

"Got it." I chuckled and also stood. "I should check on

Daisy and let you get back to work. Poor girl, I almost forgot she was out there."

"Here, let me get another treat for her. Tell her I'm sorry I kept you." Nan handed me a dog biscuit. "Thanks for listening. I feel better." She looked at her hand, then held it to her heart and smiled brightly. This time, her grin reached her eyes, creasing the corners and dimpling her cheeks. My belly warmed—I helped put the light in her eyes. "Really. I feel better than I have in a while. Maybe it's good for me to talk about it. Get it all out."

"Yeah, talking is good," I said softly, thinking about Celia.

Both Celia and Nan had been betrayed by the men they loved. But for Celia, Neal's deception and my touch left her in a dark place. I knew I could help her—I could bring her back to the light.

"Hey, Daisy-girl," I called as I stepped outside. "Nan got you an extra—" My voice dropped at the sight of a black bird perched on the bench above a snoozing Daisy. "Seriously, Liam," I muttered to myself, skipping down the steps to Daisy's side. I unhooked her leash, gave her a few good scratches as she stretched awake, then handed her the treat. "Come on, girl."

She trotted alongside me, happily munching her biscuit. The bird didn't move. I gave it a departing glare as we turned onto Charles Street.

TWENTY

Daisy and I stepped onto the veranda just in time to hear an exasperated Liam huffing into the phone.

"Not buying it. Last week it was your grandma. This week it's your dog."

Daisy, who I'd never heard really bark before, decided at that moment to use her voice when a squirrel ran across the front lawn and up a tree.

"Daisy," I whispered, pursing my lips as I held a finger up. "Shh." I leaned my ear closer to the screen door, trying to make out the rest of the conversation.

"You don't come in at four, you're fired." From the silence that followed, I assumed the conversation was done, and Dane most likely just lost an employee. Liam's stomping footsteps neared, and his voice boomed from within the door. "Cambria!"

I shuffled a few steps back, then slowly inched toward one of the rocking chairs. "Here! Yes. I mean, I'm home. What's up?"

His face appeared behind the screen. "You have a job tonight."

"A job?" I reached behind to feel for the edge of the chair to steady my wobbly legs. "I do?"

"Wednesdays are slow. Won't be anything like last night."

"Liam."

"Tips are good."

"Li-umm," I said louder, enunciating the syllables in his name.

"Short shift." He stepped onto the porch. "You need money."

I glared at him. "Did you fire someone?"

"Bella... Belle, whatever her name is, quit."

"Because you're a jerk. You don't know how to talk to people."

"She gives Dane this bologna almost every week. *I'll be late. My grandma has an appointment. My dog's been yakking. I sprained my ankle.*" Liam's attempt at a high-pitched voice had me giggling and rolling my eyes. "Dane buys it. I don't."

"Well, sounds like you now have a problem on your hands." I sank into the rocking chair and watched as Daisy circled the tree.

Liam placed his hands on his hips. I tried not to look at him.

"Your other problem is you don't ask. You order," I said with a sugary-sweet voice.

"Cambria."

"Let's make a deal. Call off the birds, and I'll help. I don't like them following me."

He narrowed his eyes and dropped his hands from his hips. "Fine."

"After last night, I'm surprised you think me going to Duffy's is a good idea—usually you're stupidly overprotective. But if you stop using your weird presider angel powers with me, then we have a deal." I shrugged and held out my hand to shake on it.

He lightly gripped my much smaller hand in his larger, calloused one. As his fingers lingered, I looked up to catch his eyes gently exploring my face. His thumb massaged the top of my hand.

Take my hand. Take my hand and don't let go.

The past whispered between our connected flesh. It murmured in the wind. It brushed my cheeks like a kiss from the breeze. Soft, gentle, comforting. Safe.

Liam's touch spoke wordless promises. I'd always be safe with him.

Regardless of whether his messengers of the divine followed me, he'd be there. He was always there, coming to my rescue.

With our hands still clasped, he pulled me up from my seat in the rocking chair and toward him, tilting his head. His jaw ticked. "I will *always* protect you."

My breath hitched. I swear my heart stopped, then restarted. I stood silent, waiting to be able to breathe again. With him so close, my brain ran slower, and my lungs didn't get the message that they needed air.

Liam released his hold on my hand but brought his fingers up to my cheek, slowly curling them into a fist. He brushed his knuckles along my jawline. I let my eyes drift shut, relishing his touch. Tingles shot down my spine, and I almost sighed from pleasure.

He then took a step back, snapping us both from the hypnotic moment. The hand that had so gently grazed my face dropped to his side. I peeked up at him. He was flawlessly handsome with an intoxicating touch. He'd already broken my heart once, and I feared he'd do it again.

"Cam," he said softly, surprising me with the ache in his voice. He always called me by my full name. "I do it because I care."

I gave a nod, lowering my eyes. "I know."

He shifted from foot to foot, then took another step back. I rarely saw Liam look uncomfortable. He held immense power—nothing fazed him.

Except you.

I wasn't sure if he said it out loud or if I imagined it, but he cleared his throat and all softness vanished from his gritty voice. "We'll need to leave around a quarter to four."

"COME ON. Won't look good if you're late," Liam called from the bottom of the stairs.

"Go ahead. I'll meet you there."

"What's taking so long?"

"Liam!" I scolded as I skipped down the steps. "If you are so eager to go, then leave. Jeez. You have no idea how women operate, do you?"

"Through the garage," he said, leading the way to the laundry room. "Daisy's good?"

"Yep. Just let her out, and I fed her a bit ago. Now she's curled up in her doggy bed. I left the TV on for her like Nova said. *Animal Planet.*"

The garage door creaked up, releasing a ray of the afternoon sun. I flipped the sunglasses down from the top of my head. Liam stopped at his Harley. I walked past him to Laverne, who hadn't moved since I arrived Monday morning.

"See you there," I called over my shoulder.

I climbed into the bug, closed the door, then rolled the

windows down. Although the outside temperature had slightly cooled from the unusual highs earlier in the week, the car's interior was stiflingly hot. I stuck the key in the ignition and turned. Nothing. I tried again with the same results. Great. Simply great. Any tips I made tonight would be going to repairs.

Sighing, I rolled the windows back up, yanked the key from the ignition, and climbed out.

"Not starting?" Liam shoved his hands into his pockets as he placed his right foot over his left foot. A small grin played at his lips.

"Yeah. Can you do your little head jerk thing and get her going?"

"No more weird presider powers." Liam shrugged and patted the itty-bitty passenger seat on his bike. "Come on."

"I'll walk, thanks."

"You'll be late."

"It's okay. I know the manager. He wouldn't dare fire me."

The bright blue sky grumbled as the clouds began to spin, swirling from powder white to an ominous gray. The smile tugging at Liam's lips lifted mischievously. "Don't want to get caught in whatever's coming. Not lookin' so good." He flipped a leg over the bike.

"Liam!" I stomped my foot and scowled.

"Listen. No time to walk. Hop on."

I eyed the motorcycle. We'd have to sit pretty close with the minuscule seats. The motor revved to life, and he jerked his chin. Sighing, I slowly walked his way, tugging at the hem of the black Duffy's T-shirt Liam had given to me earlier in the day.

"Put your hands on my shoulders. There's a peg down there for your foot."

"Easy-peasy," I muttered, gripping Liam's shoulders as I stepped on the peg and hoisted myself up.

"Put your arms around my waist." Liam's command sounded husky, even over the idling motor. "Now, relax, but hold on."

Relax? My body was on high alert, wound up like a yo-yo and ready to spiral from his nearness. I had to force myself to breathe as my arms circled him. But breathing meant smelling, and his musky scent only made my stomach coil even more.

Slowly, we moved down the drive. The bike vibrated under me, and Liam's torso hardened under my hold. He had a body made of steel, like the bike under us.

"Lean with me into the turns," he called over his shoulder before we turned onto Lake Road. I held him a little tighter, closed my eyes, and let his body guide me. The bike tilted slightly, and when I opened my eyes next, we were on the open road. A thrilling sensation of the wind whipping my cheeks as the bike sped up made my heart pound.

This must be how a bird feels—fast and free.

I pressed my cheek into Liam's back and giggled, squeezing a little tighter. One of Liam's hands must've left the handlebar because I felt him squeeze back on my thigh.

The trip was over almost as soon as it began. The bike carried us to Duffy's in a matter of minutes. Liam pulled into the same front spot as the previous day and cut the engine.

He turned and said, "Wasn't so bad, right?" The low rasp of his voice vibrated along with the bike, prickling my skin.

I flipped up my sunglasses and laughed. "That was... awesome!"

Liam grinned, and my heart pounded again. His mouth was inches from mine. I could see every crease and impression of his beautiful face. When he smiled, all he carried—the severity and gravity of his station—seemed to fall away, and he looked young and carefree, reminding me of the breathtakingly handsome man who'd turned to me and said, "Call me Liam, kid," melting away all my fears and reservations.

"Cambria?" he said, twisting. "You get off first. Okay?"

"Right." I climbed off the bike, then patted my wind-tangled hair. "I should probably run a comb through this mess."

"Not a mess." Liam's gaze roamed over my face and down my T-shirt. "I'll be inside in a minute and can introduce you to tonight's crew."

I nodded and left Liam as he hoisted himself from the bike. Duffy's was nearly empty when I pushed through the door. Only two older men sat at the bar.

The guy behind the counter gave a half-wave. "Hey, you must be Cambria," he called.

"Yes! But I go by Cami." I returned his wave and smile.

"Heard Bella got the—" The bartender made a slicing motion over his throat.

My cheeks warmed. "Yeah..."

"She was always calling in for some stupid reason or another. Dane's too much of a softie." He filled a glass with beer and slid it to one of the men. "I'm Dex, by the way."

"Nice to meet you," I said, moving to the counter and extending my hand. "I have to warn you, I'm a bit out of my element here. I've never waitressed—or whatever Liam wants me to do tonight."

"Oh, you'll be fine. Our menu's easy—burgers, pizza, bar food. Besides, Wednesdays are slow. There's a ball game that two other bars sponsor, so a lot of people hit up those places after the game. Money will still be good. Dane makes sure we get paid well even on slow nights."

Liam came through the door, and Dex yelled out a greeting. The two men at the bar also held up their hands, giving a weird type of salute.

"Dex." Liam nodded to the bartender. "See you've met Cambria."

"Call me Cami," I interjected. Being called Cambria felt weird. Besides, Liam was the only one to call me by my full name. For some reason, I wanted to keep it that way. "I told Dex I wasn't sure what I'd be doing tonight."

"Helping me take orders and deliver stuff."

"You're waiting tables?" My brows hit my hairline. "No!" Wide-eyed, I looked at Dex, who nodded.

"Yeah, he's had to step in a few times."

"Liam's good at giving orders, but taking them?"

Dex threw his head back and laughed, slapping the bar top. "Oh, that's good. Jonesy's going to crack up when he hears that one."

"Alan Jones works in the kitchen," Liam clarified. "Tonight, it'll be me, you, Dex, and Alan."

"Michelle too." Dex looked at me. "Don't call Jonesy Alan. He despises it."

Shaking my head at Liam, I muttered, "Oh, Liam."

"Wait, Michelle's on the schedule?" Liam looked up, as if searching his memory. "She wasn't on my schedule."

"She'll be here at five."

Liam scrubbed his hand over his eyes. "Guess I don't need you here, Cambria."

I looked at Dex. "I know how Jonesy feels. I go by Cami." Smoothing the black Duffy's shirt, I shrugged. "It's okay, Uilliam, I can help out as needed. Make it a training day in case there's another snag in the schedule."

"Uilliam?" Dex rubbed his palms together. "Oh, Jonesy is going to love this." He turned on his heels and nearly sprinted to the swinging door labeled "Kitchen."

I stuck my tongue out at Liam. He scowled, seeming ready to scold me when the door flew open. I whipped around to see Nan's sad stalker ex, Aaron, walking into the bar. Liam gave a single, unsmiling nod.

Aaron took a seat at the bar, then said to Liam, "Got your message. Just checked your bike. She's fine."

Liam shrugged. "Something seemed off. Leaking a little more than normal. How much I owe you?"

Aaron waved a hand. "Nothing. On the house."

"Well, how about a sandwich on this house?" Liam hitched his thumb toward the kitchen.

"Yeah, sure." Aaron plucked a menu from the condiment caddy. He studied it, then ordered a burger.

"I'll put in your order. Cambria can get you a drink." Liam pushed against the same door Dex had just disappeared through.

"Cami," I said, tapping my chest. "I go by Cami. What would you like? Although, I have to warn you, I don't know how to use the beer tapper thingy."

Aaron smiled and looked down at the bar top. He kind of reminded me of Liam. Dirty-blond hair, a plain black T-shirt and jeans. Solemn and quiet. "Water's fine. Thanks."

I pulled a glass from under the bar and filled it with ice. "Um, water." I looked around, locating the handheld soda gun. I pressed and released it, spraying water all over the counter. "Bartenders make it look so easy. Okay, let me try that again." After filling the glass, I wiped the excess water off the edges and set it in front of Aaron.

"Thanks." He rapped the bar top, keeping his eyes down.

I watched him take a sip, then I sighed. "Listen, I get that you still have feelings for Nan, and I know it's none of my business, but you're creeping her out."

Red dotted his cheeks. He pushed his glass around, leaving streaks of condensation on the counter. "I don't know what else to do. We broke up over a big lie."

Searching his face, I recognized his pain. Neal and Celia broke up over a misunderstanding, and they continued to suffer from the separation.

I promised myself I would never again meddle in a relationship, but Aaron's sad eyes tugged at my heart.

"So, what happened?" I asked, propping my elbows down and leaning in.

"This asshole we went to high school with set me up. Planted coke on my bike."

"Some guy set you up. But why?"

"Stupid high school shit he can't let go of. But the thing is, Nan believed it. She knows me, yet she thinks I'd jeopardize everything for drugs. I worked my ass off for six years putting myself through college, then another four working shit jobs at Harley so I could finally move into my dream position. I wouldn't mess any of it up over drugs. Not with Nan, not with my job. Looks like Chaz wins again."

"Chaz?" I frowned as my pulse ticked up.

Aaron crossed his arms over his chest and lowered his voice. "Yeah, spoiled asshole we graduated with. Daddy has him working at the bank. He's a mean SOB, but get a little alcohol in him, and he's violent. But Daddy always gets him out of trouble. I'm sick seeing Nan hang out with him."

"Really?"

"It might be a small town, but Chaz's dad runs a big

bank. All the area businesses from the neighboring towns bank there. That prick thinks he's invincible because of Daddy's deep pockets. Only going to get deeper when the deal for the new business park goes through."

"Why didn't you say anything?"

"Huh?"

"When it happened, why didn't you explain yourself?"

He scoffed and leaned in. "Because I was pissed. Nan and I had been dating forever. I bought the ring. I thought she was *the one*. And she believed a lie from the town asshole? She had no faith in me." He shook his head and absently made a ring around his water glass with his index finger. "But the sad thing is, I *still* think she's the one. Even though she didn't believe in me, I still believe in us."

I shouldn't get involved. I knew it'd come back to bite me in the butt.

But I wasn't the least bit surprised when I heard my own voice promising, "I'll help you make things right."

TWENTY-ONE

Dex and Liam weren't exaggerating when they warned Wednesdays were slow. A couple of boaters came in for to-go orders, but other than a few random seats taken at the bar, the tables sat mostly empty.

Michelle rushed in at five fifteen, offering a flurry of apologies for being late. I assumed she'd gotten word of Bella's dismissal.

"Guys, seriously, check the scanner. Police had part of Waverly Street closed off. Took me forever to get through." She yanked at her long ponytail, pulled it tighter, then dropped her hands and smiled when she noticed me. "Oh, hi."

"Hi. I'm Cami." Since I was behind the bar, I offered a wave.

"Bella's replacement?"

"Not really. I'm helping out with Daisy until Dane and Nova get back. I think Liam forgot you were on the schedule today, so he had me come in for backup."

"Right! I heard about you. Nice to meet you in person."

She grinned, flashing perfectly white teeth and a gummy smile. "I'm a friend of Nan's."

"Oh, she's the best!"

Michelle and I spent the next hour chatting like old friends as we filled ketchup bottles and salt and pepper shakers and wiped down the laminated menus tucked into the condiment caddies at each table. When the door finally opened with customers, Michelle and I turned to see Chaz and a buddy walk in. Both men wore polos tucked into pressed khakis. Red tinged their cheeks and forearms.

Michelle went to their table as I moved behind the bar next to Dex and Liam.

"He's such a tool." Dex rolled his eyes as he began filling two glasses. "Brandy old-fashioned, which he'll drink half of, then send back because something's wrong. Cheap-ass jerk."

"Tell him no." Liam shrugged and folded his arms over his chest. "He takes more than a few sips, he's paying for it."

"I'll leave that up to you, boss," Dex said.

Michelle walked back, rolling her eyes as she relayed the order to Dex, who already was muddling the drink.

"Wanna bet there's something off about the seltzer?" she said under her breath. "They're already half in the bag from golfing."

Minutes later, Dex, Liam, Michelle, and I watched Chaz slurp half the drink, then lift his hand and wave Michelle over.

She planted on a smile and walked away, muttering, "Jerk alert."

I had to give her credit; the smile didn't fade as Chaz complained. We couldn't hear what he was saying—maybe Liam could, but he gave no indication—but Chaz pointed to the half-full lowball and then to the bar, wrinkling his nose and shaking his head. Michelle took the glass and walked our way.

"Apparently he wanted a whiskey old-fashioned? This is brandy." Michelle tilted the cup, exposing chunks of ice and smashed fruit.

"Took him half the glass to figure that out?" Liam said, putting his hands on his hips.

"Never fails. That's his MO." Dex grabbed the glass and dumped the contents. "Dude's dad has more money than God, but he can't pay his bar tab or tip." Flipping a new lowball onto the counter, Dex started preparing a new drink.

"Hold on. Why haven't I heard this before?" Liam asked, narrowing his eyes on Chaz.

Both Dex and Michelle shrugged.

"Let me handle this."

"Liam," I said calmly. "Play nice."

Liam flashed the quickest smile and sauntered to Chaz's table. Conversation between the two men was filled with theatrical hand and arm motions. As Liam took a step back, crossing his arms forebodingly across his chest, a red-faced Chaz pushed back in his chair.

"Oh, crap," Dex hissed. "Chaz has a temper."

"Liam can handle him." I sucked in my lower lip, watching the drama unfold. I was surprised Chaz was taking it as far as he was. Liam was formidable when relaxed; he looked downright deadly when angry.

As Chaz pushed to his feet, a young guy came through the door, yelling, "Hey, who here has the convertible?" All sets of eyes twisted in his direction.

"Why?" Chaz said, balling his hands into fists.

"Flock of birds just took a dump on your front seat."

"Dammit." Chaz groaned, marching toward the door

and growling, "Come on, Sam!"

The guy at his table sheepishly apologized to Liam as he followed Chaz out of the bar.

Liam called, "Don't worry, *Chad*. I'll put this on your tab." As he walked back toward the bar, a smile tugged at his lips. "What kind of name is Chaz anyway?"

We cracked up, with Michelle clapping her hands then patting Liam on the back.

He passed me, and I whispered, "Nice one, Liam."

His smile widened, making my knees weak and my tummy flip. "My winged friends are good for more than just tailing you."

DUFFY'S HAD a mild rush around six thirty, but by eight, Dex, Jonesy, Michelle, Liam, and I were the only ones left in the bar. Michelle stretched her arms, rolled her neck, and yawned.

Liam looked at the clock above the bar. "Why don't you head out now, Michelle. You look tired."

"Thanks, Liam. That's what every girl loves hearing. But I guess you're right. I'm pooped." She yanked off her apron and grabbed her tip envelope from behind the bar. All tips went into a communal jar and were divvied up at the end of the night among the workers—including Jonesy. Since we hadn't had a patron in the last hour, Dex and Michelle had already sorted the funds. I'd refused when they offered me a cut. Spending time at the bar was more fun than work.

Besides, Michelle had a husband who was out of a job and a two-year-old at home. I had no one but myself to worry about. And Laverne.

Over the last few hours, I'd learned a lot about Duffy's and its small, close-knit pool of employees. The beloved previous owners hadn't had the energy to keep up with the bar. They had been beyond eager to retire and unload it on Dane and Nova, who'd breathed new life into the place.

Under the old management, the bar survived from the Friday and Saturday night crowd that came in to watch the bar's lineup of live music. Dane's idea of trivia and karaoke made Tuesdays and Thursdays almost as profitable as the weekends. Wednesdays were typically a dud, which meant the bar closed on time at nine sharp.

"Jonesy and I can handle the rest of the night if you want to take off too," Dex said to Liam as he unloaded clean highball glasses onto the shelves. He glanced at the clock. "Only fifteen minutes anyways."

Liam scrubbed a hand over his eye. "Okay. Ready?" he asked me.

I nodded. "Yes. So nice to meet you both. Hope to see you again before the week is up."

Jonesy, an older man with more hair on his face than his head, scratched his chin. "Dane said they'd be gone two weeks." He took a sip of his diet Coke, then a giant bite of the sandwich he'd whipped up before closing down the kitchen.

"Told me two weeks also." Dex shrugged and continued to tidy his immaculate bar space.

I groaned and looked at Liam. "You were there. She said one week. Two at most. Why not just say two?"

"Probably because *you* would have said no." Liam avoided eye contact by studying his nails.

"Looks like you're due some overtime for dog duty." Dex laughed.

More like overtime for Liam duty.

TWENTY-TWO

Liam and I pulled up to the house to find the garage door partially open. He yelled over his shoulder for me to hop off, then he cut the engine. My hands shook as I punched in the code. The door crept the rest of the way upward, revealing the wide-open interior door that led to the laundry room.

"Oh, no!" I cried, hurrying into the house. "No, no, no. Daisy-girl, you here?" I ran up the stairs and into the master bedroom, finding her doggy bed empty. When I returned to the staircase, Liam stood at the bottom. "She's gone!"

"Calm down, already have my messengers looking for her." He flipped his palms up, gesturing in a slow down-ward motion. "She's done this before."

"I know! That's why they said to make sure all the doors and the garage were shut properly." I clamped my hand over my forehead as my pulse pounded. "I can't believe she ran away. What if she gets lost? Or worse, what if she gets hit by a car?" I shook my head and leaned into the wall. "*What* is wrong with me? I can't even keep a pet safe."

"Cambria," Liam said, slowly coming up the stairs and

stopping a step below. "It's as much my fault as yours. Daisy will be fine. My messengers will find her."

"Well, I can't stand here doing nothing." I brushed past him and barreled down the stairs to the front door. "I'm going to look too."

Liam sprang to my side. "Let's go."

The yard's lamp post provided a bright, yellow-orange glow, but not enough light to see past the midway point of the driveway. A black bird flew above the house, swooping up and down as it circled the front and backyard.

From the veranda, I yelled Daisy's name.

"Be right back." Liam slipped inside and returned a few minutes later with a flashlight. "Come on. Let's check Lake Road."

I trailed him down the drive, calling Daisy's name every few steps. At the bottom, I tugged Liam's arm. "This way."

We headed north onto the country road. Every so often, we'd hear a *caw* or catch a glimpse of one of Liam's birds flying in and out of the forest. Each step farther from the house brought more trepidation to my stomach.

"Daisy!" I called in a wobbly voice. "Daisy! Come on, girl. Where are you?" We hit the entrance of the trail that followed Sully's Creek. "Which way? She could be anywhere!" The leaves above us rustled as the wind whistled. "I can't believe this is happening."

Clouds began to thicken and rumble as my anxiety notched up. Daisy wasn't a big dog; what if an animal attacked her? Raindrops fell from the sky, sprinkling our faces. My mind raced with worst-case scenarios.

"Are there bears in the woods?" My head swiveled from the trail that disappeared into the thick forest to Lake Road, which, as Liam had mentioned on several occasions, had no shoulder. The only light came from Liam's flashlight and the moon's hazy glow. "I hate the woods. I hate bears. I can't believe this is happening. Why did Nova ask me to watch Daisy? She didn't need me. I failed her. I'm always failing people. I wish she hadn't asked me to come to Collins Grove. I hate the woods. I hate bears. I hate it..." The words sputtered from my mouth.

Liam set the flashlight on the gravel. Its beams lit upward, illuminating a narrow scope of the road and tree-tops. He placed his hands on my biceps, tugging me in. "She'll be okay." His hands traveled up my arms to cup my face. Our eyes locked. He cocked his head as his thumbs gently stroked my cheeks. "Stay calm, Cambria. We'll find her."

I watched his lips form the words. His low, gritty voice seemed to vibrate through my whole body, settling my pounding pulse. The corner of his mouth lifted into a half-smile, and it stroked my soul. A wave of calm washed over me.

His voice, his touch, his presence. Liam was a ray of light in my dark skies, always leading the way to safety.

"Okay?" he asked.

I nodded, my eyes remaining locked on his as his hands continued to cradle my face. Slowly, he splayed his fingers, letting them drift over my cheeks as he lifted his hands away.

"Always saving me," I whispered.

"Cambria. I don't want to—" Bright headlights and the sharp honk of a car interrupted Liam's quiet plea. He grabbed my hand and pulled me onto the narrow shoulder, then picked up the flashlight.

An SUV pulled up beside us, and the window rolled down. "Cami!" I recognized Cathy's voice at once. *Of course,* Daisy had escaped to visit her best friend, Bruno. "Guess who I found outside my front door!"

"Oh, Daisy!" My hands flew to cover my heart as I leaned closer toward the window. "She had us worried sick!"

"I tried calling you but figured I'd bring her home in case she had snuck out after you'd already gone to bed." Cathy exited her side of the car and came around to Liam and me. "Hey there, Liam."

He returned her greeting with a nod.

A flock of four birds flew overhead, squawking into the night air, swooping low enough where I could almost feel the rush of their wings.

Cathy took a flustered step back, muttering, "Oh," as she looked up. We watched the birds circle twice, then fly out of sight with an echoing round of caws.

"They came awfully close." Cathy rubbed her arms as if she were cold. "That was a bit creepy, huh?"

"Harmless," Liam grumbled in the birds' defense.

Cathy shrugged it off and yanked open the car door to reveal a tail-wagging Daisy. Bruno sat next to her.

"Daisy! You naughty girl!" I scolded as I reached in to hug her. Her tail thumped louder and faster against the seat. "You had us worried. Did you sneak off to see your friend? What are we going to do with you?" I turned to Cathy, throwing my hands up. "Can I ground a dog?"

"These two are besties, that's for sure." Cathy grinned. "Bruno sure misses Daisy."

"We really need to plan that playdate so she doesn't do this again." My voice lowered, and my jovial tone turned serious. "Honestly, I was so scared. It was my fault—Dane warned us about the faulty latches and the sticky garage door. I don't know what I'd do if something happened to her."

Daisy hopped from the car and sat beside me, leaning into my legs and looking up with big brown eyes that seemed to be begging for forgiveness.

"Happens to the best of us. Dogs are like children. They sure can be naughty, but they're worth it. Right, girl?" Cathy scratched behind Daisy's ear, and Daisy's tongue flapped from the side of her mouth. "Don't be hard on yourself. Bruno's done the same."

"I kept thinking she might've gotten hurt. It'd break my heart! And Nova's. Can't imagine having to tell her something happened to Daisy." My past failures already weighed heavily on my chest. Any more would crush me.

"Do you two—*three*—want a ride home?" Cathy gestured toward the car.

"Think I'd like to walk. I'm a bit wound up. Is that okay, Liam?" I asked.

"Yep."

"Oh, we don't have a leash!" I said.

"She'll stay close," Liam replied with conviction. "Won't let her out of my sight."

I nodded to him, then crouched down to Daisy's level. "Don't you do that again, hear me? Cathy and I will plan a playdate with Bruno. No need to run off, Daisy-girl."

"I need to check my calendar at home, so I'll text you with times," Cathy offered as she walked around to the driver's side.

Liam and I watched Cathy's SUV taillights slowly fade into the darkness. I sighed, releasing the built-up stress of the evening.

"Daisy wanted to see Bruno earlier, but I took her to The Poppy Seed instead." Guilt seemed to continuously gnaw at me. I'd neglected to take her on a second walk of the day because Liam had roped me into the shift at Duffy's —but it was no excuse. Daisy was my responsibility.

And I'd failed. Again.

"Come on." Liam pointed the flashlight's beam down the road and started walking. Daisy trotted alongside him.

"Liam?" I said softly. He turned, and the flashlight bounced to my face, blinding me. I held up my hands to shield my eyes. "Why do you think Nova lied? Why'd she have me come here when Cathy could have watched Daisy?"

With the bright light on me, I couldn't see Liam's face, but his words were so soft and sincere, it was as if they stroked my cheeks. "Maybe she thought it'd be good for you."

"Good for me?"

"Quiet. Nature. Daisy. Caring for an animal is therapeutic. And the people around here are good. Genuine." As he walked toward me, the flashlight bobbed. Slowly, his beautiful face came into focus. The usual sharp lines and jagged corners of his formidable jaw softened under the moonlight and the flashlight's glow. He stopped in front of me. "It's been good for me. "

"Yeah. I can see that."

"I needed this," Liam said as his eyes searched mine. Over the years, his power and strength had grown, and the severity of his station had made him rough around the edges, hardening him. He looked to the ground. "Slowing down. Appreciating the beauty of humanity."

"I guess maybe I need it too," I admitted. The guilt that usually consumed me hadn't felt so heavy. Maybe it had to do with Collins Grove. The people, the peace.

Maybe it had to do with Liam.

He eyed me, pinning me with his intense gaze. "Seeing Nova and Dane... makes me realize it can happen." Liam's words hit my lips like a kiss. If I wasn't paralyzed by his eyes, I would've leaned in to feel them.

"What?" I asked breathily.

"Life after."

"After?"

"All we've seen. All we've done," he murmured.

Usually, talk of the past made me anxious, but Liam's presence calmed my inner storm. I breathed in his intoxicating scent, savoring his nearness. "Do you ever wonder what it's like to be normal? Just a regular person?"

He moved closer yet. "Every day."

His arms hung at his sides, and our bodies barely touched, yet I could feel his chest rising and falling as he breathed. Seconds passed.

"Liam?"

"Yeah?"

"Can we go home?"

It wasn't a profound question, but Liam stood statue-still for a full minute before taking my hand, intertwining our fingers, and staring at me for a few more seconds. He dropped his hold, gave a definitive nod, and answered with a simple, "Yeah."

Collins Grove wasn't my home. Dane and Nova's house wasn't my home. But walking side by side with Liam on a dark road had never felt more like home.

TWENTY-THREE

For the first time since I could remember, I had a solid night of dreamless—or more accurately, nightmare-free—sleep. When I woke the next morning to sunlight flooding Nova's master suite, I figured Liam must've had something to do with it.

"He's messing with my head," I said more to myself than to Daisy, who lifted her head, then plunked it back down. *But he's nothing like Papa.*

Most nights, Papa stormed my dreams, chasing me or Mama in the woods behind the cabin I grew up in. Or worse, he'd catch us.

I hadn't been to the cabin in decades, but my vivid nightmares transported me there nightly.

Last I heard, the piece of property I used to share with Mama had been declared abandoned and later sold. I didn't have the heart to claim a stake in it; instead, I prayed whoever bought it had created a loving home and was hopefully raising a family that could bring light back to a land that had been ravaged by dark.

Daisy wandered to my bedside and sniffed at my hand as I held it out to give her a scratch.

"Hungry?" I paused, waiting for a reply, which came through wild panting and tongue wagging. "Okay, okay. Let me go potty first."

I hurried in the bathroom, knowing Daisy probably needed to relieve herself as well. She followed me down the stairs to the front veranda where I let her out. I kept the front door open to allow the breeze into the foyer and to keep an eye on Daisy while I grabbed my phone from the living room, where I'd abandoned it the previous night before leaving for Duffy's.

Several text alerts popped on my screen—including the one from Cathy that mentioned she'd found Daisy at her front door. I returned to the veranda and cozied down on a rocking chair to read through the rest of my messages.

Nan: *Heard you got a side gig at Duffy's. The Pop needs you!*

Gwen: *Free tomorrow? I have the day off. I can come visit you or maybe we can meet?*

Vann: *Hey, hot stuff. Miss you. In Milwaukee for a gig tonight. Drinks?*

Before I started shooting off replies to everyone, I tossed around the conversation I had with Aaron the night before, unsure if I should mention anything to Nan. Aaron seemed like a genuinely good guy while Chaz gave off the jerk jock vibe, validated by his behavior the night before.

Do not meddle, I said to myself, then whispered aloud, "How do I get myself into these situations?"

"What situation?" Liam, with his bionic hearing, asked from behind the screen door.

Gasping, I nearly dropped my phone. "Jeez, Liam!"

"Cambria?" he asked in a lethal, intense tone as he stepped out. "What's going on?"

With a sigh, I flipped my phone over and set it on my lap. "What do you know about Aaron?"

"Cambria."

"Liam."

He studied my face for a minute before taking a seat next to me. Daisy wandered up the steps and plopped down in the space between us.

"Fine. Don't tell me." I started to stand, but Liam held up his hand.

"Aaron's a good guy. He's a GM at the Harley dealership off the highway. Helps me with my bike." Liam took a deep breath before adding, "And he's Nan's ex. Don't involve yourself in that mess."

"She's dating that jerk, Chaz."

Liam's lips flattened into a grim line, and he gave a nod of his head. "Yep. I heard."

"Chaz set Aaron up. Told Nan a lie to get them to break up. It's not right."

"So, you want to help right their wrongs?"

I looked away. "It's not fair."

"Life's not fair. Sometimes bad things happen to good people."

"I know that," I shot back. "*You* know *I* know that. So why is it wrong to want to help?"

"Helping is not wrong. The desire to help is embedded in you—it's the light that burns inside you. I know you want to help people. I *want* you to help people. I want you to use your gift. But dammit, Cambria, when things go sideways, you can't always take the blame."

"I don't think you understand—" I started to speak, but Liam interrupted me.

"I understand!" His voice boomed in the sky, jerking Daisy awake. She stood up and cocked her head at me, as if annoyed by Liam's outburst, then moved to the farthest part of the veranda.

Liam's nostrils flared as he took a calming breath and gentled his tone. "I understand. I was there. I was there the night it happened."

My cheeks flamed. He was referring to the night of the big fire.

"You were a child. *A child.* Young and vulnerable. Barely spoke, refused to eat. I saw your pain, and it broke my heart. I *felt* your pain, and it tore my soul. But you crawled out of that hole, only to fall back in because you couldn't forgive yourself. You can't forgive yourself for something that happened when you were a child."

"But it's my fault Celia—"

"She doesn't need you!" he bellowed, and I flinched. He jabbed a finger in my direction. "You're using Celia as an excuse. Giving your light away won't bring your mama back. It won't relieve your guilt."

I didn't answer. I didn't look at him.

"It'll be wasted, but I guess it's being wasted anyways." From my peripheral, I saw him stand. With his back to me, he looked forward at the expansive front lawn. "You want to help people? Start with yourself."

"Enough," I whispered. "Just when I see a glimpse of your humanity, you return to the arrogant angel. You have no right to judge. You don't know what I feel or the weight of what I carry."

"Oh, I feel it." He pushed from the banister and stalked to me, stopping when his shins touched my knees. "I feel you. I carry your pain. It burns my back." Bending closer, he said through gritted teeth, "You are my greatest pain. My greatest weakness."

"Stop," I pleaded, clutching the armrest of the rocking chair. My limbs burned. Lava lolled in my stomach. "Just stop."

"Celia, Neal, Nan, Aaron—they don't need you." He balled his fists, then slowly splayed his fingers over his chest.

But I do. I need you.

He didn't say the words out loud, but they whispered in the space between us, creating a tension in my tummy that shook the planks beneath my feet, nearly bringing the nails unhinged from the subfloor. Daisy whined and yelped. Liam took a step back. Remorse coated his face as his chest heaved for air. His eyes stayed glued to mine. We silently stared at one another until our breathing stabilized. I released my hold on the armrest, revealing black handprints. Liam's eyes darted to them, and my stomach churned.

Liam and I both knew the truth. I would never learn to control my gift. I was a threat, a liability. I never deserved Mama's light. In the end, I would destroy it—snuff it out—like I had destroyed my own.

I shut my eyes. "Please go. Just go."

AFTER THE CONFRONTATION on the veranda, I shuffled through the motions, getting breakfast for Daisy and me, drained mentally and physically. I crawled back into bed and napped the morning away, waking hours later to gray skies, a headache, and the buzz of my cell. Groaning, I rolled over and pinched the bridge of my nose with one hand as my other fished the nightstand for my phone.

"Hello?" I mumbled into the phone after the line connected.

"Cami? Did I wake you?"

It took me a moment to place the voice. "Oh, Cathy, hi. Sorry, no. I mean, yes, I guess. I was napping—have a bit of a headache."

"I'm sorry!"

"No problem." I released my nose and pushed to a sitting position. "What can I do for you?"

"Well, this is short notice, but my husband and I are heading to our camper for the night. It's on ten acres. I thought Daisy might want to join us. She can get playtime with Bruno."

I glanced at Daisy, who snoozed peacefully in her doggy bed. Poor girl had had a fright from my emotional display on the veranda. A night away with her best bud would probably serve us both well. "That's incredibly thoughtful. I think Daisy would love it."

At the mention of her name, she lifted her head, and her tail thumped.

"We'll pick her up on our way out of town—in about half an hour. And we can drop her home tomorrow afternoon, probably around two."

"How wonderful. Thank you, Cathy. I feel a little silly asking, but is there anything special I should pack for her? Dog biscuits? Dog food?" I hadn't noticed Daisy paying extra attention to a favorite stuffed animal or dog toy. Did she need her bed to sleep in? I racked my brain, like a mama sending her child off on her first sleepover.

"She's camped with us before. She'll be just fine."

"I think she'll be in heaven." After clicking off the call, I eyed Daisy, smiling. "Guess what, girl? You get to spend the whole day and night with Bruno."

At the mention of her friend's name, Daisy released a high-pitched bark. She scooted her butt in the air, wiggling it back and forth.

"You excited?" I pushed from the bed and walked to her side. She licked my hand while her body continued to squirm. I scratched under her chin and grinned. "Okay, okay. I'm happy for you. I'll miss you though. Let me get changed. They'll be here soon."

I brushed through my hair and splashed my face with cold water, then grabbed a stuffed duck from Daisy's pile of dog toys on her bed and led her to the veranda for a potty break before Cathy arrived. Nova had indicated on her detailed list of instructions that Daisy only ate twice a day, so I didn't worry about feeding her.

While Daisy meandered around the front lawn, I sat on the front step and searched the forecast on my cell's weather app. No rain and sunny skies for the next several days. The heat wave would continue, although not quite as hot as earlier in the week. A text alert popped up, and I figured it was Cathy, but Vann's name appeared.

Vann: *Girl, you alive? No cell service out in the country?*

Smacking my head with my free hand, I realized I hadn't replied to the messages I received earlier in the day.

Me to Vann: *Sorry! Coffee tomorrow? Laverne's dead so you'll have to come here. Hour north of the city. Inviting Gwen too.*

Me to Nan: *Duffy's was a one-time thing. Never helping Liam again.*

Me to Gwen: *Tomorrow works! Laverne dead. Want to take a short road trip to Mayberry?*

A series of replies ensued.

Nan: *Liam and you need to get it on already.*

Gwen: *Mayberry? Thought it was Collins Grove?*

Vann: *How can a guy turn down drinks with two hot yoga instructors? Send me the addy.*

Messages flew back and forth as my friends and I solidified plans for the following day. Vann would meet at the house, then we'd head to The Poppy Seed for coffee with Gwen and Nan. Excitement bubbled in my tummy at the idea of getting the group together. My soul desperately needed the boost.

A few minutes later, the same SUV from the night before crept up the long drive. The back window was rolled down almost the whole way, with Bruno's head happily lolling out. Daisy barked and ran to the car.

"Hi again, Daisy," Cathy called, climbing from the passenger side. She opened the back door to let Daisy in. "Thanks for letting her come."

"I should be thanking you—for last night and today. I owe you." I pressed two fingers against my temple. "I really appreciate a night off, although Daisy is not a lot of work."

"It's our pleasure." Cathy gestured toward the man sitting in the driver's seat. "That's my husband, Norb."

I gave an acknowledging smile. "Nice to meet you."

As quickly as the introductions were made, we were then saying our goodbyes. I stayed on the front walkway until the SUV disappeared from sight. I sighed, already feeling Daisy's loss. She'd been my shadow for the last several days, except for the few hours I'd spent at Duffy's. As much as I would miss her, a night to myself was just what I needed.

Well, a night to myself along with a soak in the giant Jacuzzi tub and a glass of wine from Nova's expensive stash.

～

TWO HOURS and an entire bottle of wine later, the stress from Daisy's escape the previous night and my spat with Liam earlier in the day drifted away in warm, lavender-scented water. Folk rock lulled from a music station app on my cell. My head rested against a bath pillow, and I was half asleep when the phone erupted with a text alert. Startled, I shrieked and bolted upright, splashing a wave of bathwater against the wall.

Seconds later, pounding sounded on the door, along with Liam's gritty voice. "Cambria?"

Before I could respond, he pushed through. My hands flew to cover myself. Liam's eyes widened, and he stood statue-still for a second before I shrieked again. Liam swung himself around and grabbed the doorframe.

"God, Liam. Can you knock?"

"I'm an angel, not a god."

"Don't try to be funny."

"Heard you yell," he said gruffly.

"I'm *fine*."

"I can see that."

"You didn't see anything." That was a lie. He saw *everything*.

I grabbed Nova's fluffy white robe from the bath's wide ledge and slid my arms into it as I stepped from the tub. "Way to ruin my peace."

"Didn't sound so peaceful." He shrugged, still gripping the doorframe.

"Will you stop?" The wine from earlier made my words a bit slurred. "Stop with the lectures. Just stop."

"Were you drinking?" His head swiveled toward the tub where he spotted the empty wine bottle. "The whole *bottle*?"

"The whole bottle. What are you going to do? Ground

me?" I tied the belt of the robe and moved toward the door, which Liam blocked. "Stop with the constant hovering and worrying and hovering and—*all* of it. I know you'll always see me as a kid, but stop."

I pushed past him, but he grabbed my arm and twisted me around. With his hand clutching my bicep, his gray eyes pinned me. My stomach clenched at the intensity of his stare.

I averted my eyes, wishing he didn't have this paralyzing effect on me. "What?"

"Where's the mutt?"

"Well, she didn't run off again, if that's what you're worried about." I wiggled out of his hold and moved farther into the bedroom. "Cathy has her." As I stopped, something occurred to me, and I glared at Liam. "Cathy said she offered to take Daisy, but Nova made some excuse that they were getting another rescue. Cathy acted like she had no idea what I was talking about. Do you know anything about that?"

He jammed his hands into his pockets and stared at the ground.

"And have you been messing with my sleep? Are you crawling into bed with me?" My voice rose with each word. "Is that why... Is that why..."

As if the bottle of wine hit me right over the head, I swayed and reached for the tall dresser, but Liam was at my side, steadying me. *Always saving me.* It only pissed me off more.

"Don't!" I swatted his hands away. "Stop trying to save me. Stop manipulating me. Stop controlling me. You're no better than Papa."

Liam's shoulders tensed as he stared at the ground.

Silence stifled the room. I shook my head, angrier at myself than Liam.

"I do it because I care," he said quietly before turning and walking out.

After the door shut, I flopped onto the bed and cried. And cried. When rain hit the windows, I only cried harder. I cried until I fell asleep.

I woke hours later to thunder and lightning, soaked bedsheets, and remnants of an intense nightmare. Papa was back, hiding in the woods behind Nova and Dane's house, waiting for me.

He'd always be waiting for me.

TWENTY-FOUR

When the doorbell chimed the next morning, I jolted upright from bed, then scrambled downstairs to the foyer. I whipped open the front door to find my gorgeous friend Vann waiting.

"Cami-bee!" he squealed, pulling me into a bear hug, then leaning back to study me. "Girl, you look like H-E-double hockey sticks. Your hair is crazy." He clucked his tongue and plucked at one of my tangled locks. "Please tell me this is *not* from a romp with Uilliam?"

I scrunched my nose and groaned. "Stop. Not only does Liam treat me like I'm still nine, we've done nothing but fight. It's terrible." I pinched the bridge of my nose. Surprisingly, even after I had a bottle of wine and a restless night of sleep, my head was clear. "You know how he is."

"Oh, yeah, I do." Vann's blond brows wiggled. He had amber-colored eyes like mine, but his always twinkled with mischief—probably because he always was up to mischief. "Still all arrogant and pompous?"

I nodded. "Yep."

"Pompous. Love that word." Vann grinned and nudged my arm. "Still hot, though, right?"

"Unfortunately." I frowned.

"He's not home, right?" Vann inched back toward the door. "You thought he wouldn't be home."

"No, he's usually out on the lake by now or at the bar checking on the construction. He's on some weird sabbatical. Fishes during the day, then—get this—at night he waits tables at the bar Dane and Nova own." I watched Vann's jaw drop. "I'll fill you in, but I should change and we should head out before our luck runs out. I don't need another run-in with him, especially after last night."

"Oh, girl, what happened?" Vann asked as he rubbed his hands together. He loved a little gossip, especially when it involved another member of the divine. Vann was also a lumineer, which was partly why I thought we bonded so tightly. We both were patrons of hope and light, but while I used yoga and meditation to spread my gift, Vann's method was music. He was usually booked for gigs months in advance, so it wasn't unusual for us to go long stretches without seeing each other. When we did, we picked up where we'd left off.

"I'll tell you on our walk."

"Walk?" Vann pointed to his pristine white leather loafers, complete with fancy tassels. "These shoes are *not* made for walking."

I waved a hand. "It's only like, a mile and a half."

The appalled look on Vann's face made me double over laughing.

"Oh, Vann, I *so* needed this." I grinned, hugging him again, but as the sliding glass door in the kitchen skidded open, I pulled back and dropped my hold. "He's back. Put your arm around me."

"What?" Vann whispered, wide-eyed.

"Put your arm around me," I repeated, inching closer.

"No way. I'm not pissing off Liam." Vann's already pale face drained of all color. "You know how weirdly protective he is of you." Under his breath, he muttered, "More like *possessive*."

"Oh, don't be a baby," I hissed. "What do you think he'll do?"

"Better question is, what the hell are *you* doing?"

Since Vann obviously lacked the balls, I wrapped my arms around his neck and leaned up to murmur in his ear, "Come on. I remember you saying how much you'd enjoy wiping that smug look off his face."

"Yeah, but he can literally wipe me off this realm, so I think you should stop." He peeled my arms away as Liam stopped in the doorframe between the dining room and foyer.

Liam's eyes grazed past me and settled on Vann. He leaned against the frame, crossed his arms over his chest, and stared. "Evander."

"Oh, hey, Uilliam." Unfortunately, Vann's voice came out wobbly and shrill, undermining his attempted cool act.

Liam stared unblinkingly at Vann, who looked like he was ready to bolt. *Bully*. Liam knew exactly how to get under Vann's skin. I watched my poor friend's throat gyrate as he swallowed.

"Okay, we have to hurry." I grabbed Vann's hand and yanked him toward the stairs. "Come on. I'll show you around later. I need to change."

Vann followed me as I took the stairs two at a time. At the top, I peeked down and caught a glimpse of Liam's face as he remained planted in place. His shoulders rolled forward, and his chin dropped. Vann asked me something—

I wasn't sure what—but Liam's head jerked up at the sound of Vann's voice, and our eyes connected. My heart paused for a beat.

A flash of torment etched Liam's perfect face, softening his intense eyes and hollowing his cheeks. The air went still. His brows turned down, and his lips parted, imploring me, pleading with me, as if he were asking for something.

But neither of us knew the question. Neither of us had the answer. We spoke to each other in foreign languages, never able to understand one another. Over and over, we played the same game with the same results.

Oblivious to my turmoil, Vann grabbed my hand and flashed a toothy grin. He repeated himself, but I still didn't hear. Liam winced and broke our connection. He turned around and walked out of the door.

But breaking free of one another would never be that easy.

SAFELY TUCKED within the master suite, Vann kicked off his loafers and plopped onto the bed. "Okay, spill," he demanded.

"Spill what?" I disappeared into the bathroom, leaving the door open so I could still hear him.

"What was that all about?"

"Oh, Liam? Yeah, sorry. He's in and out. I hoped we wouldn't have a run-in." With a flick of my finger, I turned on the faucet and stared at my reflection. Smudges darkened the sensitive skin under my eyes. Since I'd fallen asleep with wet hair, chunks of knotted strands tumbled past my shoulders. I finger-combed them into a messy, low ponytail, then splashed water over my face.

"Cami." Vann's voice came from behind. I jerked upright. "Don't pretend with me." He gave a scolding, motherly look. "Were you trying to make him jealous?"

"Liam?" I grabbed a towel and buried my wet face into it. "No. Why would I do that?"

"Because you've had a crush on him since you were a wee lumineer." He jutted his hip into mine. "If you only wanted to piss him off, my presence alone accomplished that. So why the arm around my neck? You poking the bear?"

Bears terrified me. Papa was a bear that barreled through my safe haven, destroying everything in his path. Liam wasn't a bear.

But Liam also shouldn't be poked.

Sighing, I let my shoulders sag. "I don't know what we're doing. I don't know what *I'm* doing. I'm so confused."

"Well, let's walk and talk." Vann admired his reflection as he patted a hand over his shaggy blond hair. "Yes, I just agreed to walk. Does Dane have as good a wardrobe as Nova? Let's see if he has some tennies I can switch into."

I dug through my suitcase in the closet while Vann searched Dane's side for gym shoes.

"Is it gross to wear someone else's shoes? I mean, his foot sweat is probably all dried up in there." Vann wrinkled his nose as he tossed the sneaker aside, then held up a pair of gray ones that appeared to be brand new. "These look okay. Maybe a little big on me, but better than messing up my new Gucci's. Think Dane will care if I borrow them?"

I pulled a tank over my head, then glanced over my shoulder. "No. And at this point, I don't care."

"Hm?" One of Vann's brows arched.

"Hang on." I shooed Vann out of the closet so I could shimmy into buttery-soft yoga shorts.

"Like I haven't seen that before," Vann called.

I tossed my sleep shorts and tank top onto the pile of dirty clothes. Since Nova said they'd be gone a week—two at most—I had seriously under-packed.

"Okay, so here's the thing," I said, stepping out and flipping up my hand. "Wait. Before I get into the messy details, let me check the time. I told Gwen eleven." I yanked the charging cord from my phone and tapped the screen. Notifications for three text messages from Cathy illuminated along with the time.

My heart jumped at the thought that something might've happened, but as I tapped the screen, a picture popped up. A muddy Daisy and Bruno stood side by side with their mouths open and their tongues happily dangling to the side.

Cathy: *Lots of unexpected rain in the night, but these two are having a ball! We're thinking of staying another night if it's okay, but I can certainly bring Daisy back if you're missing her too much.*

Cathy: *We promise Daisy will get a really good bath before we drop her home!*

Sighing, I twisted the phone so Vann could see. "This is exactly my point."

"Hm? What?" Vann squinted as he glanced at the screen.

"Let's get walking, and I'll tell you on the way." I tapped a reply back to Cathy, letting her know it'd be fine to keep Daisy another night. I'd miss the girl, but she'd have more fun camping than moping around with me.

Vann grabbed my arm with his free hand. The Gucci loafers dangled from his other. "Okay, but if Liam's out there, no funny business."

We exited through the garage. Liam's motorcycle was

parked next to Nova's SUV, so I assumed he was either on the lake or somewhere inside. Whatever. I was happy to avoid him.

"Let me put these in my car." Vann trotted to the Mercedes parked behind Laverne to store his loafers. She looked even shabbier than usual next to the shiny, waxed cherry-red sports car.

At the end of the driveway, Vann linked his arm through mine and said, "In the clear from big, bad Liam. Now spill. *What* is going on?"

I blew out a frustrated sigh. "So that message I showed you, the picture of Daisy with another dog? That was from Cathy—Daisy's former foster mom. Nova said Cathy couldn't watch Daisy because they were getting a new rescue with aggression issues. Come to find out from Cathy, she *offered* to watch Daisy."

"So, Nova roped you into watching Daisy? With Liam also staying under the same roof." Vann glanced at me. "Interesting."

"But I have a feeling Liam also had something to do with it."

Vann stopped walking. "More interesting."

"It's not interesting, it's manipulative!" I groaned. Vann knew a lot more of my past than most, although I'd never divulged the true horror of the fire. But he knew my father had manipulated my mama. It was part of the reason he'd been so concerned when he found out Neal had used his gift to entice Celia. "I'm tired of Liam only seeing me as the petulant child he once saved. He tries to control everything."

"Oh, Cam, I think you have it all wrong," Vann said, tugging me into a loose embrace. "I don't think Liam sees you as a child."

I looked up at the cloudless sky. I hadn't noticed any of Liam's birds since he agreed to call them off.

"Liam sees you as a woman all right. *His* woman. He looks at you like he'd rip the head off anyone else that looks at you."

My head swiveled around. "What?"

"Seriously?" Vann scrunched his face. "You really don't see it? Because everyone else in this damn world sees it. Liam wants you."

TWENTY-FIVE

For the rest of the walk to The Poppy Seed, I tossed around Vann's words. Could it be true? *Liam wants me?* What about his confession that he regretted kissing me? What about his anger at me leaving the Hark to find him? What about his lack of trust in me or the fact that he still thought I couldn't control myself?

Vann—who typically talked a mile a minute and usually about himself—silently walked next to me.

When we turned onto Main Street, I offered a smile. "When I slow down, I find it so peaceful here."

Vann smiled back. "I can feel it too."

Our tranquil quiet was fleeting. A revving engine polluted the air. My pulse raced as the motorcycle flew by.

"Was that Liam?" Vann said, holding a hand to shield his eyes from the sun.

"No, that would be Aaron. Nan's ex. Come on, I'll explain later, but let's hurry and you can meet her before Gwen gets there. There's something special about Nan. We just clicked—kind of like you and me." I linked arms with him as we stepped up the concrete stairs.

The rich aroma of freshly brewed coffee hit me as we walked in. I didn't usually drink the stuff, but I loved the smell. Two gray-haired ladies wearing cardigans and pearls chatted at the counter with Nan. The bell above the door chimed, alerting their attention.

"Hey there, Cam!" Nan called. The ladies looked at me, then to Vann—or more accurately, they ogled him, eating him up with their eyes like he was a dripping ice cream cone on a hot day. Vann could not only turn on the charm with his sweet, innocent smile, but he also had the ethereal good looks that came with being divine.

"Mrs. Humphries?" Nan tapped her fingers against the counter. "Are the coffees for here or to go?"

"Oh, I think for here," the lady who must've been Mrs. Humphries said, nodding vigorously. She took another quick peek at Vann.

"Oh, phooey," the other lady piped up. "We don't have the time. We have knitting club at eleven. That's what the brownies are for." She gestured toward the pink box on the counter, then took her turn at another peek at Vann. "Another time."

"Gosh, it's hot in here." Mrs. Humphries clutched her pearls.

"Sure is," said the other, fanning herself. "Heat wave continues."

Vann winked and grinned, causing all three women—Nan included—to fan themselves. I elbowed Vann and sighed.

They exited, slipping past Vann as he gave them a suave, "Good day, ladies," and Nan burst out laughing.

"Oh my God, that was Tori's grandma! I cannot wait to tell her how her sweet old Nana ogled your friend. I mean, I can see why, but she's nearing eighty!" She held her hand out to Vann. "I'm Nan. You must be Vann."

Vann gripped her hand as he flashed his famous toothy grin. "Vann and Nan. How cute are we?" Still holding her hand, he shot a quick raised-brow glance my way as he gave a squeeze. While I never intentionally used my gift by touch, Vann loved flaunting his. "Pleasure to meet you. My Cami-bee told me all about you."

Nan's smile faltered a bit as she flipped her hand over and gazed at her palm. I'm sure she didn't know what to make of the sudden feel-good, euphoric vibes Vann had transferred through his touch.

"Busy morning?" I asked.

"Not too bad. Hopefully, there's a lull so I can sit with you guys for a bit." Nan gestured to the chalk menu on the wall behind her. "What sounds good? Peanut butter crunch is our freshly ground brew of the day."

"Tea for me." I raised my hand. "With a little honey, please."

"Hmm." Vann sucked in his lip as he scanned the menu. "I think I'll try the hibiscus maple latte—" The bell above the door chimed as he finished his order.

"Oh, guess I'll make it two hibiscus maple lattes," Nan said cheerily as a red-faced Liam walked through the door. "Hey, Liam! I have your cookies here, too." She grabbed a white bakery bag from under the counter and wiggled it.

Liam scowled as he walked toward Nan. He grabbed his wallet from his back pocket and plucked out a twenty-dollar bill. "Keep the change."

"Not going to join us?" Nan asked with wide, innocent eyes as she prepared our drinks.

He didn't say anything in return, just made a weird

grunt noise. "Walk here?" Liam asked, looking at Vann, whose eyes darted downward. "Nice shoes."

Vann swallowed and nodded.

"Be careful. No shoulder on our road."

Vann nodded again.

I rolled my eyes and muttered, "Okay, Dad."

When Liam flinched, I immediately regretted the words. *You're no better than Papa.* My earlier insult was excessive and beyond hurtful. I sighed and stepped away from the counter to a nearby table where I plopped down and rested my chin on my hand, absently staring at the artwork on the walls.

Nan handed a drink to Vann, then Liam. He took it and left with a bristly, "Later."

The door shut behind Liam, and Vann shrugged as he pulled his cup away from his lips. "Looks like the great Uilliam and I have at least one thing in common. Hibiscus maple lattes are my new fave." He took another sip, then leaned over and asked Nan, "How the heck does he drink a to-go coffee on a motorcycle?"

"Liam has his ways," I murmured, shifting my focus to the window.

"Speaking of mopey men on motorcycles, your ex passed us on our walk here. Cami hasn't spilled yet, so why don't I get the sordid details straight from you."

"Vann!" I scolded. "Sheesh. I'm sorry, Nan."

"No. No, it's okay," she said, swatting a hand. She grabbed the two cups of tea and came to the table. Vann trailed sheepishly behind. "Aaron and I broke up a while ago. I'm over it."

Nan and Vann took the open seats on either side of me, leaving the one across for Gwen, who must've been running late.

"Well, since we're on the subject of Aaron... I think maybe you should talk to him." I took a sip of tea.

Nan placed both palms flat against the table on either side of her tea. "No. There's no use." Her eyes glistened. "It's done. Over."

Not to him. Aaron's sad eyes flashed in my memory. He still thought Nan was the one. He clung to that hope.

Sometimes, hope was all we had.

My core warmed. I could help. I felt it deep within, as if part of me knew I was meant to be here at this very moment. The little flame in my belly flickered with hope. Nan's hope. Aaron's hope.

My hope.

I couldn't help Celia and Neal, but I could help Nan and Aaron. I sucked in my lower lip, then exhaled as I placed my hand over Nan's. The warmth in my core spread to my limbs, settling in my fingertips. Softly, I said, "I don't think it's over for him. Talk to him. Give him the chance to tell his side."

As my words floated in the air, my energy seeped into Nan. The tingling sensation didn't burn or scorch. Instead, it felt... good.

Her head bobbed, and she whispered, "Okay."

I dragged my hand away and stared at my fingertips. Vann and Nan chatted on about relationships, but I hardly heard the conversation. I was too amazed and awed by what had transpired.

Our coffee date didn't last much longer. People popped in and out, keeping Nan busy behind the counter. Gwen shot a text saying there was an emergency at the studio and profusely apologized that she wouldn't be able to make it. Eventually, Vann and I finished our drinks and waved goodbye to Nan, who hadn't gotten a break from the steady stream of customers.

On the walk home, I pointed out the empty building with the for-sale sign, mentioning it'd be a dream to have my own studio.

"Okay, the building's cool and all, but what was that?" Vann said, tugging my arm until I stopped walking.

"Hmm?"

"We both know you don't use your touch."

I scrubbed a hand over my eyes. "It just felt right."

Vann nodded. "I know."

"I... I like to use my gift in other ways. Teaching yoga, helping people empower themselves, use mind and body to channel their positive energy."

"Right. You never touch people, though. So, what happened in there?"

I shrugged. "There's something about Nan. One of the first times I met her, it kind of happened then too." I swallowed and looked at my hands. "I'm afraid of my light."

"You're afraid?" Vann's eyes widened.

"I can't control it."

"You did just fine in there." Vann put his arm around my shoulders and pulled me in. "I know you have a past. We all do. But maybe it's time to let go. I know, I know. Easier said than done, but baby steps. What you did in there was amazing. You helped her. Doesn't it feel awesome?"

I cocked my head and placed my hands below my ribcage. Yes, it did feel good.

For the first time, maybe I understood how my touch could heal instead of hurt.

TWENTY-SIX

When Vann and I made our way up the drive, Liam's motorcycle was parked in the open garage.

Vann turned to me. "I'm gonna take off. I can't chance Liam seeing us together again. He might snap, and I'm kind of fond of my pretty little head."

"Oh, Vann." I giggled, hugging him. "Thank you for coming. For everything. After this morning with you, I feel rejuvenated."

Vann leaned back. His tone turned serious as he lowered his voice. "It's a true gift we possess, Cam. Don't take it for granted. We have the power to do great things."

"I think I'm starting to see that."

Vann climbed into his sporty two-door Mercedes. He rolled down the window and held out the pair of tennies he'd borrowed from Dane. I grabbed them, then watched as Vann backed out of the drive. After he disappeared from view, I stood on the veranda. Birds danced in the sky—not Liam's messengers but a flock of small birds that swirled around the trees and Nova's bird feeder. The breeze carried the scent of pine from the forest surrounding us. Peace enveloped me.

I crossed my hands over my abdomen and squeezed, giving myself a hug. The warm, tingly feeling in my core returned. My inner flame flickered, but not in a scary, anxious way. Instead, it felt... peaceful, like the candles that used to twinkle on the nightstand in Mama's cabin when she read fairy tales to me.

I live on in you. Our fire burns as one.

I'd used my gift, and the world hadn't burned. I hadn't imploded. Nothing had turned to ash.

I stretched my arms above my head and looked to the sky. "I felt you, Mama. I *feel* you."

Since my first thought was to tell Liam, I rushed inside, stopping when I heard his gruff voice bellow from the kitchen. I tiptoed to the dining room.

"No, I don't know how much it costs for a rental car. Don't care either." Liam scowled. Inaudible chatter sounded from the other side of the call. "Not my problem."

I started shaking my head, knowing where this was quickly leading.

"Listen, Dane might fall for your crap, but I am not paying you an extra four hundred because your crappy car took a dump. I don't care if you have to ride a bicycle with your little guitar strapped to your back. Honor the contract you signed or bug off."

"Stop," I mouthed silently as I placed a hand over Liam's arm. He jerked it away, as if my touch stung.

The guy on the other line's voice raised loud enough for me to hear his cursing secondhand before the line went silent.

"Guess he'd rather bug off." Liam shrugged and chucked his phone onto the kitchen counter.

"Great." I picked up his phone and tapped the screen. "Now I'm going to have to beg this guy back. And he'll probably want double."

"Don't think so," Liam said, attempting to pull his phone from my hand. With my iron grip on the cell, I stumbled against his solid chest. His arm came around. I looked up as he looked down.

"You've got to call him back," I insisted.

"Don't got to do anything." His hold on me tightened.

"Liam."

"Yeah?" he murmured. His hand rolled up my back, pulling me closer. His fingers wove through my hair.

"What are you doing?" I whispered.

His arms dropped, and he stepped back. I shivered from the sudden loss of his warmth, but stood silent, anchored in place as his gray eyes locked on mine. Seconds ticked by. Finally, he twisted toward the counter, severing our connection.

My breath came out in a long exhale. I wrapped my arms around my torso, desperate for the warm feeling to return to my core.

Liam leaned back against the countertop with his hands supporting him from behind.

"What's wrong?" I squeaked out the words, hugging myself tighter.

He tilted his chin toward me. "You really want to know?"

I paused, breathed in, then nodded.

He pushed from the counter and prowled toward me. Looking down, he growled, "I can't pretend anymore."

Red flushed his cheeks. His chest heaved. He looked like the bear in the woods that was ready to attack the bunny. I'd pushed him too far.

Don't cry. Please don't cry, I pleaded with myself.

I swallowed. "Pretend?"

"Every time I see you. Every time I'm in the same damn room as you."

I lowered my eyelids. "I'm sorry about what I said. You're nothing like Papa. *Nothing* like him. It was a horrible thing for me to say."

Silence followed, and I looked up to see Liam's jawline soften as his lips slowly parted.

"Let me finish," he said, reaching out to trace a finger along the contours of my cheek to my lower lip, gently grazing it. "I can't pretend that every time I see you, every time I'm in the same damn room as you, that I don't want to kiss you."

I sighed as my lids drifted shut. "Then why don't you?"

The light pressure from his finger on my lower lip released as his hand fell away, and my eyes popped open, locking on his. He leaned closer until his lips barely touched mine. They stayed there, unmoving, for a long second before his mouth brushed with the words, "Because once I start, I won't be able to stop."

Paralyzing seconds passed. The heat of his breath caressing my lips made my skin prickle, and my heart pounded with anticipation. I couldn't breathe, think, move. It took me a moment to realize he was waiting for me. I could either tell him not to start or not to stop.

I opened my mouth ever so slightly until my upper lip rested between his parted lips and whispered my answer. "Don't stop."

He nipped gently, pulling in my lip as his tongue slipped over it. I sighed, encouraging him. His fingers grazed my bare arms, traveling up my skin like a feather dancing in the wind, landing on my cheeks. Holding my face, he sucked a little harder. I stood still, savoring the sensation, relishing in his kiss. I'd waited so long for it.

My hands came up to rest on his solid chest. He removed his fingers from my face and settled them over my hands, pressing them into him. His heart thundered under my palm; mine soared knowing I had made his pound, realizing my effect on him.

Emboldened, I dragged my mouth from his and kissed down his jawline. I heard a sharp intake of air, then speckled another layer of kisses back to his mouth. I pulled in his lip and sucked.

Keeping his hold on my hands, he brought our arms down and around me, caging me as he walked me backward until my back hit the counter. Both hands moved under my butt, hoisting me up and over so I sat on top of the granite slab. He nudged himself between my legs as his mouth explored hard and fast. His hand wove into my hair, and he palmed the back of my head, tilting it. He extracted his lips from my mouth to place feather-soft kisses along my neck.

He then pulled away, whispering, "Tell me to stop."

I shook my head.

"Good." His mouth returned to my neck where he began a descent of kisses, stopping again when he hit the inner part of my clavicle. He breathed into my neck. "Tell me now."

"No," I whimpered.

Liam pushed his pelvis against me as he reached down to grasp my thigh. His head dipped to taste the flesh above my breastbone, and he murmured, "Now?"

I moaned in response. Words could not relay my body and soul's desperate need for him. The euphoric heat of his mouth on me and the pressure of his hard body pressed against mine blasted waves of desire to my core.

As his hand inched up my thigh, he rumbled into my skin, "I want you. I've wanted you for so damn long."

TWENTY-SEVEN

Our next parlay of kisses was cut short by the buzz of Liam's cell phone. He ignored it, but when the landline rang next, he regretfully pushed away, dazed and drunk on lust.

"This better be good," he grumbled into the phone. The corner of my lip lifted as I watched him struggle to compose himself. He rubbed his palm into his eye, then ran a hand through his hair. It was something I always itched to do—to see if his hair felt as soft as it looked. "Yep, fine. Be there in a bit."

He walked back to me and again settled between my legs. The gray of his eyes resembled storm clouds. "Do you regret what just happened?" After watching my head shake, he continued. "Good. I have to deal with something at Duffy's."

When he pushed away again, I grabbed his forearm. "Are you coming back?" I blurted out. His brow furrowed, and he tilted his head, taking a step closer to close the space between us. "Last time, you didn't come back."

Liam cupped my cheek with a calloused palm. When

his thumb brushed along my cheekbone, I instinctively leaned into his touch. "Come with."

I nodded and lifted off the counter, sliding along his body as I glided to the floor. A low groan slipped from his slightly parted lips. The primal, raw sound made my stomach flip. I wanted to hear it again.

"Cambria." His voice was sandpapery.

My lashes fluttered up. "Yes?"

"Where's Daisy?"

"Cathy has her for another night." It struck me then. Liam and I would be alone in the house tonight. No Daisy, no interruptions.

Maybe he was thinking the same thing because his eyes flittered down my body and back up, settling on my lips. He swallowed. "Let's go."

I followed him through the laundry room to the garage. Liam got the motorcycle ready and motioned to me.

"Forgot this last time," he said, grabbing a helmet from the top of a tool rack. "But you know I'd never let anything happen to you."

Gently, he placed it over my head, then adjusted and clipped the straps. I waited for him to climb onto the bike before I joined on the back. As soon as I touched his shoulders, the hard muscles under my grip tensed. I pushed up and swung my leg over, then scooted in so I was flush against his back. My arms circled his waist, and I leaned against his flannel-clad back, inhaling and relishing his unique, musky scent mixed with laundry detergent.

The five minutes it took to get to Duffy's only intensified the tension in my core. With my hands clutching his concrete abs, my thumbs made gentle strokes over his solid muscles. He was strong and hard, but his hardness was strangely comforting. I loved the feel of him. I loved his power, his strength, the overwhelming sense of security, care and protection I felt when he was close.

I loved *him*.

I'd loved him since I was nine years old when he offered me his hand and told me to not let go. I'd made a promise to myself that I would never let go. I never had.

I never would.

After Liam parked and cut the engine, I didn't release my iron grip. I kept my face buried in his back until he squeezed my thigh and called over his shoulder, "Hop off."

Reluctantly, I lifted my leg over, then watched him do the same. The loss of his nearness sent a cool shiver over my skin. I looked down to the gravel and dug in with the toe of my Converse sneaker. Goose bumps freckled my bare arms.

"Cold?" Liam asked in a calm, steady voice as he rolled his shoulders. He unhooked and lifted my helmet off.

I shook my head and wordlessly followed him into the bar. Inside, a flurry of activity centered around the men's bathroom. I recognized Tom in the mix of men working the renovation. From what I could hear, a wrong part for the plumbing had been ordered, and now the toilet wouldn't be functional by the time the bar opened that evening. For the Friday night crowd, a closed bathroom could be catastrophic.

"I guess the dudes can take a leak outside?" offered a bearded man wearing a tank top and ripped jeans.

"Most of them do it anyway," Tom said, shrugging.

"What about a number two?" the third guy asked, scratching his chin. "Could leave some TP out back, I suppose."

Liam held up his hand, and the men went silent. "Hang on. Got another box in the office." He turned in my direction. The muscles in his jaw were taut as his eyes met mine.

He crooked a finger to me, mouthing the words, "Come here."

My belly flopped. I slid off the stool and followed him to the door marked "Private." He jabbed a key into the knob and pushed the door open, then stepped aside, allowing me a sliver of space to access. When I brushed against him, my skin prickled from his proximity. He closed the door, then ambled toward me. I reflexively stepped back until my butt hit the edge of something hard—a desk. I reached behind to grasp onto the edge, steadying myself.

"Liam?" I whispered. From his squared shoulders, he looked tense. "Are you—"

Before I could say more, his mouth was on mine. His tongue darted between my lips, probing them open and kissing me with a rough, urgent passion that brought a new meaning to the phrase "weak in the knees." If I wasn't holding onto the desk, I would have melted to the floor.

Liam's exploration gentled, but I didn't want slow and sweet. I wanted to relieve years of needing and wanting and built-up tension. I needed release.

I needed him. All of him.

I hooked a leg around the back of his thighs and pulled him closer as my hands ran over his shoulders to his waist. He reached over and tugged my T-shirt over my head, then looked down at the simple pink cotton bra I'd put on earlier in the day. Lust hooded his eyes. A low groan rumbled from his lips. He looped a finger under one of the straps and slipped it over my shoulder while my hands roamed down his abs to the top button on his shorts.

His hands covered mine, and he pushed them off, panting, "Not here. Not like this." His jaw twitched, as if it pained him to say the words.

Giving a nod, I lifted my bra strap over my shoulder and

felt around for my discarded shirt. Grabbing my wrist, Liam brought my hand in front of him, twisted my palm upward, and placed a kiss in the center.

He looked at me with imploring eyes, speaking a wordless plea. This would not end here; it was just the beginning.

TWENTY-EIGHT

As I pulled the shirt over my head and finger-combed my hair back into place, Liam rummaged around the office for the missing box. From the closet, he lugged out a medium-sized, empty cardboard container. He set it down at our feet, splayed his hands over the top, closed his eyes, and breathed in and out. The air shifted, turning heady and dusty. He released his hold, yanked open the flap, and motioned inside.

"Presto!" Liam exclaimed hoarsely. I looked it over, not really knowing what the gadget was, but I assumed it must have been the missing part. "Weird presider powers save the day."

Most gods could create tangible objects using dust and their mind. I didn't know how it worked exactly, but growing up, I saw gods do it effortlessly in the Hark. Here, among mortals, it was more taxing.

"As long as they're not used on me, I'm okay with it." I ran a finger over the flap of the cardboard box, then shrugged. "I admit, it's impressive. But if I had your abilities,

I'd be filling boxes with hundred-dollar bills, not complex chunks of shiny metal."

I was joking, but Liam said earnestly, "Whatever you need, Cambria. I know you lost your job and live in that crappy apartment."

The mention of my studio and the idea of returning there soured my stomach. I had a month-to-month lease; I could easily relocate and save money with cheaper rent in this charming, small town, which apparently had lots of job opportunities. Maybe I could eventually save enough money to open my own yoga studio.

Lost in thought, I flinched when a sudden knock sounded at the office door.

"Hey, uh, Liam?" a deep voice called from the other side. "Did you find it?"

"Yeah," Liam said, keeping his eyes on me as he closed the flap. "Hang on." He leaned in, bopped a finger on my nose, and whispered, "Shirt's on backward."

Nervously giggling, I popped my arms in, twisted my shirt the right way, then popped them back out and pulled at the hem.

"Perfect." Liam lifted the box and carried it in one hand while he yanked the door open with the other. A tall guy wearing a tight white T-shirt, worn jeans, and knee pads stood grinning like the Cheshire cat.

"Here," Liam said, shoving the box into the guy's chest. He reached behind and grabbed my hand. A round of hoots and laughter erupted from the two other guys mulling around outside of the bathroom. "All right, all right. Get back to it. We open in an hour." Turning to me, Liam asked quietly, "Want to stick around for a bit? Band doesn't start till seven, but when Alan gets here, he can make us burgers."

"I thought you fired the band?"

"That's tomorrow's lineup."

"You know you have to call them back." I peeked up at him.

He scrubbed a hand over his eyes, then laid it on my shoulder, tugging me in. "Know what? I'm in a pretty giving mood now. I'll shoot them a text. So, what about dinner? Only burgers and pizza here. Rosario's delivers. If I remember, shrimp scampi was one of your favorites."

My stomach answered with a growl. "Sounds fabulous."

"Oh, I called it!" a familiar voice yelled before I had the chance to answer. "Jonesy owes me some money!"

Peeking from over Liam's arm, I saw Dex rub his palms together.

"I told him by the end of the week, you two would be hooking up." Dex put his arms around Liam and me, pulling us both into a bear hug, beaming like he'd just won the lottery. "Fifty bucks. Jonesy didn't think you had a chance with her."

I wiggled out of the bear-hug hold, then nudged Dex's arm with an innocent, doe-eyed look. "Hey, who says we're hooking up?"

"Me," Liam growled, yanking me in again. "I say it."

I squeaked from his surprise grab and from the blatant public display of affection. Liam wasn't the type. Always serious, always on guard, he rarely showed a softer side.

Dex slapped his thigh and laughed. "Well, you're a lucky man."

"I know," he replied to Dex with a dead-serious face.

But Liam wasn't a man. He was a beautiful, powerful, intense angel. And he was mine.

At least for now.

My stomach did a nervous dance. *What* were we getting

ourselves into? If we crossed that line and he left again, I didn't think I'd survive.

"So, anyway, is the bathroom all fixed?" Dex hitched his thumb toward the crew who were packing up the boxes and tools scattered over the floor. I nodded, and Dex continued. "Now that it's all new and nice, I sure hope no one pukes in there tonight—and by no one, I mean Jonny Larkin. Dude has a pukin' problem, and I'm getting a bit tired of it."

"Going to be busy. Think we have five on for waitstaff, and Amanda will help bartend. Can you guys manage if I don't stay?"

"Oh, he just can't wait to get you home," Dex said to me, wagging a finger. His smile faded when he noted Liam's dagger eyes. "Yeah, yeah. We got it. Go spend time with your lady. We're fine."

While Liam did work in the office, I helped Dex prepare for the bar's opening by cutting lemons, oranges, and limes and filling the garnish trays. A few minutes before four o'clock, Jonesy rushed in, yelling about his car and the crappy mechanic who'd overcharged him. Dex didn't even have the opportunity to throw it in his face that he'd won the bet. Jonesy disappeared into the kitchen with the warning that he didn't want to be bothered unless it was for an order.

After the bar was organized, I slipped around to the other side with a glass of white wine in hand. Staff slowly trickled in. Dex kept introducing me as "Liam's lady." With each announcement, I blushed a little warmer, liking the sound of it more and more.

Shortly after opening, the Friday happy hour rush flocked to the bar. Liam returned from the office to check on everyone, including me, before handing me his cell.

"Got to check on a few more things before we can head

out." He pointed at the phone. "Waiting to hear back from that con artist about tomorrow night. Can you answer it if he calls? Maybe you can sweet-talk him."

"Remember what I told Dane and Nova? Daisy's my responsibility, not you."

Liam lifted a piece of hair over my shoulder and leaned in to whisper, "But Daisy's gone for the night, so you get me."

The heat of his words hit my neck and radiated down to my limbs. I itched to touch him, to feel his warmth, to run my hands through his hair. But instead, I gave a nod and tried to look cool while my insides simmered.

I sipped my wine as I watched Amanda and Dex work the busy bar in harmony. A variety of people, from men dressed in white-collared dress shirts to women wearing athletic shorts and tennis shoes, mulled around, giving animated greetings and boisterous hugs like it was a high school reunion. The vibe of the happy-hour crowd was a combination of excited and relaxed—a prelude to the weekend that had me buzzing from their energy.

"Hey!" The woman sitting next to me tapped my arm with a perfectly manicured, red fingernail. A diamond the size of a gumball glistened like a disco ball from her ring finger. "Think your phone's buzzing."

"Oh! Thanks." I looked down to see a long string of numbers appear on Liam's caller ID. I slid my finger across the screen to connect the call, grimacing at my own non-painted, plain hands. I never wore jewelry. "Hello?"

"Ca—mm— Ca—" Weird muffling noises gurgled from the earpiece.

"Hang on, I can't hear you." I slipped from my seat and walked outside to find better reception. "Okay, is this better?"

"Ca—nn— You— rrr—"

I walked farther away from the front door, weaving through the rows of cars parked in the gravel lot. "Is this about tomorrow?"

"Ddd— Caa—"

"I'm sorry, we have a bad connection. Can you hear me?" After no response, I looked at the screen. The line had either dropped or the person on the other side had given up and ended the call.

I started to make my way back through the maze of cars when the distinct scent of fire assaulted my nose. Heat shot down my spine, landing in the pit of my stomach where my own flame flickered. I nervously scanned the lot, finding a group of three men standing in a circle near the front door. A cigarette dangled from one of the guy's lips.

Sweat beaded my hairline, and my heart pounded, yet my legs unwillingly drew me closer.

Another one of the guys pulled out a pack of cigarettes from his back pocket and offered it to his other buddy, who plucked one. The guy to his left, about eight feet directly in front of me, drew a lighter from his front pocket. The orange flame flickered to life.

I stood still, mesmerized and paralyzed. Since I was nine years old, I avoided being around fires, which often proved to be difficult. Usually, if I caught a glimpse of a flame or the scent of ash, I could talk myself through the immediate, reflexive panic.

But seeing the cherry-red glow of their cigarettes, I couldn't move. Bile rose in my throat.

Turn around, turn around, I coaxed myself, but my legs didn't get the memo from my brain. Puffs of smoke floated from their mouths, making my stomach churn. The scent triggered the memory.

The air sizzling and crackling, vibrating from my screams. A spider-web of fire emanating from my body. Flames flashing from my toes, zapping along the dirt, igniting the bushes. The grass shriveling into angry orange flames. Streaks of crimson traveling up the trunks of trees. Leaves wilting and turning to black.

Waves of fire rolling over and over and over…

All I could see was the red glow. All I could smell was smoke. The world around me turned red and white and orange and yellow as flames flickered behind my eyes.

"Hey, you okay?" a fuzzy voice asked. "You don't look so good."

The words blended into a ringing sound in my ears. My vision started to tunnel, and I grasped for the car beside me. *You okay… You okay… You don't look so good… so good…*

"Stay away!" I screamed as my focus locked on the tiny flame burning from the tip of the cigarette.

It dangled from the guy's lips, flipping up and down as he spoke. "Jeez, sorry. Just wanted—"

He was cut off by the banging of the front door as it smacked into the brick wall. Liam's voice boomed out a second later. "Cambria!"

My lower lip trembled from relief and mortification. I didn't want Liam to see me like this—on edge, ready to lose control.

"Put that out. *Now!*" he roared as he pushed past the three men to my side.

One of the guys immediately dropped the cigarette from his mouth to the ground and snuffed it out with his boot. The other two looked at Liam with confusion.

"Hey, man, you said no smoking in the bar. We're outside—"

"No smoking *anywhere!*" Liam's voice thundered,

echoing off the trees. His arms enveloped me, and I sank into his chest.

"Sorry," one of them said.

The other muttered, "What the hell? Whatever. Let's get out of here."

I buried my face in Liam's shirt, taking deep breaths to fill my nostrils with his soapy scent and replace the lingering stench of cigarette smoke. After my racing heart settled, I pushed away, muttering a quiet apology as I averted my eyes to the ground.

"Cambria?" Liam's worried voice was like sandpaper on my soul. "Are you okay?"

I nodded but kept my focus on the gravel.

"I know you don't want me saving you or interfering, but—" Liam cupped my cheeks, forcing me to look at him. "I won't apologize. I will always do what I can to keep you safe. Always. I will slay every monster. I will wipe every tear."

He was beautiful, so beautiful it almost hurt to look at his earnest face. Emotion caught in my throat. I desperately wished to grab him, hold him, kiss him, but instead, I hoarsely whispered his name. "Liam?"

"Yes?"

"I...." *I love you.* But my mouth couldn't form the words. Not because they weren't true, but because I was scared. "I want to go home. Let's go home."

What I'd wanted for so long was within my reach, but a great big forest separated where we were and where we were going. Until I faced my past, I'd always be the scared little girl running through the woods, afraid of the monsters.

TWENTY-NINE

After we got home, Liam called for Rosario's delivery and putzed with his bike in the garage while I ran upstairs to comb through my wind-knotted hair and check my messages. Daisy was undoubtedly fine in Cathy's care, but I hadn't seen my phone for a good part of the day and needed reassurance.

I tapped the screen, and it illuminated to life. A text message from Nan was at the top of the list of notifications.

Nan: *OMG. I heard from Michelle who heard from Dex that Liam and you are TOGETHER. What the heck happened since this morning!? Need to hear the deets...*

Nan: *BTW Aaron and I are getting coffee tomorrow.*

The speed of Collins Grove's gossip mill was faster than an F16. I rolled my eyes and shot Nan a quick reply, then noticed I had two voicemails from an unknown number. Cold-callers—I really needed to put my number on the no-call lists.

Before listening to them, I hurried to the bathroom to splash cold water over my face to wash away the lingering, pungent menthol scent of cigarettes. I could almost taste it on my tongue. I grabbed my toothbrush from the cup on the vanity and slathered on minty paste before jamming it in my mouth. As I scrubbed, I tapped my cell to play the voice-mail messages over the phone's speaker.

"*Cami!*" Nova cheerfully greeted. "*Sorry I'm just calling now—reception is terrible. We're in a remote area, but on the highway now so thought I'd try you. Give Muffin a kiss from me. Umm, so, yeah. I hope things are going okay with Liam? Um, anyways, we're heading back from Dublin. Reception sucks, but you can email. We'll try Liam's phone next. Miss you! You're the best!*"

With the toothbrush dangling from the side of my mouth, I clicked on the next message.

"*Oh! So, um, Dane said he chatted with Liam a few days ago and everything's going okay, so, um, I hope Liam relayed the message that we plan to stay another week. I promise we will pay you back big time. You're the best! Miss you!*"

I popped the toothbrush from my mouth and spit into the sink, then replayed the message. *Dane chatted with Liam a few days ago? Relayed the message... another week?*

"Liam!" I yelled, stomping out of the bathroom, down the stairs, and to the laundry room. I jerked the door to the garage open. "Li-umm!"

Crouched on the floor next to his motorcycle, he jerked up, knocking his head on a handlebar. "Ouch!"

"Did you talk to Dane?" I squared my shoulders and glared at him.

Liam's jaw twitched as he pushed to his feet and rubbed his head. He gave a nod of his chin.

I tapped my foot. "A few days ago?" I waited for him to nod again. "And they're staying another week. You didn't think to tell me?"

"Guess I figured Nova would've called or emailed you." Liam shrugged. "That it?"

"Liam!" With a hand on my hip, I wagged a finger at him. "I want to know exactly what is going on with this 'playing house' gig. Because we both know I don't need to be here. Cathy could've watched Daisy."

"Okay, but can you put that down first? Kinda feel like I might get stabbed in the eye." He pointed toward the toothbrush, which was clutched like a knife in my white-knuckled fist against my hip.

I stomped into the kitchen and tossed it onto the counter, where it skidded and landed inches from the edge of the other side. "There. But just remember, I do have nails that can still do some hardcore damage to one's eye."

That was a lie. I'd chewed them down to little stubs.

"We have to talk about this tonight?" Liam asked, running a hand from his forehead through his hair. It landed at the back of his neck. His bicep flexed as he massaged his muscles.

"Yes."

"But I was hoping…" He gave a sly smile and gestured toward the countertop, where we had our make-out session earlier in the day. A plate with a half-eaten sandwich sat next to the sink—probably his lunch that was cut short by the call from the band, then further interrupted when Liam and I kissed.

"You want to pick up where we left off?" I raised a brow.

His head bobbed up and down. "Yep. Very much."

I crossed my arms over my chest and leaned against the counter. "Why am I here?"

Liam took a step closer and eyed me. "Because of me."

"You?"

"I asked Nova to have you come."

Of all the manipulative, sneaky things to do. "Why?"

"Because you lost your job. You want to find Celia. You live in that shit apartment. You're broke. You seemed really... lost."

My heart sank. "Will it always be like this?"

"Like what?"

"You trying to control and manipulate everything I do?"

"I'm not like him, Cambria." His eyes flickered down, and he balled his hands into loose fists at his side.

"I'm not saying you are." I sighed and walked to the sliding glass patio door to look at something other than Liam. I *couldn't* look at him because if I did, I would lose my train of thought, and I desperately needed to be clear-headed for this conversation. "But you lied. You tricked me."

"I could feel you slipping away. Your light, your hope. Year after year." In the glass door's reflection, I saw Liam splay his hand over his chest. "I can feel it now."

I swallowed away the lump in my throat. Hours before, Liam and I had been lost in a sea of passion—now we were just lost.

I pressed my forehead against the cool glass. My breath hit the pane, creating a light fog. I focused on it, trying to keep my emotions in check as thoughts churned like a tornado in my head.

"I want to help you, but your healing has to come from within." The ache in Liam's voice shot down to my bones, and I winced. "I can't have you shut me out."

I stared ahead. In the glass door's reflection, Liam stood solemnly in the kitchen behind me. But as my focus shifted forward, out of the darkened pane, I could make out part of the lawn and trees in Nova and Dane's yard. Dense woods separated their property from their neighbors', cocooning the house. Sheltering us. Monsters could be lurking anywhere out there in the deep, dark forest.

Anchored in place, I thought about what was in front of me, behind me, around me. The past, the present, the future.

Liam was my safe haven, always there, waiting to swoop in and save me. My hero, my savior. But he was right. I needed to heal. I needed to save myself.

Lost in my thoughts, I jumped when Liam's strong hands snaked around my waist and pulled me into his solid chest. His chin dropped into my hair.

"Don't shut me out," he murmured. The thick cording of his arm muscles tensed as he pulled me tighter, and I melted into him with a breathy sigh. I never had a fighting chance when it came to Liam, but surrendering to him was a battle worth losing.

As I relaxed, he twisted me around to face him. My hands came to rest on his chest, where his heart thumped heavily, and the sensation was oddly comforting. He was formidable, strong, and powerful, yet he had fears and worries and pain and passion.

He could be hard and unyielding, but soft and vulnerable.

We stood for a few minutes before the muscles under my fingertips tightened as Liam spoke. "When you were younger, I'd see the way you looked at me. Like I was your hero. Like you needed me. I didn't know if I liked it or not. But eventually, I craved it. The feeling of being needed by you. You grew up, and you started to look at me differently. And I began to crave that feeling too."

I hesitated for a split second, then asked the question that had bothered me for decades. "After we kissed, you sent me to the Hark. Why didn't you ever come back for me?"

"I shouldn't've kissed you. You just lost your mama. You were too raw."

"But you didn't come back."

He dropped a hand from his hold and used it to lift my chin. "When we kissed, I felt your passion. And your pain. You needed to heal. It felt wrong, like I took advantage of you."

"And now?" I stared at the top button of his black, blue, and gray flannel that was undone, exposing his white undershirt.

"Nothing felt wrong about what we did earlier." His growly voice vibrated over my forehead, shooting tingles over my skin. "You regret it?"

Regret it? I wanted to relive it. Over and over.

Reaching up on my tippy-toes, I pressed my lips against his as I grabbed the collar of his soft flannel and pulled him in. It was my turn to show Liam just how much I wanted this, how long I'd waited.

I kissed him slowly and sweetly. Liam held still, allowing me to set the pace. As my mouth explored his, the fire in my belly ignited, stroking the flame to my soul, yet I maintained control. Heat pulsed through my veins, electric shivers that radiated through my body. After several blissful seconds, right when the world began to spin, Liam pulled away with a low groan.

"Cambria." He said my name like a prayer and a plea, and it was the sweetest thing I'd ever heard.

I waited for him to continue, but when he didn't make

any effort to move or speak, I asked with a shy flutter of my eyelashes, "So what do we do now?"

His eyes blazed with desire as he inched closer and spoke softly. "I want you. I want all of you. But I don't want anything between us. No secrets." I blinked, unsure where this was leading. "Last I heard, Celia was staying in the Hark. She's with Lucille. Cambria, she's okay. She's more worried about you and what you'd do if you found her. She thought she was protecting you by staying away."

I drew in my lower lip as my stomach did a weird flip. Suddenly, it clicked. I'd been looking for Celia for years, but the Hark was the one place I couldn't easily access.

Liam took my hand and softly said, "I also thought I was protecting you, but in doing so, I wasn't taking my own advice. I wanted you to heal, but I kept trying to shield you, protect you. Healing comes from within. Not from me, not from Celia. I should have supported you, trusted in your abilities. Moving forward, I want to go into this with one hundred percent trust between us."

"I... I also trust you. I've always trusted you. From the moment you offered your hand and told me to never let go. I've never let go." I watched Liam's throat gyrate as he swallowed, then I continued. "For the longest time, I wanted to give away my light, pass on my gift to someone deserving. I thought it'd rid me of my guilt, and that's how I'd heal. But now, I think I understand. It's Mama's gift to me, my way to stay connected to her."

Liam brushed a knuckle against my cheek. "You have no idea how long I've waited for this moment, to hear you say you understand."

"But I'm scared. I'm afraid I can't control it..." I trailed off and shrugged, then turned toward the counter. My arms dropped to my sides, and I sighed. "I need to face the fire, but I'm afraid."

Liam grabbed my hand, pulling me around to face him. Clutching my fingers, he said, "I will hold your hand. I'll be by your side. When you pass through the waters, I will be with you; and when you pass through the rivers, they will not sweep you over. When you walk through the fire, you will not be burned; the flames will not set you ablaze."

"That's on Mama's grave," I whispered as tears smarted behind my eyes. "Was it you?" I didn't need his confirmation; in my heart, I knew. "It's beautiful."

"She's with you. She lives on in you. Her light burns in you."

A tear dripped down my flushed face. I sniffed and dragged a hand over my eyes. "Earlier today, I *felt* her."

A small smile crept up Liam's face. I didn't want to see it fade, but I needed to tell him the rest—the reason why I felt Mama and how I gave Nan a little nudge. With our recent proclamations of trust, I couldn't hold back.

"There's more. I promise I didn't meddle... Well, technically speaking." The sudden dip of the corners of his lips made my heart stop, then restart with a loud thud. I inhaled sharply, but he gave a reassuring nod, as if telling me to go on, everything would be okay. "I used my gift today. I spoke with Nan about Aaron and urged her to give him a chance. To hear his side. Nothing more. I did it without attaching my emotion, other than hope. When I did, it felt good. The little fire inside of me was warm, comforting. Not scary. I realized how precious it is."

As soon as the words left my mouth, Liam's lips were on mine. He held me tightly against his powerful body. Taken by complete surprise, I yelped, then whimpered, giving in to the eruption of desire. In between his kisses, he murmured, "I know. I know."

I grasped his hard, broad shoulders to steady myself. His hands came under my butt, and he hoisted me to the top of the granite counter, then wiggled between my legs again. All the while, our mouths remained connected. As his tongue tangled with mine, I gripped his collar, then traveled to the second button of his shirt, undoing it and moving down the line until I pushed the flannel off his shoulders. Our eyes locked as I stroked down his concrete chest to the hem of his white undershirt. I started to lift it—

Ding-dong!

We both flinched. Liam pushed back, half in a daze. His gray eyes swirled like molten metal as they locked with mine. I might have feared fire, but I wanted to burn in the heat of his eyes. He kept his intense focus on me as he took a step back.

"Must be Rosario's," he said in a calm voice before placing a finger on my swollen lips. He turned to answer the front door.

After his eyes left mine, I blinked a few times before bringing two fingers to my breathless, parted lips to replace his. Chatter sounded from the hall, but I couldn't make out the words over the sound of my thumping heart. As if Liam's kiss took me up a mountain, the air felt thin and crisp. I took several calming breaths to bring myself down from the high.

Liam reappeared seconds later with a giant brown bag. His arm muscles rippled as he set our food on the counter. When he turned toward me, there was a hard look on his formidable face.

"What's wrong?" I whispered.

Taking slow, prowling steps to me, Liam stopped when

his legs bumped against mine. He caged his arms around me, placed his palms flat against the granite, then leaned over until his nose brushed my forehead. "Lost my appetite."

"Oh?" It came out half-moan, half-question.

"For dinner."

"You... you lost your appetite for dinner?"

His nose grazed along my hairline as he nodded. "Hungry for something else." He made a trail of soft kisses down the side of my face to my neck.

"Oh, God, Liam," I croaked as he nipped under my ear.

"Not a god," he muttered against my neck.

I wrapped my legs around his waist and squeezed him in closer. "No, not a god."

An angel. My angel.

Liam growled, sounding not so angelic. "Let's go upstairs."

I nodded, and he effortlessly lifted me, then shifted me around so I was cradled in his arms. He took the stairs two at a time, not the least bit winded as he hauled me up. At the top, my heart, which already had been working overtime, thudded so hard, Liam took notice.

"Too fast?"

I didn't know if he referred to the pace of my heart or the pace at which things were moving between us. Maybe he meant both.

"I don't think so," I answered honestly. "I want this."

"Want it too, but..." He placed me at the edge of Nova and Dane's bed, then shifted my legs so they dangled off the side. The mattress dipped as he sat next to me. "It doesn't have to be tonight."

"Suppose not. They'll be gone another week." I

absently ran two fingers along the silky comforter as I stared ahead.

"Doesn't matter if they're back tomorrow, next week, or in a month. This is between you and me." Liam pointed a finger at me, then tapped his chest. "I'll wait an eternity if that's how long it takes. Whenever you're ready. I've been patient, and I'll continue to be patient." He glanced at me, giving a sexy grin. "But it will happen."

THIRTY

Need, want, and desire tangled with caution, anxiety, and fear. What I'd wanted for so long was right in front of me, touching me and making it difficult to breathe, let alone think coherently. But intimacy wasn't easy for a lumineer. Passion fueled our fire.

Intimacy with Liam? I'd possibly combust.

Liam didn't say more. We gave in to the silence, sitting next to one another with our thighs pressed together. The soft sound of his breathing calmed me. As I leaned into his shoulder, he scooted back against the headboard, bringing me along with him and tucking me into his hold.

"Quite the day, huh?" he murmured as he brushed away a few stray strands of hair from my forehead. His calloused hands then wove into the thick mess.

"Liam?" I whispered.

"Hmm?" He stroked my head, soothing me until my eyes grew heavy. Whatever question I was going to ask melted away as I fell asleep in his arms.

The next morning, I woke alone, but unlike the other nights when Liam had snuck into my bed, his side was unmade. I smiled, considering it a deliberate message that he had no regrets, no doubts.

After a quick shower, I shot off a few messages, including one to Cathy. She and her husband planned a day of hiking with Bruno and Daisy, then the trip back to their house to bathe the dogs before she'd drop Daisy home.

I slipped into a clean cotton tank top and shorts—loungewear since I had no plans for the day and a heaping load of laundry to do. Back in the bathroom, I slid off the turban-style towel wrap from my head, finger-combed through my white trusses, then applied a layer of face cream.

Leaning closer to the mirror, I studied the amber color of my unusual retinas, searching for any trace of Papa. Swallowing, I put my hand on my belly and closed my eyes. Heat tingled deep in my stomach. I breathed in and out, controlling the flame and its flow, pushing it into my limbs. It felt good, like sunshine warming me from the inside out.

It felt so good that I sighed and swayed, bumping my forehead against the glass. My eyes popped open. In my reflection, I saw a kaleidoscope of yellows, golds, and coppers—nothing like the fiery-red rage in Papa's eyes.

Instead, my eyes were the color of a summer sunrise, like liquid honey straight from the hive. They looked beautiful. Pure, sweet, innocent. Like Mama's.

DOWNSTAIRS, I found Liam in the kitchen dumping the contents of our forgotten Rosario's delivery into the garbage.

"Morning," he said as he flipped on the faucet and washed his hands. "Hungry? Eggs?"

"Starving. Seems I missed dinner last night."

"Interesting. Me too." He rifled through the refrigerator, pulled out a carton of eggs and milk, then used his hip to shut the door. Grinning, he caught my eyes. "Was distracted. Someone couldn't keep their hands off me."

"Me?" I asked innocently, batting my eyes and placing a hand over my heart. "You practically *mauled* me!"

He set the food on the granite countertop and faced me. Crooking a finger, he called in his gritty voice, "Come here."

"Me?" I asked again. This time, the word came out a little choked.

"Hmm." He pulled in his lower lip and nodded.

My heart ticked a few beats faster. I slowly went to him, getting a whiff of Irish Spring bar soap mixed with laundry detergent, clean yet somehow intoxicating. I stopped in front of him, keeping my eyes down, focusing on the fresh white T-shirt that stretched across his broad chest.

Liam lifted a wet lock of hair off my shoulder, then traced a finger over the damp spot it'd left on my tank. The lone fingertip gingerly trailed up the fabric, then over the strap. When he came to the top of my shoulder, he slipped the strap down. A shiver danced over my skin.

His fingertip lingered on my arm as his liquid eyes speared mine. I took a ragged breath, and his gaze dropped to my chest. His fingers began to roam again, taking a sweet, seductive tour back up my arm, over my shoulder, and down my chest to the ribbed collar of my low-cut tank. With focused intent, he watched my chest rise and fall, like a vampire readying for a bite. I closed my eyes in anticipation.

"I want to touch you," he mumbled.

My tongue darted out to moisten my upper lip. I swear Liam groaned, but it could have been me. Regardless of who made the noise, Liam took it as an answer. His index finger swept lower, over the fleshy part of my breast, where his hand moved to cup it.

Another low moan sounded. This time from me. Passion ignited my core—an entirely different heat than my lumineer fire. I wanted to make it burn brighter; I wanted to feel it detonate.

"Say you want this." He caressed my flesh. "Say you want it as much as I do."

A whimpered "Yes" fell from my lips, and in a flash, Liam's mouth pressed to mine, kissing me possessively. His hands gripped my butt, lifting me up and over his shoulder. I watched dazedly as the kitchen tiles gave way to the dining room's hardwood floors, up the carpeted stairs and hallway, to the cream-colored plush rug in Nova and Dane's master suite.

He set me back down and placed his hands firmly on my shoulders as I gained my bearings. "Okay?"

I nodded, and he was kissing me again, pushing me up against the wall as he grabbed my wrists and lifted them over my head, pinning them as his mouth traveled down my neck to my collarbone. His leg came between mine, wedging them apart. Pleasure radiated down my body like flashes of lightning as I surrendered to him.

With his lips pressed against my upper chest, Liam released a low grumble, and I sighed from the vibration.

"Cam?"

"Yes, yes," I half asked, half answered.

"Tell me." He took both of my hands in his one, keeping them pinned above me. With his freed hand, he tugged at my tank, pulling the stretchy cotton up, exposing my smooth, tanned midriff below my bra. His palm flattened over my rib cage and inched up as I hoarsely whispered an answer.

"I want this as much as you."

He released his hold and took a step back. Watching my reaction, he tugged his shirt over his head and tossed it to the floor. My eyes fluttered down, taking in the pink-and-white welts that scarred his body. I went still.

Liam tilted his head and looked at me with hooded eyes. "Touch them," he commanded softly.

I took a breath, stepping closer as I bent to study the beautiful swirls. My fingers hovered for a few seconds before I gained the courage to touch him. He tensed, and I dropped my hand.

"It doesn't hurt. I promise."

"Then why...?"

"Because you touching me feels good."

I chanced a look at his face. His eyes were slits of melted steel. I resumed my explorations with my hands, soon followed by my lips. I gently kissed the pink-and-white ridges, moving up and down his scarred flesh until Liam grasped my wrists and pulled me up and over to the bed. He flipped me onto my back and positioned himself on his knees between my parted legs.

Shirtless, Liam was magnificent. A living statue, carved from the most exquisite stone. He was so breathtaking, so beautiful. Tears prickled my eyes.

"Cam? Is this okay?" Concern softened his chiseled jaw as he peeled my hands away.

I shook my head furiously and whispered, "It's... everything I've wanted."

A small smile twitched his lips. He gave a knowing nod, then ducked his head to kiss me. His hips moved against me as his hands gripped the hem of my tank, tugging it off and flinging it to the floor. He stared for a few seconds—long enough for me to take notice, but not long enough to make me self-conscious. Instead, I felt emboldened by his appreciative attention. I reached for his jeans, and he shifted to give me access. Together, we shed all remaining clothes.

Both bare, we went still, absorbing one another's bodies. The tension between us thickened, turning the air heady with lust. I inhaled deeply, filling my lungs with the mingling scents. Desire shot through my veins as the heat in my core bubbled like a volcano ready to erupt.

When I reached for him, all preamble was lost. We turned frantic, touching and exploring with a loss of control that titillated and thrilled me. The rough stubble of his chin and his calloused hands set my skin on fire—hot, tingly firecrackers exploding over my body.

Liam paused, catching my eyes before slowly sinking inside me. I watched in pure wonder as he filled me, making me feel complete and whole, as if a part of me was lost and finally found.

I had seen the power of fire, the heat of its flame, but the warmth that flooded me as Liam and I became one burned hotter than a million suns, brighter than the fiercest lightning bolt. He began to move in a slow, steady pace, still holding my eyes. Pleasure burst from my core to every minuscule cell and fiber of my being. My body was a bomb, and the friction between Liam and me was about to set us off.

Melting, blending, fusing.

As he moved faster, the pleasure became too great, too much. I closed my eyes, but Liam hoarsely groaned, "Open your eyes. I want to see your eyes."

Obeying, I looked at him. Our gazes locked. We burned hotter, brighter, until we detonated together, bursting in waves of pleasure, scorching the bedsheets, searing our skin, melding our souls. I gasped in surprise, my eyes widening, then refocusing on Liam. I was lost in an explosion that shook me to my soul.

As our quaking limbs slowly settled, pieces of my soul floated along with pieces of his, dancing like ash after a fire. Our bodies cooled in each other's arms, and I knew I never would feel whole again without Liam by my side.

THIRTY-ONE

"So, about those eggs." Liam's chest vibrated against my cheek as he spoke.

Rolling away, I fidgeted with the corner of the silk sheets. "Eggs? I'm more concerned with this." Chunks of the material had shriveled or blackened. With warm cheeks, I asked, "Does this happen every time you... you know?"

Liam chuckled. "First time it's happened to me. You?"

"Definitely the first time."

"Hopefully not the last?" Liam cocked his brow and gave a sly, sexy grin.

My smile matched his. "Definitely not the last."

"Good."

I sucked in my lower lip as I sank back into the bed. "So. What now?"

Liam propped himself up on an elbow. "Are you asking literally, as in what do we do next this morning? Or do you mean figuratively? In the grand scheme of things because we just, you know..." Liam wagged his brows.

"Both," I answered, shivering as his finger brushed my shoulder.

"Okay." He pushed to a sitting position and held out his hand, ticking off on each finger. "First, we eat breakfast. Then we do *this* again. After that, shower. Watch a movie. Make dinner. Do *this* again. Fall asleep. Repeat."

"It's Saturday. Don't you have to go in to the bar?"

"Those fools can manage themselves for a night."

"What about the band?"

"Taken care of. Duffy's is closed Sundays and Mondays, so we have nothing to worry about."

I sat up and yanked the sheet to cover myself. A burnt scent drifted to my nose, yet it didn't bother me in the least. Shrugging, I said, "Okay, what about figuratively?"

Liam tucked a piece of my hair behind my ear. "Remember what I said. Once I start, I won't stop."

"So, you won't stop... kissing me?"

"Kissing you. And this." He pointed to the sheets. "But we do need to figure out how to do *this* without destroying all of Nova and Dane's linens."

My cheeks flamed. "Well, it's never happened to me before, the sheets and all. I mean, I've done *it* before, but *this* hasn't happened."

Liam held his palm up. "Stop. Don't want to think about what you've done with others."

"Liam?"

"Yes?"

"There haven't been many others. I've, um, been afraid, so I've held back. But I don't want to hold back with you." I glanced at the fireplace. Liam squeezed my hand, encouraging me to continue. "I want to let go of my fear. But first I need to face it. This... this heat between us... it was intense, consuming, almost too much, but it was beautiful. It was amazing. I want to see the fire in me the same way. I want to know all the good things it can do. I don't want to look at it and think of Papa. I was thinking maybe later we can drink wine, sit by the... fireplace."

There, I said it. It was out, and even if the idea made my tummy queasy, part of it also bubbled with excitement. What if I could really, possibly free myself of my fear? Free myself of Papa?

What if when I looked into my amber-colored eyes, I no longer feared I'd see evil? What if I only saw Mama instead?

"You're brilliant." Liam grabbed my shoulders and planted a sloppy kiss on me. "And you're mine."

"Yours?" I stuttered.

Liam's mischievous eyes shifted to a steely, stormy gray as his jaw set. "You're mine. And I am yours." He grabbed my hand, taking me back to a time when he first made his grand proclamation.

You have a place. You have a home. With me. I will be yours, and you will be mine.

LIAM and I held true to the schedule he'd ticked off on his hand, except for the repeated romp in the bed—instead, it was a blistering shower together. The water went from warm to steamy to scalding, yet it couldn't hold a candle to the heat between our bodies.

While I dried my hair, Liam ordered pizza from Rosario's for delivery and picked out a movie on Netflix. We picnicked in front of the unlit fireplace with a blanket on the floor in Nova and Dane's massive bedroom. Just as I was about to sink my teeth into a slice of the veggie supreme, my phone ignited with a text notification.

I read it, then flashed the screen to Liam. "Cathy will be

bringing Daisy home soon. Do we have time for our little fireplace exercise?"

Liam glanced at the cold fireplace, then to me. He gave a firm nod.

"Should I get wine or mix some cocktails? People in the movies usually drink while sitting by a fireplace, right?"

"Cam," Liam said, looking at me like I was crazy. "Alcohol is highly flammable. We already scorched their sheets."

"Right." I blushed, then cocked my head and glared at Liam. "Hey, what's with calling me Cam? I've been telling you for years to stop with your surly *Cambria,* and now I'm suddenly Cam?" I used a gruff, low voice when I said "Cambria," imitating Liam. He rolled in his lips, trying to suppress a laugh. "Oh my God, Liam! You've been doing it just to irritate me, haven't you?" I nudged his rock-hard bicep, which didn't budge in the least. "Bully."

"Bully? Me?" Liam flattened his palm over his chest. "You've done everything in your power to drive me insane for the last, I don't know... hundred years? A little surliness is nothing compared to the torture you've put me through."

Insecurity flooded my chest. I always felt like a burden to Liam, but *torture?* Wide-eyed, I whispered, "Torture?"

"That came out wrong." His brows drew together, and he tossed his slice of pizza into the box. "I might have met you when you were just a kid, but it wasn't long before you turned into a woman—a stunning woman I could not get out of my mind, no matter how hard I tried. And believe me, I tried. But there you were, ruining every other woman in this world—and the worlds beyond. I wanted you and *only* you, yet you infuriated me. You had a precious, irreplaceable gift you were bent on giving away."

I listened to his earnest words, feeling their raw honesty.

So much time had passed, so many seconds, days, months, years, decades. Both of us wanting and longing but unable to move forward.

"When I came from the Hark to find you, you knew. But you sent a bird." I spoke quietly without emotion or accusation.

Liam looked away. "I thought if I could keep you in the Hark, you'd be safe, sheltered from the pain and ugliness of this world. Eventually, I realized you needed to find peace with the past, find your place and purpose, appreciate your gift, and know the power you hold. You still had growing to do."

He stared at the fireplace, causing a small cherry-red light to flicker and ignite the logs inside. My pulse picked up, and Liam faced me. "Does that bother you?" I gave a shake of my head. "If I wasn't here, would it bother you?"

I didn't answer because I didn't know. Two days ago, I would have been terrified, even with Liam by my side. Now, the fire held me captive, fascinated me.

The flame in my belly simmered from my uncertainty, and the log in the fireplace crackled and hissed. Yet I wasn't afraid.

"Cambria, you needed to be whole before you could give a part of yourself to me."

I studied the fire, watching the yellow, red, and orange colors swirl and dance, like lovers in a heated tango. They swooped and sizzled, mingling then retreating. The flames moved in and out, becoming one single flame, then blowing and drifting apart.

"It's beautiful," I whispered with awe.

"Love is like a fire. It simmers and roars, contracts and expands. It can be hot and hurtful, or calm and soothing. It can feel like a hug, or it can scar the flesh." Liam looked at me, piercing my heart with his eyes. "I knew love the moment I knew you."

Tears dripped down my face. I swiped them with a shaky hand and looked away.

Liam palmed my cheek, then brushed his thumb over my lower lip. "I saw your mama's love for you. I saw your love for her."

"But I ... I was a monster. Out of control. I scarred you. I stole Mama's light."

"*He* was the monster, Cambria. And I proudly carry this scar, a reminder of the warrior child who slayed the beast. You *saved* this world from a monster. Did you ever think of it that way?"

I shook my head, scattering a flurry of tears.

"You saved this world from a beast, and your mama saved you."

THIRTY-TWO

The heavy conversation came to a quick and sudden end when the doorbell chimed.

"Oh, it's Daisy!" I exclaimed, scrambling from the floor as I scrubbed a hand over my drippy nose and tears. "I'm a mess. Can you run down there?"

"Yep." Liam casually lifted from the floor and padded downstairs.

Alone, I watched the fire, apprehensive but not afraid. It hummed and whistled, glowing softly. I squinted, looking for any signs of evil, for red-hot fiery rage. Orange-and-yellow flames continued to dance.

Soft murmurs sounded from the lower level, along with Daisy's high-pitched yap. I hustled out of the bedroom and to the top of the stairs, suddenly eager to see my furry friend.

"Hey, Cami!" Cathy called. Her smile faded when her eyes landed on me, and I realized I must've looked like a wreck. Her gaze darted to Liam, then back to me. She probably thought he was the cause of my red eyes and nose—which was true technically. "You, um, okay?"

"Oh, gosh, yes," I said, swatting a hand, making light of my splotched face. She looked unconvinced, so I blurted out the first plausible lie I could think of. "Liam and I were just watching a movie—a real tearjerker. Don't let him fool you. He was crying too."

Liam chortled and pinched the bridge of his nose. "Not true."

"Oh, that's so sweet. It's okay. Men cry too," Cathy said as she patted Liam's muscly bicep.

"Nope, didn't cry." He made small shaking motions as he scrunched his nose.

"You're right. It was more like full-on sobbing. I had to cradle his little head," I said, rocking an imaginary baby. Laughter rocked his shoulders.

Cathy's head swiveled between the two of us. "Okay. Well, I think it's sweet, Liam, to show your softer side. But, um, anyways, not to add any additional emotion to your evening, but, well, there's no easy way to say this. I think Daisy is pregnant."

"What?" Liam and I simultaneously yelled.

"Daisy!" I smacked a hand over my mouth.

Liam crouched next to Daisy and lightly rubbed her fluffy belly. He obviously recovered from the shock much quicker than me because he grinned and muttered, "Bruno, that dirty dog."

"I'm guessing she's in her second month. We can bring her to the vet on Monday. I'll go with you. I feel terrible laying this burden on Nova and Dane, but it must've happened during one of their doggy playdates."

Liam rubbed the corners of his mouth. "Can't wait to see Killbane's face."

"Liam!" I jabbed him in the rib. "This is serious!"

Cathy chuckled. "It's serious, but it's also nature, I

suppose. Puppies are a lot of work. Thankfully, I have no fosters, so I'll be able to help."

"This is crazy," I said in awe, gently running a hand over Daisy's belly. "Puppies?" Daisy laid her head down and looked at me with big, brown eyes. "Wow. What do we do now? Do I do anything differently? Should she be taking prenatal vitamins or is that just for human mamas?"

"Let's chat with the vet, but usually you move to high-energy dog food at some point during gestation and add a little more. I haven't cared for a pregnant pup in a long time."

We solidified a plan for Monday. I'd call the vet to schedule an appointment, then Cathy could accompany us for the visit.

As she departed, her head dropped. "I really feel bad laying all this extra responsibility on Nova and Dane. They have this new house, the bar..."

Instinctively, I squeezed her arm, releasing a small jolt of positivity. Tingles radiated through my limbs to my fingertips. Cathy sighed breathily, and I dropped my hold. When she looked up, cocking her head, her eyes sparkled and her lips lifted into a small smile.

"I think Nova and Dane will be very excited," I said with hope and conviction.

After Cathy left, Liam shut and bolted the door, then turned to me, rubbing his palms together. "Can't wait to see his face."

"Liam! Jeez. What kind of angel are you?"

"One nearing retirement." He pulled me into his arms. "I'm ready for 'the after.'"

The little fire in my belly flickered. I swallowed. "Oh... um. What happens in 'the after'?"

"I can feel your pulse." He chuckled and tightened his

hold. "I'll tell you what happens in *my* after. I settle down with my lady. In fact, I already have the perfect place. Bought it a while back, just been waiting for the perfect time to do something special with it. It has a cabin, a lake, a big forest in the back. Lots of fishing. Very peaceful."

"W-wait," I stuttered. "You mean Mama's cabin? *You* bought it?"

Liam drew back. "For you. Bought it for you. But I was hoping it would be for us. Weekend getaways."

I crushed my mouth against Liam's, putting all the love I felt for him into the kiss. "I can't believe it. I can't believe everything that has happened in the last week."

He chuckled. "Me either. Life changes quickly, even for an old angel like me." Lifting my chin with a finger, he looked into my eyes. A deep line creased his brow. "I'll have to give up some of my divine energy, and I won't be able to procreate."

I nodded. A delicate balance of energies meant gods of different realms were forbidden from bearing children together. Dane and Nova had already made the same sacrifice to be together.

"I can see your brain twisting and churning. I don't really look at it as giving anything up. I'm getting everything I've always wanted."

I glanced at Daisy then whispered, "Maybe we can be... puppy parents?"

THIRTY-THREE

The next morning, Liam rowed us to his "secret" spot on the lake where he claimed fish practically jumped into the boat. We proceeded to unsuccessfully fish for hours. And hours. In the early afternoon, I finally caught something—a tiny bluegill that looked no bigger than our bait.

By midafternoon, I had a sunburn and a newfound hatred of fishing.

"Please tell me you usually have more luck." I stretched my legs, then folded them back under the hard metal bench in the rowboat. "I have to pee. Can we go home? I'm starving, and poor Daisy looks as miserable as I feel."

He cast out a line, then frantically reeled it in, pulling up an empty hook. "Your negativity is scaring away the fish."

"My negativity is going to knock you right off this boat."

"Fine," he grumbled.

When the boat glided next to the pier, I hopped off, then reached to grab Daisy from Liam's arms. She padded alongside me up the lawn and to the porch.

"Going back out. Catching dinner," Liam called, hitching his thumb toward the lake.

"Knock yourself out," I yelled back over my shoulder. Patting Daisy's head, I smirked. "Remind me to never, ever get back in that thing with him." Her tongue lolled out of the corner of her mouth. "Right. You got my back. I got yours, girlfriend."

In the kitchen, I filled Daisy's bowls, then poured a big glass of ice water for myself. I grabbed my cell from the counter before sinking into a chair to catch up on messages.

Nan: *Holy cow, has life flipped upside down the last few days!*

"You don't say," I muttered before continuing.

Nan: *Aaron and I are back together. I can't believe everything that's happened. I'll explain when I see you. At The Poppy Seed till four. Back tomorrow morning at eight.*

A happy grin stretched my cheeks. I felt its glow tingle down my spine and settle in my tummy at knowing I helped restore Nan's and Aaron's hope.

It gave me hope for Celia and Neal. Maybe I could help —not *fix*—but *help*. As Liam said, healing needed to come from within. I couldn't do it for them, but I could be the light in their stormy, dark skies, the beacon that guided them to second chances and new hope.

Glancing back at the screen, I noticed the late hour. The Poppy Seed would be closing in the next thirty minutes. I didn't have time to make it. I shot Nan a reply, promising to come in the morning.

Looked like we both had a lot of explaining to do.

~

THAT EVENING, Liam and I fell asleep curled up together with me tucked under the heavy, secure weight of his arm. A vivid dream filled my sleep. I was at Mama's cabin—*our* cabin. The wooden cross I'd whittled for Mama dangled from the wall on a shiny amber peg. I ran a finger down its smooth finish as a floral-scented breeze floated through the open window. I was alone in the cabin, but I wasn't afraid.

Crunching sounded from outside the window. Liam was probably back from fishing. He wanted to catch something for dinner. I chuckled, musing we'd have to order takeout again when he came back empty-handed.

I missed him, even though he was nearby—out on the lake. The crunching sounded again. Footsteps? Maybe he was back. I rushed to the front door, throwing it open to find the sky filling with gray, stormy clouds. They reminded me of Liam's eyes. But as they rolled faster, churning to an ominous black, the temperature dropped at least fifteen degrees. I shivered and ran onto the lawn, calling Liam's name, urging him to come back before the storm hit.

The wind picked up, smacking my cheeks. A musky combination of rain and soil floated from the thick, green grass. I darted toward the lake, but the rustling sound came again—from behind me.

"Liam?" I called, whipping my head around, scanning the yard. My eyes settled on the forest beyond our cabin. Leaves rustled from the force of something big and strong.

"A bear!" I yelled and ran toward the cabin to grab the rifle that sat inside the door.

But instead of a bear, a terrified Nan burst through the thick foliage with tears streaking her face and blood caking her lips. Behind her, a rush of energy parted the trees—

"No!" I screamed and bolted upright. White-knuckled, I clutched the bedsheets.

Liam tightened his hold on me. "A nightmare?" he asked, brushing a hand through my hair, instantly calming me.

I swallowed and nodded. "It was terrible. Nan was being attacked. I think it was... *him*."

"He's gone, Cam. Dust, ash. He can never come back for you. I made sure of that." The deadly tone of his voice made me wince.

"You?"

He nodded, and I relaxed against his unyielding hold. "You slayed him in this world. I brought him to the next to face final judgment."

Papa was gone. *Really* gone. We lay motionless for a long while until Liam twisted his head to check the alarm clock. The red numbers illuminated the time—just past six in the morning.

"Think you can fall back to sleep?" he asked.

"I'm up. Think I'll do some yoga. It'll help calm me. Want to join? I can teach you some easy poses."

"While I truly appreciate your flexibility," Liam said, raising a seductive brow, "no. Nothing about it sounds fun."

"Seriously?" I poked his arm. "I fished with you on that stupid little boat for hours."

He snickered and rolled from bed. "I should get to the bar. I gotta work out the schedule for the next pay period, and it's easier when nobody's there bugging me. People keep messaging me, requesting days off." He rolled his eyes and pulled on a pair of athletic shorts.

An hour later, we parted ways with Liam heading to the bar and me to the back porch. I worked through an hour of breathing and stretching exercises. As I rolled up my mat and tucked it under my arm, I'd never felt stronger, more alive, more connected. Around me, nature—the grass, the wind, the trees—buzzed with positive energy, feeding my flame.

With renewed hope in my step, I grabbed Daisy's leash from the laundry room and called for her. "Come on, girl. Let's go see Nan. I'm sure she has a biscuit for you!"

She lifted her head lazily, then set it back down. "Oh, Daisy! How could I forget? I need to call the vet!"

I located the number on Nova's meticulous list, scheduled an appointment for the following day, then shot Liam and Cathy a message to let them know the details. I tossed around the idea of emailing Nova but figured it would add unnecessary stress to their vacation.

As angry as I'd been with her for tricking me into dog sitting, I now owed her a giant debt of gratitude... But I'd still make her pay. The idea of opening my own yoga studio lingered—and I'd need every cent possible.

Halfway through our walk, my phone vibrated in my canvas crossbody bag. I pulled Daisy off to the side of the road and yanked it out.

Liam: *Will join tomorrow for Daisy's apt. Be home in a bit.*

His mention of "home" made my stomach flip. It wasn't our home, but his use of the word felt intimate—a subliminal message.

Me: *I'm halfway to The Pop with Daisy. Want a hibiscus maple latte?*

Liam: *Meet you there—will stop & get the car. Should run to Target or Bed Bath and Beyond...*

I groaned, thinking of the scorched sheets we had to toss. They were high-end Egyptian silk—probably costing everything I'd make from my dog sitting stint. At least Nova had a linen closet full of replacements to use in the meantime.

I sighed and tugged the leash. "Come on, Daisy-girl."

At the foot of the concrete stairs to The Poppy Seed, a wave of unsettled energy flowed through me, making my legs wobbly and weak. I stumbled, nearly falling to my knees as I grasped the banister. Daisy cocked her head and whined.

"I don't know, Dais," I whispered, panting as I tried to fill my constricted lungs. I flattened a hand over my abdomen and took long, deep breaths. Gaining my bearings, I blew out a puff of air, sending a few strands of hair flying around my face.

"Let's get some water." I tried twisting the knob at the top, but it didn't budge. I leaned in, squinting through the spaces between the etched writing on the pane. The lights of the back room were illuminated, but the front of the shop was dark. I knocked.

Dread crept over my shoulders. Sweat beaded my forehead. I knocked again, harder.

Denise popped out from the back room. It was hard to see, but her face seemed contorted. She moved closer, and recognition lit her eyes. Something was definitely wrong.

The door flew open, and she tugged my arm, dragging Daisy and me in. She bolted the lock again.

"Oh, thank God. Maybe you can help." She wrung her hands. "Oh, Cami, it's bad. It's so bad."

"What?" I said, gripping her arm. "What happened?"

"Come with me." Denise led me to the back room, where a bloodied, bruised Nan sat on a stool.

"Nan?" I covered my mouth with my hand and took a step back. "Oh, Nan!"

"He had her back there—" Denise pointed to the rear

door. "Had her face pressed against the brick wall. I swear he was going to kill her." Tears streamed down Denise's face. "If I didn't get here in time..." She shuddered.

My heart pounded, shooting hot, electric sparks through my veins. Lava rolled in my stomach. *What have I done?* I'd encouraged Aaron back into her life, and he.... attacked her?

Denise gently pressed a wet cloth against Nan's forehead. "She won't let me call the police. Says it's no use because of Chaz's parents. They have deep pockets."

"Ch-chaz?" I stuttered.

"That animal attacked her because she got back with Aaron. He's a *monster*."

Bile bubbled with the lava in my stomach, and my hand again flew to cover my mouth. I swallowed it down and tried desperately to calm myself. This wasn't about me—it was about Nan.

She sat statue-still with dirty tears streaking her face. Dried blood caked her lips, purple marks bruised her neck, and scrapes marred her cheeks. Dropping to my knees, I clutched her hand. Her eyes darted to meet mine.

They were hollow.

Summoning the heat in my core, I inhaled and pulled energy up from my belly and into my limbs, fingertips, and cheeks. I blew out and squeezed her hand, releasing a wave of what Vann called spiritual endorphins—pleasure, hope, peace, and positivity. It slowly seeped into Nan. Her skin pinkened, and I released my grip. Resting back on my heels, I sucked in air to fill my winded chest.

Nan blinked, as if something in her had reset, then she gasped for air, taking desperate, sobbing breaths. "Oh, God," she said over and over as Denise and I held her until her shoulders finally stopped quaking.

"Shh!" Denise popped to her feet, on high alert. "Did you hear that?"

We all went still. Fists pounded at the front door. Was he back to hurt Nan more? Denise's eyes widened as she curled a hand around the doorframe that separated the front and back part of the coffeehouse.

"It's Liam. Oh, thank God. I thought that monster was back." Denise turned to Nan. "Should I tell him to go?"

When the pounding resumed, I stood up and sighed. "He won't go away. Is it okay, Nan?"

She nodded. I kept her hand in mine as Denise left to let Liam in.

"You'll be okay," I whispered. She nodded again.

"Cambria!" Liam bellowed as he rushed in, stopping when he saw Nan. "What happened?"

I compressed my lips and said in a low, calm voice, "Chaz hurt Nan. She's going to be okay."

Liam gave a nod. "Have you called the police?"

"She's worried." My eyes darted from Liam to Denise, then back to Liam. I closed my eyes, again summoning the warmth in my core, bringing it to my limbs and fingertips. I set my hand on Nan's knee. "I think you should talk to the police. I have hope that justice will prevail."

Liam tilted his head, eyeing me with a combination of pride and awe. He nodded. "I think you're right."

THIRTY-FOUR

L iam and I went with Nan and Denise to the police station and stayed while they took statements. Since there was a witness to the incident, it looked likely that Chaz's dad would not be able to get him off so easily this time. Liam and I drove home in silence.

As he navigated Nova's BMW into the garage, I spoke. "I can't help but think it's partly my fault. I encouraged Nan to talk to Aaron. Had I not interfered, none of this would have happened."

"Had you not, Nan wouldn't know what a monster Chaz is."

The mention of monsters made me think of Papa.

"Why does it seem, no matter my intention, when I try to help or step in, something bad comes of it? I can't help but think it's because of *him*. Because part of me was created from evil."

The thought sent a chill over my skin. What if it was true? Trouble did seem to follow me.

Liam squeezed my knee. "You okay?"

"It's just... scary. Scary to know people like Chaz are out

there. His dad might not get him off scot-free, but he'll get what—a slap on the wrist, a few days in jail, a fine? Is that justice?"

"You want me to snuff him out? I'll rid you of him if that's the justice you need." The lethal coolness in his voice sent another chill dancing over my skin. "Say the words, and it will be done."

I shook my head. "No, no. It's not what I want."

"*That* is what makes you different from your father. *That* is the good in you."

We climbed from the car, and I let a very tired Daisy out from the backseat. She toddled around to the veranda and settled at the far end, away from the rocking chairs.

I plopped down in one and stared at the trees. "I can't get the image of Nan's sad, hollow eyes out of my head." I shuddered as I wrapped my arms around myself. "She was so traumatized. If only I had gotten there earlier, I could have saved Nan from him. I failed her."

"You're taking the blame?" Liam walked up the stairs and stopped in front of me. I picked at my stubby nails, avoiding his question. "The night of the fire, had I arrived a few minutes earlier, things would have been very different for you. Do you blame me for what happened?"

I waved my hand. "That's silly."

The night of the fire, if Liam hadn't arrived when he did, Mama wouldn't have survived. He healed her mortal body after she fed me her light and lost her divinity. His timing saved her, and ultimately saved me.

"Exactly," he said softly, taking the chair next to me.

"It's a miracle you arrived when you did," I whispered.

"Not a miracle." He looked at me. "Fate."

I blushed and smiled. Mama always used to say fate had

brought Liam to us. I wondered what she'd think if she saw us now.

Nothing would make her happier.

My chin tilted toward Liam. A knowing grin spread across his handsome face as he rubbed my arm.

Later that evening, I readied for bed in the privacy of the giant master bath. The quiet let me absorb the palette of emotions from the rollercoaster of a day—fear for Nan, anger at Chaz, gratitude for Denise and Liam, hope for justice. When I thought of myself, the same array of emotions filled my core, mingling with the pride and awe I saw in Liam's eyes when he watched me use my gift.

After a quick shower, I slipped into Nova's fluffy robe and glanced in the mirror. Droplets dotted my lashes. My amber eyes blinked back, warm and comforting. No sign of Papa.

He's gone, Cam. Dust, ash. He can never come back for you.

I'd seen and felt Mama's presence. I'd faced my fear of the fire. I'd used my gift with control. Maybe I was truly and finally free of the past.

When I opened the bathroom door, Liam was sprawled in the middle of my bed, lounging with his hands casually clasped behind his neck as if it were an old habit. The TV hummed with a sitcom I didn't recognize. I paused under the doorframe, mesmerized by the sight of him.

In a blink, Liam's body language shifted from relaxed to tense.

"Come here," he commanded.

"Sure getting bossy with your come-heres." I heard myself speak, but the husky voice sounded foreign. I gazed at him for a few more seconds before he pushed from the bed to stand in front of me.

Reaching for the tie on my robe, his hands grabbed both sides of the knot and pulled me against him. "Gonna get a whole lot bossier in a minute."

"You are?" I croaked as he bent his head to kiss my neck. He untied the knot and pushed the robe off my shoulders, letting it fall in a puddle at my feet, leaving me naked before him.

He unlatched his lips from my neck. "Yep." As he took a few steps back, his eyes blazed with desire, roaming over me with pure lust. He took his sweet time inspecting every curve, line, and angle of my body. "You're perfect."

With warm cheeks, I lowered my eyes. I'd never been stared at in such a way by a man, and that it was coming from Liam only made it more impactful.

"Embarrassed?" he asked, tugging my chin. "Don't get shy on me now, Cam. I want you. All of you. The innocent side. The passionate side. I want to know every bit of you." He pulled back, and a finger slid down my side to my hip. Liam whispered into my parted lips, "Every inch. Every sweet spot."

Tension and excitement buzzed in me. Liam raked my hair from my face, then kissed me slowly, thoroughly, inspecting every curve, line, and angle of my mouth. One of his big, strong hands glided down my spine. I tangled my hands in his hair.

I'd already made a vow to take his hand and never let go. Now, I'd give him everything—my heart, my body, my soul.

I focused unblinkingly on him as my hands worked from his hair, down his chest, and to the hem of his white undershirt. I tugged it off and tossed it on top of my discarded robe. My hands returned to Liam's chest and slowly inched down to the band of his shorts. I started to slide them over his hips and butt when he took hold. He yanked them the rest of the way off and stepped out of them.

When he stood upright, I let my eyes take their fill of Liam. His body was perfect, even with the scars. I ran a finger along the side of his hip and up his back, following one of the ridges.

"You're perfect, too," I whispered.

Liam grasped my cheeks with both hands and pressed his lips to mine, walking me backward until my butt hit the wall. He pressed the length of his body against me, and I writhed from the out-of-control ache inside me that demanded more. My hands raked his back while he cupped my bottom, tugging me closer against his hardness. A groan erupted from Liam, sounding a lot like the rumble of his motorcycle. His mouth unpeeled from mine to nip down my neck to my breasts.

With his hands still cupping my bottom, he lifted me, and I instinctively wrapped my legs around him. In three long steps, Liam set me down on the bed. He crawled over me and tugged at my calf to bring it over his back while pushing into me in one fluid motion. I moaned at the flood of pleasure shooting through my body as he began to rock back and forth. Each thrust brought more sweet friction, sparking the fire in my core.

We moved in sync, grinding faster and deeper, pushing one another to a sweet release, so in tune, it didn't take long to get there. Waves of hot, pulsing pleasure shuddered our bodies as we came undone together. Primal sounds mingled in the heady air—moans and pants escaping from our connected lips.

Once the shudders subsided, Liam collapsed against me, but I hardly felt his weight. My body was still humming, still tingly. For several minutes, we savored the feeling of being together, being one, until Liam rolled off. He tugged me into his side and nuzzled his face into the back of my neck.

"Perfect," he whispered. "This thing between us, you, me... everything is perfect."

Liam's breathing evened as he slipped into sleep. I closed my eyes and savored the feel of him against me.

I was far from perfect, but Liam was right—together, nothing felt more perfect.

THIRTY-FIVE

The next morning, I woke with two soft brown, soulful eyes inches from my own.

"Daisy!" I squealed, jerking from Liam's hold, but he tugged me back in and grumbled something incoherent. "Liam, let go. What time is it?"

"Early, too early," Liam groaned. "Kept me up too late."

The red letters of the alarm clock illuminated behind Liam's tousled hair. "It's almost ten!" I screeched as I pushed him off using both hands and sat up. Daisy watched with a look of annoyance. "Oh, you poor thing! You're probably starving!" My feet hit the plush carpet, and Daisy's nose went into my shins as she whined. "Right, potty first. Come on, girl."

She followed me down the stairs to the front. I let her out and watched from the veranda as she quickly found a spot to relieve herself. The landline rang shrilly through the screen door, causing me to jump.

I answered the phone in the kitchen with forced cheer. "Hello?"

"Hi, this is Izzy from Dr. Meele's office with Collins

Grove Animal Clinic. We had Daisy on our schedule for this morning at nine thirty. Cathy Hansen's waiting here too. She suggested I call this number to reach you."

I smacked my forehead. "Oh my gosh, I'm so sorry! I—I didn't set the alarm." *And I had a night of mind-blowing, soul-altering sex that kept me up way too late.* "I'm so sorry."

"If you're able to make it here in the next half hour, Dr. Meele can still see Daisy."

I offered another round of apologies and promised we'd be there as quickly as possible.

"Liam!" I yelled, skipping up the stairs two at a time.

Through the open bathroom door, I saw him leaning over the sink as he splashed cold water over his face, momentarily making me forget my urgency. I stood dumb-founded with a silly open-mouthed stare, paralyzed by the sight of him.

"Stop looking at me like that or we'll be even later," he called.

"Like what?" I asked breathily.

Liam turned and faced me. Excitement bubbled in my core. He prowled toward me, his jaw twitching and his eyes heated. "Like you want to set my world on fire."

THE VET CONFIRMED what Cathy suspected—Daisy was pregnant. From an ultrasound, we learned she was past the halfway point of gestation, which typically was around sixty days, with four pups in her litter. We received instructions for ongoing care, including a change in her diet to pet food specifically formulated for pregnant dogs and no strenuous exercise, with shorter playtimes and walks.

We left the office with a print-off of things to watch for, when to be concerned, and what to expect in the coming weeks, although we explained Nova and Dane would be returning well before the final phase of Daisy's pregnancy. Liam and I agreed we'd hold off on messaging them. It already was Tuesday afternoon, and the last time Liam had spoken with Dane, he said they planned to return on Sunday. Daisy would be well cared for by us in the meantime, and the two lovebirds could enjoy their trip without guilt or worry about their fur-baby.

On our way home, we stopped at The Pop to see Nan, who I'd checked in with a few times since we'd parted ways at the police station. Although Chaz's assault hurt her to her core, she was adamant that she wouldn't let fear or shame control her. She would not let Chaz have that power over her.

Aaron was a different story.

"I don't want Aaron to do anything stupid," Nan said as she handed Liam a dog biscuit for Daisy, who was patiently waiting outside. "I told him to let the police handle Chaz. That monster might've gotten away with crap before, but I have to believe justice will be served."

Part of me hoped I'd played a part in Nan's strong, brave stance.

"Aaron may have a knee-jerk reaction to act, but he seems like a levelheaded guy," Liam said, taking a sip of his hibiscus maple latte. "Gonna sit out front with Daisy. Thanks for the drink, Nan."

When it was just the two of us, she asked about Liam. "So. You and Li-yum, huh?"

Her eyes danced, and I committed them to memory, erasing the dead, hollow look from the previous morning. While she still had a scraped cheek, bruises on her neck, and a crusted cut on the side of her lip, she appeared unfazed by the assault.

"Yep. I'm as surprised as you."

"Surprised? Girl, we all saw it. The tension between you two was almost painful. When he looked at you..." Nan hollowed her cheeks and blew out, then fanned herself. "Explosive."

If she only knew. "Well, what about you and Aaron?" I said, nudging her hand down and giggling.

Her face pinkened, and she bit her lip. She palmed her cheek and sighed. "Oh, Cam. We picked up right where we left off, as if the last few horrible months never happened. As soon as he walked through those doors with his sad puppy eyes, it was as if he looked into my soul, and I understood. I can't believe I was so blind—thinking Aaron would jeopardize our relationship for drugs, thinking Chaz was a good guy." She gave a little shudder, then gripped my hand. "I can't thank you enough. I don't know why I was so stubborn, but you opened my eyes."

"I'm happy for you. I'm glad you guys cleared the air." I clenched my to-go cup and sighed. "But I wish I would have gotten here earlier yesterday. Maybe if—"

"You came right when I needed you. Sure, if Denise or you showed up sooner, maybe Chaz wouldn't have taken things as far as he did, but eventually, something would have set him off down the line. With that type of temper and his loss of control, I can't help but worry—maybe he's hurt other women, someone who didn't have the support system I have. I don't know what's going to happen to him yet, but it felt good taking back my power. Hopefully, it's a wake-up call to him and his parents. He has serious problems. He needs help."

"You truly are amazing. I'm lucky I met you."

"Ditto, friend."

I wrapped my arms around Nan and pulled her in. As she hugged me back and warmed my core, I felt the gentle embrace of my new, dear friend, but I also felt Mama.

I live on in you. Our fire burns as one.

Pulling back, Nan grinned. "So, you'll be at trivia tonight, right? I mean, I know I had to drag you last week, but I—"

I cut her off. "Oh, Nan! Did I not tell you—Daisy's pregnant! We just came from the vet. I'll need to stay with her tonight."

"Pregnant? Oh, yikes. I hope Nova and Dane are paying you some cha-ching. Way above and beyond the usual pet sitting duties."

"Well, Daisy won't be having the puppies anytime soon. They'll be back before she goes into labor."

"So, you *can* come tonight?"

I shrugged. "Kind of feel guilty leaving her."

"When my friend Gabby was pregnant, she loved her alone time. Relished it. Daisy might appreciate some quiet, especially after all the 'noises' that might be keeping her up at night?" Nan made air quotes and wiggled her eyebrows.

After the instant, deep flush of my cheeks, she threw back her head and laughed.

I glared at her and wagged my finger. "Don't you *dare* say anything to Denise, Tori, Michelle, or the rest of this gossipy little town!"

AT HOME, a clearly exhausted Daisy beelined to her doggy bed in the kitchen and fell straight to sleep. Liam and I ate a late lunch of leftovers on the back patio.

"Gotta go in tonight," Liam said in his gravelly voice. "Need you to come."

"Someone called in again?"

"Don't need you to work. Need you with me."

I blushed and glanced toward the kitchen. "I should stay with Daisy."

"She'll be fine. I'll take her on a walk before we go, then she'll need to rest." He tapped his chest, causing mine to pound in sync with each thump against his hard pec. "Need you with me."

"Need?" I cocked a brow.

He nodded. "Don't want to be away from you. Not for a minute."

How could a girl say no to *that*, especially when *that* was a man—an angel—with heavenly looks and sinful touches?

"We can swing by during the shift and check on her," he promised as he gathered our plates.

"Okay," I relented. "Oh, it's trivia night."

He nodded. "Will be busy."

A week ago, I'd begged Nan to avoid Duffy's because I'd chance encountering Liam. Now, I'd be riding on the back of his bike there and going home to his—or more accurately, Nova's—bed after.

Upstairs, I rummaged through Nova's closet for something to wear. With all the activity of the last few days, I hadn't had time to get to the heaping pile of dirty laundry. My suitcase had been depleted of everything but a pair of black yoga pants, a cardigan, and a thong. I'd have to do a load, or I'd be scavenging her underwear drawer next, and I refused to stoop that low.

I yanked a ballerina-pink cashmere sweater from a hanger and paired it with my remaining clean yoga capris, which were thankfully a nice, thick fabric, making them appear more like casual pants than workout clothes. In the bathroom's full-length mirror, I fluffed my white, long waves, applied a layer of shiny gloss, and made a kissy face.

"Better be saving those for me," Liam called from the door.

Startled, I yelped and whipped around, clutching my heart. "Why are you always sneaking up on me?"

He sauntered toward me, eyes pooling with desire. I gripped the counter behind me as my pulse immediately began to race. Liam planted both hands around me, caging me like a trapped animal. His lips lowered, grazing my forehead before traveling to my ear.

"Pink looks good on you." He kissed my neck as his hand traveled under my shirt and up to my bra, where he cupped me. "But it'd look better off you."

I moaned against his cheek. "Don't we have to leave soon?"

"Hmm," Liam murmured, turning his head and catching my mouth, kissing me possessively. The hand under my shirt lowered to the hem and tugged upward just as his back pocket exploded with noise.

"Dammit," he muttered into my parted lips. He took a step back and yanked out his phone. "Crap. You make me forget everything else." He eyed me with a sly, sexy smile tugging at the corner of his luscious lips. "We got to go. Daisy's been walked and fed. I'll turn on *Animal Planet* for her. Oh, your lipstick's smudged."

Two fingers flew to my lips as I twisted to see my reflection. Shiny pink gloss streaked my cheek. I shook my head and groaned. "Thanks. I look like a mess."

"The best kind of mess." He winked and walked out of the bathroom.

THIRTY-SIX

G ossip traveled fast in Collins Grove, and the news of Nan's assault was no exception. Liam and I stepped into Duffy's with our hands tightly clasped, not seeming to draw a single raised brow from the patrons crammed at the bar and tables. Obviously, we were old news while Nan and Chaz were the front-page headline.

Dex rubbed the bridge of his nose and averted his eyes, looking very uncomfortable as he said, "I heard. Everyone's heard. Can't believe that asshole. I know I'm not management, but he's banned. His ass is not welcome here. I refuse to serve him."

Liam gave an approving nod. "Not welcome within one hundred feet of here. Or me. Or her." He drew me into his chest and whispered into my hair, "Gotta check the delivery that came and get it inventoried before things get crazy. You okay out here or you want to help me in the back?" Before I could answer, he threw out, "No, never mind. I can't think straight with you around. Stay here." He kissed the top of my head and turned on his heels.

"Damn. That man is po-zess-ive." Dex whistled, giving

me a wide grin. "Chaz better get the memo he's not welcome because the way Liam looked when he said that—" Dex whistled again. "He'd be dead meat."

"Speaking of meat," Michelle called from behind, tapping my shoulder. "Oh! Sorry, didn't mean to startle you."

"Well, you snuck up on her talking about meat. What did you think would happen?" Dex rolled his eyes at Michelle and waved the rag in his hand. "Also, what the hell do you need to talk to Cami about meat for? That's weird."

Michelle laughed and tossed her ponytail over her shoulder. "Yeah, okay, I didn't mean *meat* meat. Meatballs and Matt are over there. They'd like for you to stop over if you get a minute, Cami."

"That dude goes by Meatballs? How did I not know this?" Dex screwed up his face. "And why 'Meatballs'? You know what, I don't think I want to know."

I had no desire to talk to Chaz's friends, but when I turned around, Nan and Aaron were beelining from the front door to Matt and Meatballs' table. Both men rose as they approached with Meatballs drawing Nan in for a hug while Matt shook Aaron's hand and patted his back. I couldn't hear the conversation, but Nan gave a limp smile and nodded as Matt pointed to the chairs around the table.

Michelle leaned in to my ear. "Chaz is done. Toast. Even if Daddy gets him out of legal troubles, this town won't tolerate him. We're close-knit. We take care of each other. Everyone feels terrible his bad behavior has gone unchecked for so long."

"Wow," I whispered.

Over the last week, Collins Grove had opened my eyes to friendship, love, honesty, responsibility, respect, and community. I realized in that moment that I never, ever wanted to leave Collins Grove. It'd become *home* over the last week—my landing place, my safe haven with my hero.

I had Liam, and I had a home.

A few minutes later, I made my way to their table. When I'd met Meatballs and Matt the week before, they seemed like cocky jocks with big muscles and bad attitudes. Looking at them now, I saw kind smiles and round, sincere eyes. Again, Meatballs stood upon my approach and drew me into a hug.

"Heard how you helped Nan," he said softly, drawing back. "Can't believe that dick attacked her. I mean, he's had his issue with anger, but..." He trailed off and looked at Nan, then back to me, leaning in and lowering his voice. "Heard he got kicked off the board at the bank, maybe even fired. I don't know if his dad would have done it if it weren't for this big project coming to town, but I'm glad he's feeling the squeeze. It's not enough, but it's a start."

Matt chimed in, also pushing from his chair to stand. "I don't know why we haven't cut ties earlier. He's so negative. Brings the whole group down."

"Guess while we're at it—thanks for encouraging Nan to talk to me," Aaron said quietly as he looked from me to Nan, his eyes lighting with love. "I owe you."

"You don't owe me anything." I swatted a hand as someone pressed into me from behind. I didn't have to turn around to know it was Liam. I not only recognized his scent, but my body recognized his touch, relaxing instead of tensing when his arms snaked around my waist and pulled me in.

His lips nuzzled my neck as he murmured, "You okay?"

"Hey, Liam." Nan giggled. "She's fine, jeez."

Aaron put his arm around the back of Nan's chair. "Hey, man. Bike looks great, but you should know, when we came in, there was a big, and I mean *huge*, black bird sitting on your seat like he owned the place. Tried swooshing him away, but the thing wouldn't move."

"Oh my God!" a feminine voice exclaimed, cutting off Aaron. I twisted to see Tori as she joined our group. She jabbed a finger toward Liam and me. "I knew it! I called it. Didn't I call it last week?"

"We all did," Nan said, rolling her eyes. She looked gorgeous with her chestnut curls framing her sweet face. Although she wore eye makeup, she didn't use cover-up to conceal the scrapes on her cheek or the bruises on her neck. I wondered if it was deliberate—to show she wasn't ashamed or embarrassed, to use it as a symbol of her courage and strength. She showed the world she could get knocked down but would get back up again, stronger than ever.

I'd always thought of Liam's scars as horrid and ugly; they were a reminder of the traumatic night I lost control. But Liam wore them proudly as a reminder of me—the warrior child who slayed the beast. I glanced at him, feeling more than lust and desire. I felt pure, perfect love.

"I gotta finish taking inventory. Next round's on the house." Liam tilted his head. "You know what? *Tonight's* on the house. Get whatever you want. Top shelf, whatever. Need to celebrate."

"What're we celebrating?" Meatballs rubbed his hands together and smacked his lips as if he already could taste the fried appetizer platter.

"Strong women," Liam said, looking warmly at Nan, then me. He dropped his hold on my waist, grabbed my hand, and wove our fingers together. "Okay, I gotta get to work."

Nan mouthed, "Thank you," to Liam, then said, "Hey, game's starting in a couple minutes. Cami, you're going to sit with us, right? That is, if Liam doesn't cave-man carry you over his shoulder to the stockroom and have his way with you."

"Not in there. Too much glass." He pointed to the office door and said with a straight face, "Couch in there."

"Liam!" I squealed. Heat rushed to my cheeks. I pushed away and covered my face. "Guys, he's joking."

"I'm not," Liam said, dead serious, but then his face softened into a smile that stretched across his cheeks, lighting his gray eyes into shiny orbs of steel. His breathtaking transformation was so intense, I swear the room went silent.

Liam pressed his lips together, seeming to realize the ethereal effect his smile had on the table. He waved a sheepish goodbye before walking away. I watched him talk to Michelle en route to the back, motioning to our table before continuing to the stockroom.

I slipped into the seat next to Meatballs. He flashed the tablet and grinned at me. "Getting us logged in. What's your strength?"

"My strength?" I asked, scratching my chin. "What do you mean?"

"For trivia."

"Oh. Well…" I strummed my fingers against the table-top. "Guess I'm good at history."

"Cool. Things get serious here."

"Well, before they do, I've been dying to know. What's with the nickname?"

"I can answer that," Matt interjected, putting an arm over his friend's shoulders. "Back in high school, the night before football games, we'd have pasta parties—load up on carbs. Meatballs here holds the record of thirty-three meatballs. Think it took him, like, eight minutes too."

"It was nine minutes, fifteen seconds, then I puked them up. Haven't eaten a meatball since." He shuddered.

The group erupted into fits of giggles. The happy sound of my own laughter mingled with theirs. Most of them had known each other since grade school with inside jokes and stories, a history that went back decades.

I may have been the outsider, but I was no longer the outcast. In fact, I'd never felt more like I belonged.

THIRTY-SEVEN

Michelle rushed over to take our order, explaining all drinks and food were on the house. Apparently, Liam promised the bar staff a bonus if they gave our table expedited attention. She eagerly scribbled on her pad and left to relay the order to Dex, only to return empty-handed minutes later.

"Hang on, guys. Something wrong, Michelle?" Aaron asked, waving a hand to hush Nan and Matt, who argued vehemently over the answer to one of the questions—who was the first gymnast to receive a perfect ten in Olympic history?

Michelle nervously wrung her hands together. "Daisy's running loose. Someone called saying they spotted her on the trail following Sully's Creek, somewhere between Nova and Dane's house and here. They couldn't catch her, so she's still out there."

"Oh, no!" My stomach dropped as I pushed from my chair. "Oh, gosh. Guys, I gotta go. Nan, can you tell Liam?"

Berating myself, I flew out of the back door of the bar without grabbing my bag. I should not have left Daisy. She probably wanted to see Bruno. How could I have let this happen? *Again.* She was pregnant, slow, tired, and now wandering somewhere in the woods where she could trip, fall, or worse—a wild animal could attack her. A bear or—*Stop!*

I skidded to a halt to calm myself. Taking a deep breath, I waited until my heaving chest leveled, then plucked a few wedged rocks from the bottom of my ballet flats before I started walking again on the trail at a deliberate, steady pace.

"Daisy!" I called, scanning the woods. "Daisy-girl!"

About halfway down the path, I stopped again when I heard the crunching and swooshing sounds of footsteps coming through the shrubs. Holding my hand to my ear, I listened intently for more movement. Twigs snapped from behind.

"Daisy! You stinker!" I whipped around with a huge sigh of relief.

But it wasn't Daisy who'd stepped from the forest onto the path. Chaz scowled at me with hate-filled eyes. His ruddy cheeks were puffed, and his lips were pinched like his face had gotten stuck blowing up a package of balloons.

"Where's Daisy?" I asked. When he didn't answer, I took a step back and swallowed. "It was you. *You* called the bar."

His jaw ticked, but he didn't move.

"What do you want?" I squeaked. Chaz's eerie quiet was more disconcerting than if he'd shouted or yelled. "Well, then I'm going to go."

I turned to walk away, but I knew there was no chance I'd get off so easily. His footsteps pounded over the gravel trail, quickly growing louder as he neared me. I sucked in a breath, then bolted, running as fast as I could, knowing he was bigger, stronger, and fueled with anger. Rocks tore into the soles of my ballet flats as I darted down the path.

Maybe the weight of his rage slowed him down because I got farther than I thought I would before he caught up to me.

"You dumb, lying bitch!" Chaz yelled as he crashed into me.

We tumbled off the path, rolling onto a patch of tall grass mixed with wildflowers. I quickly pushed to a sitting position and wheezed to catch my breath. Chaz effortlessly jumped to his feet and towered over me, stretching out his thick, bulging muscles to send a message—he could easily overpower me.

Fear jolted my vision, but through teary eyes, I made out every vein popping in his thick neck. I clutched at the dirt behind me and slowly crept backward, although any chance of escape was futile.

Chaz wagged a finger, slowly inching closer. "Think you can ruin my life and get away with it? Spread lies about me? Put ideas in Nan's head? My dad took me off the board, demoted me. Says I'm a liability because of your big mouth."

I sucked in a greedy breath and felt for the warmth in my belly, desperately summoning it. I was too stunned and frightened to think, but I knew I had to keep myself in check, maintain control. I closed my eyes, and Chaz said something, but I didn't listen. Instead, I focused on the little embers deep down within my belly.

My eyes popped open, and I calmly held up a hand, staring down the monster in front of me. With an even voice, I asked, "Did you hurt Nan?"

Rage twisted his lips into a snarl. "I took pleasure in smacking that bitch."

Fury replaced my calm. The embers crackled and sizzled. A small whining nose sounded, and it took three slow seconds for me to realize it was coming from my throat. My jaw clenched, and I swallowed away a rush of lava-hot bile.

"Cami!" a frantic voice called. "Cami?" Aaron stumbled into the clearing, going silent when he spotted Chaz and me.

"Oh, this is perfect," Chaz said in a voice so cold, it almost didn't sound human.

"Aaron, please go. It's okay," I croaked, scrambling to my feet, but I knew Aaron wouldn't leave me alone with this monster.

"What the hell is going on? Chaz?" Aaron took one look at Chaz, and his face paled. "You on something?"

"Please, Aaron, listen to me. Turn around. Go find Liam and tell him to come. I'll be okay. Chaz and I are just talking."

"Chaz?" Aaron held his hands up with his palms facing down, pulsing them in a calming motion. "Let's go back to Duffy's and talk about it. Okay?"

Chaz stalked toward Aaron. Based on his bulky line-backer build, Chaz easily would overtake him. I had no choice. There was no way I could help Aaron unless I fueled the flame in me.

Chaz pounced, pummeling Aaron. I watched in horror until the sharp crack of a fist hitting flesh freed me from my silence.

"Get off him!" Summoning my inner fire, I screamed louder, "I said, get off! Get off him!"

The sounds exploded from my soul. Shrieks pierced the sky, so shrill Chaz rolled off Aaron to cover his ears. My eyes burned with lava-hot tears that welted my cheeks. I cried with primal, animalistic noises that shook the ground. The air sizzled and crackled, vibrating from my out-of-control emotions. I hated the feelings churning in my stomach—the fear, anger, and rage. I took a step back, but my legs wobbled.

The whole world seemed to wobble.

"What the—" Chaz stopped, turning to face me.

"Get Liam!" I screamed to Aaron, who jumped up and ran at my command.

Stunned, both Chaz and I watched as he disappeared down the path. Once Aaron was out of sight, Chaz snapped out of his stupor. He lunged for me and captured me around the stomach with one swoop of his arm. He yanked me against his body, and his free arm circled my neck, crushing my windpipe.

"I'm going to kill you, you bitch." The hold on my neck tightened. My eyes bulged and watered.

With all my strength, I kicked behind, landing a blow to his shin and startling him into loosening his hold long enough for me to take my chance at escape. I dipped down and wiggled free, then ran as if the devil himself was chasing me. Because in that moment, Chaz was as close as I'd come to the devil since Papa.

Still, I was no match for Chaz. He threw himself into me like a linebacker making the game-saving tackle. I flew forward several feet, then crashed against a tree with Chaz's bulky body landing on top of me. Several dazed seconds passed before I heaved air into my lungs.

Chaz looked me in the eye with pure hatred and rage. I lost sight of the man; I only saw a monster.

Chaz's meaty limbs enveloped me. He shifted to again grasp my neck. Even as a demigod, I lacked the physical strength to wiggle from his iron-clad hold. The air started to thicken and shake, tunneling to black as Chaz squeezed tighter, cutting off my air supply.

My eyes fluttered closed. I thought back to the day Papa came for me, reliving every detail of the horrid night that destroyed my childhood. The bear in the woods. Papa's raging-red eyes. Mama's limp body.

The spider-web of fire emanating from my body. Flames flashing from my toes, zapping along the dirt, igniting the bushes. The grass shriveling into angry orange flames. Streaks of crimson traveling up the trunks of trees. Leaves wilting and turning to black.

Waves of fire rolling over and over and over...

Electricity sparked in my veins, and lava rolled from my stomach to my throat. My eyes popped open, burning with red-hot rage at this man who'd hurt my friends, who wanted to hurt me. I choked out a cry as the energy in my tummy erupted, shooting through my limbs and into my fingers and toes. I didn't want to feel my fire this way; I never, ever wanted to feel it this way again. Searing tears dripped down my cheeks.

I needed to maintain control if I wanted to survive, but my fury was taking on a life of its own, unleashing the darkness in me. Heaving and panting, I roared, exhuming all my rage, all the years of despair, fear, pain.

Chaz jerked as shocks of energy emanated from my torso. When his hold loosened, I wiggled free and fisted my hands, punching blindly. My blows blackened his shirt to shreds and singed his skin. He rolled off me, screaming and flailing in pain.

I scooted back and stumbled to stand up as he slowly turned to face me. Before he could attack again, I held up my hand and splayed my fingers, shooting a jolt of energy into the air and knocking him back like a physical punch to the stomach.

After recovering from the blow, he stared at me, wide-eyed and horrified. "What the fuck are you?" A combination of fear, shock and anger crossed his face. He made a slight movement—and I reacted in self-preservation.

I screamed, and a wide circle of fire orbited him. He was trapped. Tears simmered in my eyes, and the flames encircling Chaz seethed along with me, heaving with every labored breath I took.

A flock of black birds swooped in. Their wings violently flapped around Chaz like ravens circling a carcass. He flailed his arms over his head, protecting himself, until they flew up into the darkening sky. Their caws echoed in the woods, bouncing off the trees in a guttural signal. If they were here, it meant Liam was close.

My chest heaved up and down, desperate for air, desperate for reprieve.

Desperate, desperate, desperate.

I fell to my knees and sobbed. The flaming ring around Chaz fizzed and hissed.

"What the hell are you?" he shouted.

I cried into my hands. "Stop! Please, stop!"

"What the fuck is wrong with your eyes?" Chaz asked. "What *are* you?"

My eyes snapped to Chaz, and I only cried louder when I saw his face. Pure horror replaced his earlier anger. He looked at me like *I* was the monster, the beast. I wept, and the flames surrounding Chaz shot upward.

"What kind of freak are you?" he yelled with revulsion. "Help! Someone help me!"

A gust of energy swept through the clearing, making the fire encircling Chaz rise and retreat in a menacing dance.

The air shuddered. An echoing round of *caws* boomed in the sky. I didn't have to look up to know Liam had arrived.

"Liam," I whispered between sobs, looking to the ground with shame. My hands dropped to the dirt, and I rocked on all fours. "Please don't look at me. I don't want you to see me like this. I'm a *monster*."

Liam took a step forward. As he drew closer, I couldn't help but look up. His formidable presence made everything around us go still, as if nature itself was holding its breath, waiting for him to act.

"You always thought there was a darkness in you." Liam lifted his arms, crooking them at his elbows. "But you're nothing like your father. *Nothing*. I feel your remorse, your shame, your fear. I see how it's tearing you apart." The lightness of his words floated over my heated skin. "Look into yourself," Liam gently commanded.

My eyelids fluttered closed as I breathed in and out. Behind my lids, orange and yellow flames flickered against a backdrop of pure white. *My* light. *Mama's* light. The two flames waved and sputtered, rising and falling, until they finally merged into one.

I pushed back to a squatting position and squeezed my hands around myself, weeping as I felt the fire in my belly. I hadn't snuffed out my gift. The realization quenched the circle of flames surrounding Chaz. He stood in the center, blinking at us with wide, bewildered eyes.

"You didn't want to harm Chaz, but you needed to protect Aaron. You needed to protect yourself." Liam took slow, deliberate steps until he reached my side. He gently laid a hand on my shoulder. "Just like you needed to protect your mama. You're no monster. You're strong and brave and smart and kind and beautiful."

I gulped between sobs, shaking my head as Liam pulled

me into his chest. He nuzzled my hair, whispering, "Most importantly, you are mine. You are mine, and I am yours."

～

SIRENS WAILED IN THE BACKGROUND. The sounds felt oddly comforting considering the storm of police infiltrating the path.

Liam had already cleaned up my mess. The torched grass and shrubs surrounding us grew plush and green with a nod of his chin. That same nod sent Chaz flying against a tree, knocking him unconscious. When he woke, I knew the last half hour had been wiped from his memory, replaced with a story Liam embedded in his mind.

Most of the events were true—Chaz called the bar to lure me with the intent to do me harm. I had the bruises, cuts, and scrapes to prove it. The cocktail of drugs Chaz had taken before he attacked me had made his mind foggy regardless, but he had no memory of the divine intervention that took place during the altercation. Instead, Chaz thought he'd hit his head against a rock in a scuffle with Liam when he tried to stop the attack.

The police found a large number of pills on Chaz, adding another infraction to his long list of charges. There was no way the golden boy or his rich father would get him out of the trouble he'd landed himself in this time. Justice would finally be served.

Liam and I stayed by Aaron's side as he was loaded into an ambulance. He had a concussion from Chaz's tackle, rendering his recollection of the night fuzzy too. I felt terrible seeing him in pain, feeling responsible for the injury. When I had stormed out of the bar, Aaron followed to make sure I was safe since he knew Liam wouldn't want me walking through the woods alone. After Liam finished inventory and returned to the bar, the table had filled him in on the phone call. He'd sent his messengers out to locate us as he frantically searched the path and ran into Aaron along the way.

Once our statements were taken, Liam and I were cleared to leave. We walked the rest of the trail home in silence. At the bottom of the long, winding driveway that led to Nova and Dane's house, I collapsed against Liam. He effortlessly lifted me into his arms and carried me the rest of the way. Using divine energy wiped me out. I fell asleep before we even made it through the front door.

That night, I dreamed I was in Mama's cabin. The wooden cross dangled on the wall, and I smiled tenderly at it, remembering Mama's pride when I surprised her with the whittled gift. A lavender-scented breeze permeated the room through an open window. I walked to the door and looked outside to the sparkling lake in the distance. Mama stood at the shoreline, no longer the old woman who slipped into eternal sleep while I held her crepe-paper wrinkled hand. She was young and beautiful again, with snowy white hair and amber-colored eyes. Like looking in a mirror, I saw myself in Mama—her hair, her smile, her eyes. A warm, comforting flame flittered in my belly. I placed my hand over it, feeling Mama as I watched her move closer.

Although I wanted to run to her, I worried any sudden movement would wake me from my dream state, and I desperately needed more time with Mama.

Instead, we gazed at one another. Love, peace, and—most importantly—hope floated in the vast space between us. I understood her message. She was in another world, but distance, space, and time could not keep us apart. She lived on in me.

As I lifted my hand to wave goodbye, I woke with a small, sad smile on my face and Liam's eyes inches from my own.

"I saw Mama," I whispered groggily. "She was so beautiful, Liam."

He studied my sleepy face. "She's proud of you. So proud. We both are."

Twisting loose of his hold, I asked, "I want to see the cabin. Can we go sometime?"

"Anytime, sweetheart." A finger brushed my lips.

"It's really mine?"

"Name's on the deed."

"What about property taxes?" I had no extra money or job and a car in desperate need of repairs.

"Taken care of."

"Liam."

"This is nothing compared to what I want to give you." He leaned in and kissed me, momentarily transporting me back in time to our first kiss, landing us in a place of pure perfection.

The sun, the moon, the stars.

Hope. Beauty. Peace.

A field. A lake. A kiss.

Passion. Desire. Fire.

He pulled away and placed a finger over my kiss-swollen lips. "A place, a home with me. I am yours, and you are mine."

THIRTY-EIGHT

"Come on, pokey-pants! The Pop closes in thirty minutes," I yelled over my shoulder.

"Not getting into that clown car," Liam called from the veranda.

I rolled my eyes and kept walking toward Laverne. Today was the first time I'd had the energy to leave the house since the incident in the woods two days before. I'd promised Nan we'd see her before her shift ended. Not only were we already behind schedule since I'd slept in obscenely late and taken a long, relaxing bath, but Liam now fussed about taking my car.

"Cam, love you and all, but no. Rather walk the two miles than ride in that thing."

I whipped around. "What?"

He stepped down onto the sidewalk, stopped in front of me, and grabbed my hands. "You need a new car."

"Maybe I need a new boyfriend."

"Not a boy. Or a man."

"Right." I rolled my eyes again. "So, what *will* I call you in retirement?"

"Once an angel, always an angel." Liam shrugged and shot an innocent smile, transforming the sharp lines and edges of his rugged, handsome face to the softest, sweetest face—the face of an angel.

"You're too much." I shoved my palm into his chest. "But let's circle back to my question. What did you say?"

He pointed at my bug, which Aaron had helped him fix that morning, then to Nova's BMW SUV in the garage. Thankfully, Aaron's concussion was mild. Or more likely, Liam had helped his healing process along. "No. Yes. Or walk."

"No, what you said before that—before the bit about how you'd rather walk."

Liam scratched his chin, then threw up his hands. "What're you talking about?"

"Gah, Liam!" I squealed, throwing up my arms, mocking him. "The 'love you and all' bit!" I imitated his growly voice.

He shook his head. "Oh, that. What about it?"

"You do?"

"Of course. Don't you?"

"Well, yeah, but... I like hearing it. Think it's the first time I've heard you say it out loud." It was the first time someone had said those special words to me since Mama. Words I longed for. They only sounded sweeter coming from Liam's lips.

"I love you, Cambria. I've loved you from the moment I caught sight of the strong, brave little girl who stood up to the monster and saved her mama. I loved you when you grew into a stunning woman who stole my breath and my heart. My love for you has changed over the years, from protective to passionate, but I loved you then, I love you now, and I'll love you for eternity."

"Wow."

"Was that good? Can we take the Beamer now?"

"Li-umm!" I smacked his arm but relented. "Fine. We really need to get going."

"Yeah, yeah." The keys to the Beamer dangled from his index finger. "Why don't you drive? Test her out."

"Because Laverne is just fine. All fixed. And I'd never be able to afford a BMW." Nor would I want one. Not my style.

"Come on. Humor me?"

"Fine."

Liam dropped the keys into my outstretched palm. We climbed into the car, and I adjusted the seat, then began to back out.

"Look, there's a camera," Liam said, pointing at the rearview back-up cam. "Nice, huh?"

"Liam."

"Just try it."

I rolled my eyes but glanced at the little screen as I backed out and made a Y-turn to face forward on the drive. The BMW glided down the driveway, then onto Lake Road.

"Like butter," Liam muttered.

"Surprising comment coming from the guy who drives that rumbling mass of steel."

"I don't fit in the clown car." Liam eyed me. "Gonna need something to lug around a pup."

"A pup?" I squealed. "Seriously, you want a puppy?"

"For you and me. A puppy for us. Figure if you don't want a bird tailing you, a watchdog's the next best thing."

I turned onto Charles Street with a smile stretching my cheeks. We soon passed the packed park. Kids played soccer in the fields beyond the playground. A mom waved as she passed, pushing a sleeping baby in a stroller. Liam lifted his hand, and I smiled at the community that welcomed us—me, the outcast, and my surly angel boyfriend—with open arms.

"I love it here," I murmured. Although I was excited to visit Mama's cabin, Collins Grove was home. Our landing place. Our safe haven.

Liam gripped my knee. "Me too."

On Main Street, he signaled for me to pull over at a vacant parking spot on the opposite side of The Poppy Seed. He climbed out and stood still, facing away from me. I was halfway across the street when I turned and called to him.

"You coming?" When he didn't answer, I skipped back to his side and tugged his arm. "What're you doing?"

Following his stare to the vacant building, I noticed a new sign had replaced the "For Sale" notice on the window.

"Welcome Home." I read the words out loud. I knew the building would sell well before I saved enough to buy it, but it still sent a pang of hurt to my chest. "That's weird. Thought it was a commercial building, not a house."

"There's a two-bedroom apartment above it."

"Oh. Wonder what they'll put in the storefront."

"A yoga studio."

"Oh, wow." I shrugged. "That's a coincidence. Maybe they'll be hiring."

"Think they probably will. Heard the owner is one of the best, most dedicated yoginis."

"Yoginis?" I giggled at Liam's use of the title, impressed he knew the proper term. My surprised smile turned to a curious frown. Cocking my head, I slowly turned in Liam's direction just as a sly grin twisted his lips. "You seem to know a lot about the building."

He rubbed his palms together, then grabbed my hand and linked our fingers. "Welcome home, Cam."

"Seriously?" I gawked at Liam in disbelief. "Really?"

He nodded. "Until we find something on the lake. Then we can rent out the apartment for a little extra income. But the building is ours. You'll have your own studio. Your own business."

I slowly covered my wide-open mouth with my palm, absorbing the beautiful building in front of me. "I... I've never... I don't know where to even start. How will I get clients?"

"I believe in you. You start a studio, they will come." The corners of his eyes crinkled when he grinned. "Your gift needs to be shared." Liam and I stood silently for several minutes before he tugged my hand. "Want to see it?"

I nodded. Liam fished in his pocket for a key. Together, we walked up the three steps to the heavy glass door where he jabbed the key into the knob. As I stepped inside, my hand again crept up to cover my mouth. Shiny wooden floors, brick beams, and high ceilings made it the ideal space for a yoga studio.

"Seriously, Liam, this is perfect. It's beautiful. I can't believe you bought it. It's... so perfect." Tears smarted behind my eyes as I clasped my hands in front of my face and slowly spun around, taking in every bit of the expansive room, already envisioning how I'd create a relaxing, inviting atmosphere to invite clients. "It's almost... *too* perfect." I cocked my head and looked at Liam, studying the flawless features of his handsome face. I'd never get tired of looking at him. "Did you have something to do with this? I hope you didn't use divine intervention."

"Nope."

"Wow. Must be fate or something."

"Yep. Fate works in mysterious ways."

No truer words had been spoken. The force of fate created a series of events that had led a powerful angel to save a scared little girl as she faced the monster in the woods. But until she learned to save herself, fate would pull them in different directions even as it wove their stories together.

Hand in hand, Liam and I walked through the building. I fell in love with each brick, beam, and wooden plank of what would soon be my very own yoga studio. We stopped at the bottom of the stairs in the far back of the room. Before making our way to the apartment above us, I looked at Liam with love, hope, peace, and promise.

I have a place. I have a home. With Liam. I am his, and he is mine.

THIRTY-NINE

As soon as I woke Sunday morning, I turned up the ringtone volume on my cell to its highest setting. Nova and Dane weren't due to arrive at Milwaukee General Airport until the afternoon, but the anticipation was killing me. After breakfast, I began to obsessively check my phone every couple minutes. When it finally erupted, I jumped up from my seat on the back porch and yelled to Liam, who was tinkering in the shed. "It's them!"

"Nova!" I squealed after connecting the call. Liam came up the stairs and wrapped his arms around my waist. I leaned back into his hold. "Welcome back!"

"Cami! We landed a bit ago. How is everything—how are you? And Muffie? And Liam, of course? Is our house still standing?"

I chuckled and shook my head. "Oh, I have a lot to fill you in on, but I'll wait until you get here."

"Well, it won't be long. We're hurrying to catch the shuttle for our car now. I can't wait to hear about your stay in Collins Grove." Nova's words came out in heavy breaths, as if she were winded from walking and talking. "I have some big news for you."

Inaudible chatter from Dane sounded in the background. She returned her focus to our conversation only to end it with an abrupt, "I gotta go—sorry! See you in about an hour!"

I tapped the screen of my cell and twisted in Liam's arms to face him. "They're on their way. Want to wait out front? I'll grab our drinks."

Earlier, Liam and I stopped at The Poppy Seed to pick up a box of pastries for Dane and Nova's return. Liam couldn't resist getting his usual—the hibiscus maple latte.

After a quick stop in the kitchen to grab our to-go cups, we sat on the rocking chairs. Daisy rested between us. She perked up at the sound of an engine, which was soon followed by a flash of red as Dane's Audi wound up the driveway.

Liam pushed to his feet. "Ready for this?"

I nodded. He'd have no problem keeping a straight face, but we both worried I'd quickly crumble under pressure. The Audi came to a stop at the top of the drive. Liam gave me an "it's go time" nod of his chin, then leaned against one of the pillars with his arms crossed over his chest. In true Liam fashion, his face shifted into a scowl.

"Cami! Muffie! Liam! We're back!" Nova cheerfully cried as she climbed from the passenger side. She smoothed her crisp trousers, then patted imaginary stray hairs from her face.

Daisy's tag wagged wildly, but she remained seated by my feet. Pregnancy had hit her hard the last few days. Nova stopped at the bottom of the stairs. "Cami? You okay?"

My eyes darted to Liam. He stepped forward and said in his deep, gravelly voice, "Need a word with you guys."

"What's wrong?" Nova's brows rose as she kneeled beside Daisy and nuzzled into her furry head. "Mama missed you, Muffie."

"Let's wait for Dane," I said, lifting from the rocking chair and moving beside Liam.

"Ohh-kay." Nova's eyes rounded as she called to Dane, who was lugging suitcases out of the trunk of his sports car. "Dane! Leave those for a second and come up here!"

"Guys! Looks like you survived!" Dane yelled as he jogged to the veranda. He also crouched beside Daisy to give her a rub. When he looked up, a mischievous grin dimpled both sides of his cheek. "We had a wager."

"A wager?" I asked, cocking my head.

"Yep. Nova thought we'd come back to a divided house. She literally thought there'd be tape down the middle of the floor." Dane wagged his brows. "I said you'd be hooking up. So, who won?"

"Dane!" Nova nudged his arm, but she also gave a sly smile. "Ignore him. What's going on? You have something to tell us?"

Liam nodded and reached for the small bakery box on the table between the two rocking chairs. Nan and Denise thought our idea was brilliant so they'd eagerly gone along with our devious plan. "Apparently this is called a reveal."

"A what?" Nova asked, taking the box and examining the ribbons tying it shut.

Somehow, I kept a level tone as I nodded my head and said, "A reveal. Pink and blue ribbons. There're cookies inside." *This* was the part of our plan where Liam was certain I'd crack under pressure.

"Are you kidding me?" Nova exclaimed, wide-eyed and open-mouthed. She tucked the box under one arm, grabbed

Dane's arm with the other, and took a startled step back. "No way. No freaking way."

"Just open it. We're finding out along with you," Liam said gruffly.

Dane's head jerked from Liam to Nova. "What's going on here?"

I took a big breath and blew out. "We gave Denise the sealed ultrasound pictures, and she made the cookies. They're inside."

The message finally got through to Dane—which was apparent by the slow-motion parting of his lips. After several seconds, he asked in a low voice, "How is *that* even possible?"

Liam shrugged while I struggled to keep a blank face. "Go on. Pink for a girl, blue for a boy."

"You're... you're..." Nova stumbled over her words before she trailed off and stared at the box. Finally, she gave Dane a reluctant shrug. He pulled the ends of the bow, then lifted up the lip of the box. Inside, four large cookies in the shape of bones were glazed with a light, pastel frosting. Three of the cookies were pink while the fourth was blue.

Nova blinked rapidly, studying the cookies. "Shouldn't they be all pink or all blue?"

I bit my lower lip as Liam said, "There are four."

Dane's head jerked up. "Four!"

"Four?" Nova asked slowly. Her widened eyes didn't leave the cookies.

"These are weird looking baby rattles," Dane said as he reached into the box and pulled out the blue frosted cookie. He held it up. "Well, guys, wow. Congratulations? Guess I won the bet then, huh?" He chomped into the cookie.

Nova set the box on the table and took a step toward me. "Really?"

Dane stopped chewing. "Hey, these taste a little off."

"Because they're dog biscuits, you idiot," Liam said.

Nova added in a voice filled with awe, "They're bones, not rattles." She slowly turned toward Daisy, while Dane looked down at his hand, clearly debating whether to spit or swallow.

Liam rolled his eyes and elbowed Dane. "It's not going to kill you. Just swallow it."

"Congratulations!" I squealed as I pulled Nova into a hug. "Daisy had quite the surprise for us. The sexes might not be accurate, but there are definitely four pups due to arrive next month."

"Had to do a lot of convincing to get the vet to do another ultrasound," Liam added.

After the incident with Chaz, I couldn't stop worrying about Daisy. We took her to the vet for another checkup and insisted on an ultrasound, even though it cost more than my monthly rent. I justified the expense by promptly giving my landlord notice to vacate my studio in Milwaukee.

With Daisy's news sinking in, Dane slapped a hand against his forehead. "Four *puppies*. I think I'm going to be sick."

"Congratulations, Killbane. You're going to be a grand-pa." Liam grinned and put his arm around me. "Told you he wouldn't get the joke. We had our own bet going."

AFTER THE EXCITEMENT of Daisy's announcement died down, rounds of hugs were given. We helped unload the Audi, then settled on the back porch. Liam and I took turns rehashing the events of the past two weeks, sharing certain parts while keeping the intimate bits between us.

Dane and Liam left the table to inspect the lawnmower, which Liam thought was on the fritz, leaving Nova and I alone together.

"I have something to tell you," Nova said, nervously strumming the glass tabletop. Her eyes darted to her lap, then back up to meet mine. "I invited Neal to visit. He needs something—a change, direction, goals. He's so lost." She sighed and looked at me. "I can't help but think Collins Grove will be good for him. I know what he did was wrong, how he used his gift to manipulate Celia. After all you've done for us, I don't want you to—"

I cut her off. "That's wonderful."

"Really?" Nova asked.

"Really." I nodded. "I hope he takes you up on the offer."

Nova stopped the tapping on the table, yet her shoulders remained tense. "Any news on Celia?"

"Yes, actually." I smiled and lifted my lavender honey tea to my lips. "She's in the Hark. Liam and I will soon be making the rounds to visit family and friends, including Celia and Lucille."

"The Hark?" Nova grabbed my free elbow, nearly causing my drink to slosh over. "You're going to *see* Celia?"

"Yes. My mama too. Well, her final resting place. She's buried by the small cabin where I grew up—before I came to the Hark. It's only about two hours from here. The property is mine, actually. I own it." It felt weird saying it out loud. For as long as I could remember, the only item of real permanence I owned was a beat-up VW bug, fondly named Laverne, who—although repaired—still remained very close to a sudden and real death. Now, I had a piece of property that held my most precious memories—good and bad.

I also had a community, a place to call home.

And most importantly, I had Liam.

"Eventually, Liam and I will restore the cabin, but we plan to make Collins Grove home. You're right—there's something special about this town. It's changed Liam and me. Maybe it'll help Neal too."

The hold on my elbow dropped away. Nova leaned in closer and cupped her mouth. "Okay. I have to know. *What* is the story with you two?"

"Our story. Where to start?" I giggled and turned to find Liam in the yard. As if sensing my stare, he looked my way. Our usual contest ensued, but unlike our games in the past, heat and desire pooled in Liam's eyes as he stared me down. Dane nudged him, hijacking his attention.

"I win," I mouthed to Liam.

As my attention returned to Nova, I pulled in my bottom lip in thought. "Okay, our story. I'll give you the condensed version. Once upon a time, a grumpy angel stumbled upon a little girl as she faced a monster in the woods. He spent decades trying to protect her, but she grew up and learned to protect herself. She learned she's strong, capable, and worthy." I clutched Nova's hand and squeezed, infusing my divine energy into her skin. "She learned the power and beauty of her gift."

Seconds later, when I released my hold, a low gasp fell from Nova's parted lips. She stared at me in amazement.

"I didn't use my gift the right way when I was young either, but I was given another chance." I folded my hands, rested them on my lap, and said with hope and conviction, "Maybe this place will bring Neal his second chance too."

EPILOGUE

The text messages from Neal started on a Monday. At first, they only included a letter or two, yet Josie found them immensely remarkable. Her young friend hadn't been able to read or write in over a decade, not since he'd been stripped of his words.

"Something's happening," Neal said with a mixture of awe and apprehension when they spoke on the phone. "I'm sorry for all the texts, but I can't stop. I can't stop, Jojo."

On Thursday, she had twenty messages by noon. Each time her cell pinged with an alert, the screen illuminated with the same plea.

Jojo come now.

They talked again on Saturday. Josie had known Neal for almost ten years, and in all that time, he'd been a solemn, lost soul who only showed any semblance of joy when he was singing or strumming his guitar. Now, over the phone, excitement and hope thickened his voice.

"I don't know what it means, but you have to come."

"We'll see," she said reluctantly.

A cross-country trip from California to Collins Grove,

Wisconsin, was unfathomable to Josie, even for Neal, who she thought of as a son. Maybe he didn't realize the severity of his request. Maybe he didn't know she hadn't left the small seaside town of Half Moon Bay in almost a century—not since her fall from grace. Not since Jake.

Neal's messages continued. *Jojo come now. Come now.* Thirty, forty messages a day. *Jojo come. Come now. Come Jojo.*

"What can it mean?" Neal asked when they spoke again the following Wednesday. "It has to mean *something*, right?"

"Maybe." There was no maybe about it. This was big. Josie sighed, knowing she couldn't lie to Neal. "Yes. There must be a reason, darling."

Neal hadn't been able to recognize or write a single letter in ten years. Now, his hands seemed to be working of their own volition, typing the same three words over and over.

Jojo come now.

Color of the Clouds
Of the Gods - Book Four
Coming Soon!

ALSO BY GINA STURINO

Of the Gods

Fruit of the Land (Book One)

Light of the Sky (Book Two)

Fire of the Flesh (Book Three)

Color of the Clouds (Book Four) Coming Soon!

ABOUT THE AUTHOR

Gina Sturino has been devouring romance novels since she was a teenager. After marrying her very own Prince Charming, she found the inspiration to write her debut novel. While her husband isn't a god (like Nick in Fruit of the Land), he's pretty darn close (he may or may not have told her to write that), and helped inspire the character. They've lived in cities coast-to-coast and have settled in their hometown outside of Madison, Wisconsin, where they are raising their daughter.

You can find author Gina Sturino at:

www.ginasturino.com

www.facebook.com/ginasturino

Sign up for her super exciting newsletter at:

https://ginasturino.com/newsletter/

Gina loves to hear from readers! Email her at:

gina@ginasturino.com

Made in the USA
Middletown, DE
12 October 2021

49887683R00182